Undead and Unsure

Anthologies

CRAVINGS
(with Laurell K. Hamilton, Rebecca York, Eileen Wilks)

BITE
(with Laurell K. Hamilton, Charlaine Harris,
Angela Knight, Vickie Taylor)

KICK ASS
(with Maggie Shayne, Angela Knight, Jacey Ford)

MEN AT WORK
(with Janelle Denison, Nina Bangs)

DEAD AND LOVING IT
SURF'S UP
(with Janelle Denison, Nina Bangs)

MYSTERIA
(with P. C. Cast, Gena Showalter, Susan Grant)

OVER THE MOON
(with Angela Knight, Virginia Kantra, Sunny)

DEMON'S DELIGHT
(with Emma Holly, Vickie Taylor, Catherine Spangler)

DEAD OVER HEELS

MYSTERIA LANE
(with P. C. Cast, Gena Showalter, Susan Grant)

MYSTERIA NIGHTS
(includes Mysteria *and* Mysteria Lane, *with P. C. Cast, Susan Grant,*
Gena Showalter)

UNDERWATER LOVE
(includes Sleeping with the Fishes, Swimming Without a Net,
and Fish out of Water*)*

DYING FOR YOU

UNDEAD AND UNDERWATER

UNDEAD AND UNSURE

MaryJanice Davidson

BERKLEY SENSATION, NEW YORK

THE BERKLEY PUBLISHING GROUP
Published by the Penguin Group
Penguin Group (USA) Inc.
375 Hudson Street, New York, New York 10014, USA

USA | Canada | UK | Ireland | Australia | New Zealand | India | South Africa | China

Penguin Books Ltd., Registered Offices: 80 Strand, London WC2R 0RL, England
For more information about the Penguin Group, visit penguin.com.

This book is an original publication of The Berkley Publishing Group.

Berkley Sensation Books are published by The Berkley Publishing Group.
BERKLEY SENSATION® is a registered trademark of Penguin Group (USA) Inc.
The "B" design is a trademark of Penguin Group (USA) Inc.

Davidson, MaryJanice.
Undead and unsure / MaryJanice Davidson.—First Edition.
pages cm
ISBN 978-0-425-26343-3
1. Taylor, Betsy (Fictitious character)—Fiction. 2. Vampires—Fiction.
3. Paranormal romance stories. I. Title.
PS3604.A949U5274 2013
813'.6—dc23
2013011552

FIRST EDITION: August 2013

PRINTED IN THE UNITED STATES OF AMERICA

10 9 8 7 6 5 4 3 2 1

Jacket illustration by Don Sipley.
Jacket design by Lesley Worrell.
Interior text design by Kristin del Rosario.

For Mom and Dad and Yvonne,
who paid me the sizeable compliment
of never being unsure I'd make something of myself.
And I almost have!
Made something of myself, I mean.
Any day now this writing gig will start to pay off. I can feel it!

And for Tony,
who didn't care if it ever paid off,
as long as I was doing what I loved.

Author's Note

It's not advisable for anyone to play in traffic. Even if they're a vampire king. It's a bad idea for anyone. It just is.

Also, Tina and Betsy's mom discuss Clara Barton's Missing Men project, specifically the Office of Correspondence with the Friends of the Missing Men of the United States Army. After the Civil War, so many did not make it home. They left grieving parents, spouses, siblings, and friends, all trapped in the unique agony of assuming someone they love is dead, but not knowing for sure and maybe not *ever* knowing for sure.

Ms. Barton started the Office of Correspondence to try to help shattered loved ones find (pardon the twenty-first-century patois) closure. She received tens of thousands of letters, responded to over sixty thousand of them, and tracked down over twenty thousand men. She did this without the Internet, the information highway, television, the "have you seen me?" backs of milk cartons, or—oh yeah!—funding. That is because Clara Barton *kicked ass* in pretty much everything she did. More info on her Missing Men project can be found here: http://www.civilwarmed.org/clara-bartons-missing-soldiers-office-museum/about-clara-bartons-missing-soldiers-office/.

Sinclair's definition of *priceless* comes from *Collins English Dictionary*, via *The Free Dictionary* at http://www.thefreedictionary.com/priceless.

Summit Lookout Park in St. Paul is a real place, with a real extraordinary view, and marked by a real marker that reads, in part, "This park was originally the site of the Carpenter's Hotel, a towering wooden structure of the late 1850s . . . Projecting three stories above grade, the hotel was crowned with an open observation deck. It is believed that the hotel burned."

Okay, *believed*? A towering wooden structure three stories high burned, probably, but no one's sure? I get that this was over a century ago, but I'd think someone might have made a note. "March 17, 1865. Still pretty friggin' cold, but spring is a mere twenty weeks away. Also, the gigantic hotel at the end of the street burned flat. As a direct consequence, there were a *lot* of pissed-off out-of-towners milling around while the inferno raged. I've got a splinter, too, so I'll probably be dead soon. But I found a five-dollar bill yesterday so I'll die rich!"

See? Easy.

Author's Note

Anyway, the Summit Lookout Park is a real place, but I don't think people should have sex there. There's not much cover.

There are B&Bs (bed-and-breakfasts) where guests are not only expected to help with the chores, but to pay for the privilege. I'm not as infuriated by those as Betsy's mother is, but I still think it's weird.

There is such a thing as Dinkytown, and such a place as the Historic. Dinkytown will forever have a place in my heart, as it's where the first Khan's Mongolian Barbecue popped up in the Twin Cities. When I moved to Boston from the Midwest, I missed my friends, my family, and Khan's (I'm gonna pretend it was in that order). It's no coincidence that in *Undead and Unwed*, Betsy gets attacked outside Khan's, which inadvertently leads to her becoming queen.

Freudian Slippers are a real thing. I'm so jealous I didn't think of them. Find them at the Unemployed Philosophers Guild at http://www.philosophersguild.com.

Finally, although it describes Betsy perfectly, I didn't come up with *genius ditz*. For that I must thank the tireless juggernaut of pop culture minutiae that is Television Tropes and Idioms (TVTropes.org). I've found it an invaluable (and time-slurping) resource and was startled and thrilled to find my own work mentioned in several categories. Anti-Antichrist, Our Vampires Are Different, Fluffy the Terrible, Answers to the

Author's Note

Name of God, Fantastic Racism, Ironic Name, and A Chat with Satan are just a few of the places Betsy, Jennifer Scales, and other characters have popped up.

Warning: this site is beyond engrossing. Do not visit unless you've got thirty-six hours you don't know what to do with. You have been warned.

I heard that you were feeling ill
Headache, fever, and a chill.
I came to help restore your pluck.
'Cause I'm the nurse who likes to—

—*FERRIS BUELLER'S DAY OFF*

To the last I grapple with thee; from hell's heart I stab at thee;
for hate's sake I spit my last breath at thee.

—HERMAN MELVILLE, *MOBY DICK*

If her own family thought she was hard sometimes, it was
because they didn't understand that when you went through
hell you came out baked by the fire. And when you had to burn
to have your own way, you always wanted to have it.

—STEPHEN KING, *CHRISTINE*

To stay in shape, the brain needs to work out.

—"HOW TO KEEP A SHARP MIND,"
MARTHA STEWART LIVING

I have an almost complete disregard of precedent, and a faith
in the possibility of something better. It irritates me to be told
how things have always been done. I defy the tyranny of
precedent.

—CLARA BARTON

Undead and Unsure

The devil's dead, and the Antichrist is pissed. That's pretty much the whole thing right there.

Well . . . there's one more thing: I killed the devil. And the Antichrist is my half sister. (Two more things.) Because Christmas isn't stressful enough, right? Take it from me: if you trick the devil into granting a wish and then kill her while the Antichrist screams at you to stop, family get-togethers thereafter are uncomfortable.

But I was up for the challenge! Of course, the trick is making the family get-together happen at all. Luckily I'd married rich (and dead). And even if I hadn't married rich (note I'm not saying married well), my best friend and gestating roomie, Jessica, was also rich. It's weird that I was dead and lived in St. Paul in a snowless winter with two zillionaires, right? Never mind.

I used to be so heavily dependent on Hallmark. It had a card for almost everything. Even better, it had a *funny* card for almost everything. But I couldn't depend on a faceless corporate entity to convey my good wishes, condolences, birthday wishes, Mother's Day howdies, and happy holidays in general, since there were some occasions the good people at Hallmark Cards, Inc., didn't figure anyone would need to cover.

And even after the make-your-own-card phase popped up, there were some cards that just couldn't be made, no matter how much money got pissed away at Archiver's.

Side note: this DIY crap has gotten out of hand. Cards first, but followed by make-your-own pop (which is soooo hard to find, so of course people start making their own), make-your-own beer (see above, re: pop), make-your-own cheese, and make-your-own eggs by raising chickens. In the middle of cities, people are raising chickens! If you don't believe me, check a Williams-Sonoma catalog sometime. Honest to God. It's all right there: make-your-own vinegar pot, $89.95. The Reclaimed Rustic Coop with Painted Chicken, $399.95. (I assume the chicken was painted on the side in case there was any doubt that the coop surrounded by chickens was a chicken coop.) A Backyard Beehive and Starter Kit, $89.95, so you can start your own bees ("Gentlemen! Start . . . your . . . *bees*!"). Make-your-own butter kit: $29.95.

Who makes their own butter? When did we all decide we were living in *Little House on the Prairie* reruns?

All this to say there wasn't a card at Hallmark or a sticker at Archiver's to convey "Sorry I killed your mom, who was also Satan. Also, Happy Thanksgiving." I didn't even bother looking. Instead, I turned to more sinister methods of getting my "again, so sorry I killed your mom!" message across.

Balloon bouquets. A minstrel greeting (good to see that the Renaissance festival weirdos are employable the rest of the year). Cookie bouquets. Singing telegrams (yep, they still do those, and for a surprisingly reasonable price).

Comedy Central sowed the seeds of my sinister plan by running a John Hughes marathon. Remember when the slutty nurse went to Ferris Bueller's house to cheer him up and he was at a Cubs game so she ended up singing to his crabby sister instead (played by Jennifer Grey, who went on to ruin her career with a nose job)? John Hughes: creative genius and comedy demigod.

That was why the Antichrist was in my driveway, panting and glaring and stomping up the walk in her awful Uggs (what year did the Seed of Satan think it was? Also, even when Uggs were in they were not in) and shaking a fistful of balloons at me. "Stop *sending* these. They're *following* me."

Success! Family reunion, take one.

CHAPTER TWO

The Antichrist stood fuming on the—wait, that was just her breath showing because it was cold. And also, she was super pissed at me. So, literal and figurative fuming.

"You weren't answering my calls or replying to . . . to my . . . my . . ." I nearly gagged on the word, then coughed it out: ". . . texts." I hate that half the planet has become enslaved by their cell phones. I swore I wouldn't fall into the sweet sticky trap of tech. But it's like fighting a slow roll down a slope: you'll eventually get to the bottom. You can go easy or you can go hard, but eventually you will text. "I've been trying to get you for days and you haven't answered."

"Because I'm not speaking to you!"

"I know! So I had to resort to texting and you know I hate it. In a way, I'm kind of a victim, too."

Now she wasn't just fuming; I could hear her perfect teeth grinding together. The Antichrist had never needed braces and had a cavity-free kisser. They must fluoride the hell out of the water in Dinkytown.

Laura Goodman (yep, you read that right and yep, the irony wasn't lost on . . . well . . . anybody . . .) began to stomp up and down the cement walk just in front of the porch, the dozen helium-filled Mylar balloons trailing behind her. Early December in Minnesota could be awful, but we were enjoying a balmy stretch of low thirties. There'd been snow a few days before but it was melting. Not that it made a difference to Laura: with her feet cocooned in Uggs, she could have been scrambling for Noah's Ark and her feet would have stayed dry. And why was I thinking about her feet? Answer: because they were pretty little feet trapped in huge ugly boots, and I felt sorry for them.

"I don't want to talk to you," she explained. Pace, pace, turn, pace. She turned so fast I couldn't see her for a second until she batted the balloons out of her face. I bit the inside of my cheeks so I wouldn't smirk. "I don't want to see you. Thanks to you, I have to make some major decisions about my life. Thanks to you, not only my life but the lives and/

or afterlives of millions might have changed or will change. I've lived with the fact that I am the Desolator since I was thirteen. Now I have to decide if I'll take up my mother's sword and I'm not even legal drinking age. Bad enough that I have to tolerate the situation at all. I won't tolerate you, too."

Don't say anything about how "the Desolator" sounds like some kind of super food processor. Want your veggies pureed in a jiff? Try the Desolator!

When I was pretty sure that wasn't going to come out of my mouth, I began. "Look, I'm sorry—"

"You aren't."

"—about the situation. You're right," I added with what I hoped she saw as a sympathetic shrug. "I'm not sorry I killed the devil. But I'm sorry you had to see it. And I'm sorry you're stuck now. Yeah, it's my fault. I'm owning it. I want to help you."

She barked a laugh. "Help me?" She shook her head, and perfect blond waves obscured her eyes and then the blue headband forced it to fall back into place, framing her perfect face. "You've helped enough."

I must, I must discover what she uses for conditioner . . . and moisturizer . . .

She stepped up, stepped close. Her grip on the balloon strings was white-knuckled; when she moved there was the sinister rustle of Mylar rubbing together. I'd come off the porch and was standing in our muddy driveway, cursing my cold feet but far too badass to bitch about my cold clammy wet muddy feet. When I'd heard her drive in I'd sprinted for the front door, which meant the neighborhood was treated to me in my tattered RenFest sweatshirt ("Dragon Bait") and equally shredded purple leggings (it was laundry day, which meant if you thought my clothes looked bad, you did *not* want to see my underwear). And that was all. Since I'd already died I couldn't freeze to death, but I was cold even when the temps were Texas hot. Standing in the cold with muddy feet was agonizing, but Laura had even bigger problems.

She was wrong to say I'd helped enough. I wasn't done yet.

"Stay away from me," she said evenly, her baby blues glaring into my baby blue-greens. Even though I knew what she was capable of, it was hard to take her seriously in her cream-colored merino wool sweater, jeans that were so faded and comfortable they probably felt like silk, Uggs (but I won't go into that again), and the balloons streaming behind her. Completing the picture of corn-fed angelic innocence and beauty, her shoulder-length buttercup-colored hair was held back from her face with a thin powder blue ribbon. It was a lot like being menaced by a conservatively dressed Victoria's Secret model (holding balloons).

She looked gorgeous but it was impossible to fear her (even without balloons).

"Stay away," she said again, "and *keep* away."

"I think that's redun—"

"I'll be back when I know what I'll do about you."

"Well, don't worry about calling first. Just pop on by anytime. Literally, even." The Antichrist could teleport. But I, who hated the pop-in, was generously letting her know it was okay. See? I was trying, too!

She turned on her Uggy heel and started for her car, a used but well-cared-for ginger-ale-colored Fusion. Because the Antichrist was all about green, and gas mileage. Except, now that the devil was dead, did that mean Laura was the devil?

"But what about Thanksgiving?" I called after her. My trump card! Laura would turn down charity work before she'd turn down mashed potatoes and gravy, especially on a family holiday.

"What *about* Thanksgiving? It was days ago."

"Yeah, we postponed it." As she turned and her glare got ever more pissy, I continued. "Because it's not Thanksgiving without blood relatives. And Jessica. And her boyfriend whom we've known maybe a year? And Marc, who's dead." Ah! My loyalty to friends both living and dead would show that deep down I cared about her, we all cared about her, and this latest awful thing would blow over and our bond as sisters would be ever more strengthened. It was just a matter of—

"You lying bitch."

"Whoa!" Usually Laura's idea of foul language was to pepper her exclamations with *dang*, *darn*, *doy*, and *ish*. "That's cold. Like my poor frozen feet. Which you shouldn't even think about because us working this out is way more important than my blue shriveled feet, which have gone numb in an agony of coldness."

"You're postponing Thanksgiving because you hate Thanksgiving," she snapped, and dammit if she didn't have a point. "Not because you're waiting for us to be friends again. Not that we ever were."

"My hatred is only one small factor," I protested.

"You stay away." She stepped back (to my relief, because she had a real Close Talker thing going, and I made it a rule never to give way to a Close Talker) and turned, and this time I knew there was no point in trying to call her back. Her blond hair twirled and swirled around her shoulders as she headed for her car. The balloons bobbed in her wake.

Wait. Blond? Huh.

One of Laura's odder traits (and consider the source who called it *odder* for an idea of how weird it was) was, when she got super pissed, red-hot furious, her outside matched her inside, a soul trying so hard to be good when all of its instincts were to be bad. When she was angry her hair deepened to the color of blood on fire, and her eyes went poison green.

Not today, though. And I wasn't sure if that was good or bad. Her coloring was a litmus test to gauge her temper. Blue eyes and blond hair meant that no matter what she said or how she said it, the Antichrist wasn't furious. There was strong emotion there, sure, but it wasn't anger. She was afraid.

Of me? Herself? Both? The latter probably, yeah. It struck me as a sensible reaction, and I had to face the knowledge that things between the (new) devil and me were gonna get worse before they got better.

CHAPTER
THREE

"I bet it was the minstrel greeting," the zombie said from behind me. "That would have sent me screaming over the edge, too."

I turned and looked at my friend Marc and at first didn't know what to say. I went through a dizzying mix of emotions whenever I saw him these days: relief and surprise and joy and fear and pity and exasperation and the simple gladness that after all he'd been through and seen and heard, he still wanted to be my friend.

Or he was too afraid of what might happen to him (he'd kill himself again?) if he left. But that didn't bear thinking about.

"You're one to talk." I shivered as my sister raced to her car, wrestled the balloons into the backseat, leaped into the driver's seat, started the engine with a roar, slammed it into reverse, and shot out of the driveway, then turned, popped it into drive, and howled down Summit Avenue, leaving a smoking tire trail behind her.

Naw. The Antichrist left like she always did: she carefully snapped on her seat belt, checked her rearview and blind spots as she started the car (took a while with the balloons), cautiously backed out of the driveway, paused to let a car a block away drive past, then pulled out, turned left, and headed for home via the speed limit.

"I'm telling you," he insisted. "That's what did it."

"Nuh-uh." My personal bet was the singing telegram. "And like your suggestion wasn't a thousand times worse?"

"What?" My friend Jessica waddled out the front door and stood on the porch, one hand on the small of her back as she stretched and fanned herself with Marc's *Entertainment Weekly*. "Ugh, it's so hot."

"It's really not," I pointed out, then sadly gazed down at my frosty blue toes.

"I'm sleeping out here tonight, it's so hot."

"It's not hot!" Easy, girl. Jessica was wrong, but she was also crazy. As a rule I tried not to fuck with crazy people. Unless I wanted to, or didn't like them, or was bored, or felt needy, or was looking for a rush, or was in pursuit of justice, or needed to kill time between sample sales. "It's

December," I added, trying for calm. "It's the polar opposite of hot. Literally. Polar opposite."

Jess was a thousand months pregnant—at least, going by the size of her belly. Marc and I privately referred to her gestating fetus as the Belly That Ate the World, because we are catty and also love Daenerys on *Game of Thrones*. We talked about the Belly with furtive glee tempered with deep terror that she'd find out and make us die screaming. And also, show-Daenerys was almost as terrific as book-Daenerys. I was pretty sure. I was almost all the way through the first book. Okay, halfway through. The things are friggin' doorstops and I've got this queen-of-the-vampire thing going on; don't judge. Also it's quicker for me to just follow along in the graphic novel. Marc must never know about that.

And me liking Daenerys didn't mean anything, right? It wasn't some commentary on my own experience as a nobody who has run from responsibility my entire life only to find out I was suddenly the queen of a bunch of people, some who loved me and more who didn't, trying to bring change, hold my own, and fend off assassination attempts and also dying a few more times?

No. To paraphrase Freud, sometimes a made-for-cable book series is just a made-for-cable book series.

"Laura finally had enough, huh? Too bad I missed the

scene. Takes a while to get to the front door when you're . . ." She trailed off and gestured vaguely at her gut. "What did it? Dial-a-balloon-bouquet?"

"I think it was a combo. Hey, my choices were limited. Hallmark doesn't cover 'Sorry I killed your mom before she could kill me, and also, good luck with your new job!'"

"So you Said It with Flowers?"

"And strip-o-grams?" my zombie asked hopefully.

Argh. I've got to stop referring to him as *my zombie*. He has a name, dammit. *Two* names. Zombie Marc. Dammit! Marc Spangler. "Naw. The Antichrist is kind of a prude." A virgin prude, the worst kind. But still. The important thing to keep in mind . . .

"The important thing," I said, finishing my thought aloud, "is that she came over. We were talking, even if it was only for a minute. If I got her to do it once—"

"Aggravated her to do it once," Jessica said while Marc nodded so hard he almost fell off the porch.

"—I can get her here again. We *will* have a family Thanksgiving, dammit!"

"That reminds me," Jessica said. "I had turkey for lunch."

"That's fine." But I had a bad feeling her casual news meant I'd be hitting the grocery store again.

"All of the turkey."

Thought so. I didn't dare make eye contact with Marc. He had a hand up in front of his mouth and coughed. Since zombies didn't have to cough, I knew he was worried he'd crack up.

Jessica seemed to sense our restrained mirth, because her beautiful dark eyes got squinty and the beauty was replaced with suspicion. "Does anyone have a comment about my lunch?"

"Nuh-uh," I lied, wondering if getting terrified would be an overreaction.

"It's good that you're eating lots of protein," Dr. Marc Zombie added. In life he'd been an ER doc (though he always corrected me; apparently outside of TV they're called EWs, which is just hilarious: "Ew, I've cut the whole thing off by accident! Ew, I've gotta get to the EW!"), but in death he considered himself an able medic.

He wasn't movie-zombified. There was no shambling after us while moaning about his desire to partake of our delectable brains, he didn't stink and wasn't all gooky and covered with rotting slime, but he still didn't trust his new-and-unimproved reflexes. "You need at least sixty grams of protein a day. And that entire turkey was . . . uh . . ." His eyes rolled up and he thought about it. ". . . just over fifteen hundred grams of protein." Pause. "So you've definitely hit your protein intake for the . . ." Pause. ". . . the day."

She relaxed and smiled. Marc and I relaxed and smiled. I knew he'd been rejecting finishing his sentence with: for the week, the month, the decade, the century. He had made the wise choice, and lived to not live another day.

Besides, all anyone had to do was look at Jessica and know all was well. She was brooming with health! No, that was wrong. Blooming, that was the cliché I was groping for. I'd gotten mixed up because when she wasn't pregnant, Jess was normally the shape and weight of a broomstick. Her collarbones were so sharp you worried you'd cut yourself if you fell on her. We'd known each other since our training bra days and she'd always been super slender and annoyingly pretty. Lovely brown eyes, with smooth dark skin that glinted with reddish undertones, which meant the jerk could wear shades like fuchsia and orange, lipsticks that would make me look a) like a bitchy circus clown, b) embalmed, and/or c) an embalmed bitchy circus clown.

She'd been (and still was) rich, too, but I did *not* envy her that. Not if it meant enduring what she had: a father who wanted to bang her, and a mother who didn't much care *what* he did as long as he paid the bills. Jess was the richest person in Minnesota (not the richest woman, not the richest African American—the richest mammal) and I didn't envy her that, either.

Content that we hadn't been ready to snigger over her turkey intake, Jessica did that hands-on-the-small-of-her-back stretch thing again, then asked (I think rhetorically), "What do you get for the Antichrist who has nothing?"

"A family," I replied at once. I'd been thinking about it a lot. Laura and I had several things in common. Dead fathers, ghastly white complexions that tended toward dryness in winter, shitty tempers, an inability to rock coral lipstick, inappropriately judging people, powers we feared and didn't understand, a tendency to sunburn on cloudy days, and fractured families. "We'll show her she's not alone. That just because her mom—who she only met a couple of years ago anyway—is dead, that doesn't mean she's alone. She's got me! Us, I mean."

Now Marc and Jessica were trading glances.

"What? It's true. Just because I killed her mom doesn't mean we can't be there for each other. One of her moms," I corrected. The (late) devil was Laura's mom (who had looked weirdly like Lena Olin); but my stepmother, the Ant, was the one who had been impregnated (by my dad) and carried the baby to term. Her body, I mean, because Lena Olin possessed the Ant for the pregnancy and birth. I know. It's complicated bordering on idiotic. "Both her moms are dead, but only one by my hand. That's something. Right?"

(. . .)

I sighed. "I knew you'd say that."

"We didn't," Marc began, but I rushed to cut him off.

"Like I said, all that stuff's bad, but that doesn't mean we can't be a family again. Or for the first time."

"Bets, I love you, but I'm pretty sure that's exactly what it means."

I was too polite to argue with her. Also, I worried she was dead-on. Plus, she was smarter than me, so I'd lose the debate, unless she got tired or hungry and left before blitzing my half-assed argument. So I let it drop, and thought how nice it was to see Jess and Marc conspiring about anything, even if it was their mutual belief that I was off my rocker.

Not long ago (maybe two weeks?) Jessica had been all *Keep back, vile creature of the lamented undead!* I couldn't blame her, as glad as I was to have Marc back. The prejudice against zombies ran deep, and there were no support groups for the living impaired. It took Marc days to convince her he wasn't going to lurk around waiting for the chance to chomp on her baby's brains. And before she could make it clear that, nothing personal, but *I won't have you help me deliver; glad you're back but keep the hell away from me once my water breaks*, Marc was the one who told her that though he remembered everything about being a doctor, he didn't trust his new-and-unimproved hand-eye coordination.

"That's why I was practicing surgery on Betsy's dead cat!" he had explained, beaming, and added, "Oh, shit. Sorry. That was disgusting. Right?"

Yep.

He might talk about disgusting things, and sometimes do them, but Marc himself wasn't at all disgusting. Like I said, he didn't shamble and he didn't stink. He was a little quieter, a bit more thoughtful. Sometimes when he paused before starting a complicated task, you could almost feel him willing his zombified neurons to fire, and when they did, he'd go about whatever it was—doing a crossword, making a playlist, rereading an anatomy text, building me more shelves in my closet (love the mansion, but the woeful lack of closet space was a real *problema*)—with a calm care that was reassuring. He wasn't the same man, no. But I didn't think he was a worse man . . . just different.

Sometimes his lively green eyes would cloud over and, again, you could almost hear him thinking, *C'mon, c'mon, you know how to do this, remember how to do this*, but other than that his appearance was unchanged. He was still lanky and cute, with brutally short black hair, a sharp, aquiline nose, and pale skin—because he hated outdoor activities and thrived under blaring hospital fluorescents, not because he had a hankering for braaaaains.

In fact, when I looked at my friends these days I was struck by how different they were now: Jessica, eating for seventeen, Marc, cutting up dead things to keep his brain limber. Both had undergone incredible changes only because they were my friends.

CHAPTER FOUR

I was hip-deep in velvet clogs and last year's pumps, simultaneously cursing this timeline's lack of Louboutin while admiring Marc's shelf-building skills, and heard what was becoming a near-daily sound: someone on Summit Avenue had stomped on their brakes right outside our house. There's something about the shriek of brakes and the creak of fingers tightening on the steering wheel that kicks adrenaline from "Ho-hum, should I have breakfast *and* lunch at Burger King?" to "I'm going to be killed any second and I should do something right now!"

Even before I died that was a stressful sound, and as a vampire that hadn't changed. It could mean anything—an undead drive-by, the cops showing up to ask about any of the people I'd killed, somebody racing home ahead of a hit squad, one of my subjects warning of an impending IRS audit, another of my subjects whining about why couldn't we all just get along, still another of my subjects informing me that I wasn't cut out to be queen and then being amazed when I agreed . . . like that.

It wasn't any of those things, though; I knew that without leaving the closet. These days that sound meant one thing: Eric Sinclair, the king of the vampires, was playing in traffic again.

With a groan I lurched to my feet, not as sorry as I should have been to leave the closet. The velvet clogs were just awful, and I had thirty-eight pairs. (You're thinking, *Then why buy them?* And I'm thinking, *Then why not shut up?*)

Since there wasn't a Christian Louboutin in this reality, all my really terrific shoes didn't exist and (alas!) would never exist. I'd been able to fill the yawning void in my (black) soul with Manolo pumps (the Perpeta Silhouettes helped assuage my agony) and Feldman flats (ditto the Diamond 4-Ever red multi), but that didn't mean I didn't wish for what I once had. You could admire a cheetah and a golden eagle, but still regret the extinction of, I dunno, the dodo? The passenger pigeon? (Analogies are not my strong point.) I had made Christian Louboutin extinct when I tinkered with my timeline, and it haunted me, and would for the rest of my death. Unlife. What-have-you.

But I had more pressing pains in the ass to deal with.

Unwilling to suffer further frostbite, I grabbed the shoes closest to me, which happened to be the two-tone green Bloch snake-print flats. Snake-*print*, not snake*skin*. I'd quit PETA around the time they decided it was okay to encourage people to euthanize entire breeds (pit bulls, we're talking about you) in the name of protecting animals, but before they announced they were going to do porn to protect their furbabies. (This is true! Unbelievable but true! This is per *their own data*.)

Say it with me: ???? Makes me crave a *WTF* stamp, so I could just walk around stamping *WTF* on everything that freaks me or scares me or just plain puzzles me.

Anyway, I jumped ship after the breed-wide euthanasia train started up; it reminded me of those whack-job freedom fighters who scream things like, "Die, pig oppressors! Fear not, repressed villagers, we're here and you're safe and we'll kill you to save you!" Definitely one of those "wow, I got clear of that car crash just in time" moments.

But that didn't mean I condoned widespread snake murder. You could make all kinds of gorgeous footgear without shedding blood except that of the designer working her fingers to the bone. In fact, starting with material that was already dazzling struck me as a cop-out. Start with something wretched and make it beautiful—that was much more challenging.

Alas, no time for further shoe rumination. Wait, would

it be *ruminations*? Was that right? Anyway, I galloped down the *Gone with the Wind* staircase, zipped past a couple of parlors, and was out the front door in time to see the vampire king standing on Summit, cuddling Fur and Burr to his (broad) chest and waving a cheerful good-bye to a rattled driver who was not lingering. "I am certain that will buff right out!" he called, and the car lurched as the driver stomped the gas pedal. "It was lovely talking to you!"

"Ah, man." I fought the urge to slap myself on the forehead or grunt "d'oh!" "Again with this?" Among other things, my favorite vampire liked to dart into traffic without looking.

Eric Sinclair spun toward me, Fur's and Burr's long silky ears flaring out as he did. Identical bundles of fluff and teeth, Fur and Burr were black Lab sisters, with the soft short coat and large liquid brown eyes of the breed. They also drooled prodigiously. Fur wore a red collar with matching leash; Burr had the green one, also with matching leash. Unless it was the other way around. Who could tell? Who wanted to?

"Ah, my own, a glorious sunny day rivaled only by your beauty."

"It's cloudy," I pointed out as he came up the driveway. "And what was the other thing? Hmm, it's on the tip of my tongue, why'd I come sprinting out of—oh, right! Stop playing in traffic! Stop! Playing! In—"

"Traffic?" he guessed.

"I can't believe I've had to say that even one time to a grown man. A *very* grown man in your case—certainly old enough to know better."

"I am warmed by your loving concern. As much as I am warmed by the sun as it—"

"Lurks behind a cloudbank." I tried not to smile. My husband was a pile of contradictions, which I found as sexy as I did interesting/annoying/infuriating. Tall, dark, and— there was no other word—foreboding, with big hands capable of killing, hands that *had* killed—but he'd never hurt an innocent. Immaculately dressed, but walking around in a cloud of dog hair. Old enough to qualify for social security, but forever in the taut, toned, sleekly muscular body of a young man in his physical prime. An unstoppable satyr in the bedroom and veteran of more threesomes than Charlie Sheen, but faithful to me. Glittering black eyes capable of forcing anyone's will to his, but when he looked at me it was with sweet, sappy luurrrrv. I suppose a staid, predictable mate would be boring. Sinclair was never boring.

Yes indeed, he was my husband and my king, and together we (sorta) ruled the vampire nation (such as it was . . . no borders and no border patrols or citizenship tests or patriotic bumper stickers or taxes) and were feared and loathed by many, and bugged by many more, and there

King Puppy Love was in all his insane puppy-cuddling glory.

And it was *still* damn near impossible not to gape up at him and grin and grin, because his unalloyed joy at his new freedom was contagious.

I stomped on my happiness. One of us had to be the responsible adult, dammit, and the cosmic joke of it all was: that meant me. Setting an example. Or something.

"When I asked the devil to fix it so you could run around in sunshine, I had no idea the downside was you'd drop fifty IQ points." I was going for scolding and not pulling it off. "Is it asking too much to want you to retain some self-respect? Because you're capable of at least that. If memory serves."

Fur and Burr answered for him with puppy yaps. The little black dogs had begun squirming like hairy worms when I'd come out. They adored him, they lived to be near him, they cried on the infrequent occasions he left them, but they loved getting their fur and slobber all over me almost as much. Sinclair thought they were perfect in all ways, but I could only take their incontinent cuteness in small doses. I was a cat person whose cat was dead. So I had pretty much the same relationship with Giselle as I'd had when she was alive: we ignored each other while going about our lives. Which had suited us both fine, so don't even start with the judging.

"Where's my badass vampire king?" I complained. Unlike most rhetorical questions, this one was answerable. *Temporarily replaced by the farmer's son* was correct. Sinclair had grown up on a farm and been around swarms of dogs his whole childhood and adolescence (though he was a teenager before the word *teenager* was invented). After he became a vampire, he decided it would be cruel to try to keep a dog or dogs when he could never take them for a walk during the day, and when at any moment he could be killed again. Kind of a grim tale, right? Yeah, well, I accidentally changed that. I also accidentally changed the timeline and accidentally killed Lena Olin. Because that's me in a nutshell: accident-prone.

Not only had I made a (literal) deal with the devil for Sinclair's soul (sorta), I'd picked up the puppies and brought them home for him, a "hey, great to have you back in the sunshine!" gift. Again, in my defense, I had no idea it would leave him clinically insane.

"You were once a badass but now you're the undead Dog Whisperer," I teased. "Where's the cold, ruthless vampire I loved and loathed?"

"Right here! Isn't um badass vampire king wight here, li'l woogums, yes he is! Yes he is!"

Dear God. "Well, we had a good run, but it's time for our divorce now. I'll have my people call your people. Which will be easy since my people *are* your people."

"Oh no, not ever," he replied, confident in my love and

27

horniness. He grinned and I smiled back—just could not help it. He only talked the baby talk to Fur and Burr when I could hear him; he knew it set my teeth on edge. Right?

Please, God, that's why he's doing it, that's the only reason he's doing it, to get a rise out of me. The alternative is unthinkable!

"Come walk with me," he coaxed over the puppies' whimpering. They were trying as hard as they could to get down so they could put muddy paws on my dark purple leggings. Purple leggings that matched my slightly less purple sweatshirt, and pale green flats on my feet . . . what had I been thinking? I looked like an upside-down eggplant.

"Pass." I stepped close to pet them, which only increased the wiggling and yelping. "Bad enough to have these two always wanting to climb all over me; I don't need the neighborhood dogs chasing me home again." One of the perks of being Elizabeth, the One (gah, I know, sue me; I didn't make up that dumb dumb dumb title), is that I'll be pretty cute forever. One of the not-perks was that dogs were drawn to me.

"How can my true love say nay," he sang, "on such a beautiful d—bbllech!" He'd been cut off as Fur had licked his face and accidentally Frenched him. Heh. That *alone* had been worth running out of the house for. "No, no, you dreadful hound," he scolded in the same tone people used for "I love you and everything you do is wonderful." Yeah, that'd show those two who was boss. "Just for that, whee!"

"Please stop doing the Mary Tyler Moore twirl."

"Never!"

I'd always assumed that when I met the right vampire, we'd settle down and live with a houseful of weirdos and *I'd* be the embarrassing one. *Oh, life, must you always teach me lessons?*

But Sinclair had had enough, both of the sunshine and making me nuts, since he gently put the puppies on the ground and kept a tight hold on their leashes. "I saw your sister on my way back," he said, all traces of play gone. "You had words?"

"At least three or four of them." We fell into step together as we let the dogs lead us up the walk and around the side of the house. "I'm getting somewhere with her. At least she came over and yelled at me for a couple of minutes. It's sad that I'm taking that as a positive, isn't it?"

"It is optimistic," he decided. "Not sad. Was it the singing minstrel? I have a wager with Tina." He opened the kitchen door and held it for me. I scuttled past him to beat the puppies inside.

"No, I think the balloon bouquets pushed her over. She had a big one in her car when she showed up."

Sinclair snickered as he shrugged out of his black wool coat and unleashed the dogs, tossing both coat and leashes into the mudroom just off the kitchen. If I needed further proof that things were different now that my hub was a pet owner, the sight of him tossing a six-hundred-dollar-plus Ralph Lauren cashmere overcoat onto a dirty counter, then closing the door on the whole mess—ta-dah! all gone!—would have done it.

The mudroom was aptly named. It always looked like someone had thrown a mud grenade, then slammed the door. Ker-*bloosh!* Mud all over. Mud in places you can't get mud out of. Mud in places mud was never meant to be. The girls, knowing the routine, dashed past the door to their corner and started frisking around their food dishes.

"I have every confidence you shall wear her down with your incessant singing telegrams and refusal to acknowledge that killing her mother was a bad thing."

"Yeah, I—wait. That almost sounded like you think—"

"Followed by your insistence that, like, you're totally a victim, too." His emphasis on *like* and *totally* was pointed yet shrill, as if he were channeling a cheerleader from the early '80s. Any cheerleader, actually. I could feel my eyes squeezing into slits while he grabbed the canister kept on the puppies' part of the kitchen counter. Yeah. The dogs had their own section of counter. *I* didn't have my own section of counter.

"This is not funny," he concluded.

"I know!" I cried. "Your bitchy and inaccurate impression of me aside, none of this is funny. All right, Laura yelling at me with a fistful of balloons was funny, but not much else."

His piercing gaze met mine for a moment and I felt hot and cold at once. Cold because although Sinclair would set himself on fire before hurting me, he was pretty much the baddest vampire on the planet; you didn't break his gaze without giving something up. Hot because he was pretty much the baddest vampire on the planet and you didn't break his gaze without giving something up. Yum. Yum *squared*.

His lips parted. I felt myself leaning toward him . . . now that I thought about it, we hadn't had sex in almost seventy-two hours. The horror! Unimaginable.

"Tina!" he bawled, and I jerked back. That wasn't the name I'd expected him to shriek.

We heard feet pounding down the stairs, we heard someone galloping down the hall to the kitchen, and then— whoosh! Tina was sliding to a stop in front of us. She loved fuzzy socks, but bemoaned their lack of traction . . . most days, anyway. Also, her socks were yellow with black stripes, making it look like she had bee feet.

"Majesties." She wasn't panting, because she had no breath to be out of, but she'd wasted no time coming on the run. "How may I serve?"

Sinclair, meanwhile, had twisted the lid off the puppies' canister o' treats. "This is unacceptable."

"My king?"

He held the canister upside down and shook it. "It is not to be borne!"

31

Tina blinked slowly, like an owl. She loved my husband; she had loved him for decades before I was born and I confidently expected her to love him for centuries more. But her love didn't threaten mine. She had been a friend of the Sinclair clan for generations; she was the vampire who had turned my husband from a grieving brother and son to a coldly infuriated predator. She was devoted, had killed and (at least twice that I knew of) almost died for him, and her love for him was utterly maternal.

Which, given how she looked, was as hilarious as it was touching. Tina had been a prime hottie in her day and still was, in mine. Her dark blond hair was pulled back into a thick braid, which brought attention to her pale face, making her dark eyes and bristly lashes even more striking. Pansy eyes, my mom called them. She was regularly carded when she tried to a) drink and b) see an NC-17 movie. This was partly because she was a vampire and partly because she liked dressing the part of a lecherous senator's fantasy: plaid skirts, usually in a green or red tartan; crisp white blouses; little to no jewelry; no makeup. In life, she must have driven the other Southern belles out of their teeny tiny minds, and trust me, their minds were having enough trouble grasping the fact that Daddy's slaves had nutty ideas about how it sucked to be owned. (Yeah. She was *that* old. Her full name was Christina Caresse Chavelle. Ha!)

All this to say she was a creature of contradictions, just

like my insane husband; and also like my insane husband, she loved and protected us. That didn't mean we didn't drive her bugshit sometimes. Like now, for instance. Sinclair was shaking an empty canister and I could tell she wanted to roll her eyes but wouldn't indulge. Thus the slow blinking.

After a few seconds while Sinclair practically tapped his foot waiting for her answer, she said, "I must apologize, my king."

"How could you let this happen?"

"I foolishly let the budget, the management of our offshore accounts, an audit on the nightclub the queen keeps forgetting she inherited, a conference call with Michael Wyndham and Dr. Bimm to lay groundwork for possible alliances, and the monthly newsletter take precedence."

I wanted to sigh with admiration. Only Tina could have gotten away with it: a perfectly serious response, with terrific undertones of *Because it's not my fucking job, nimrod, now how about you go play with your dogs and let me get back to the grown-up stuff?*

"It's nothing to freak out about. We're not out." I figured I'd toss Tina a save, not that she needed one. "There's a whole pack of those Chew-eez puppy treats things in—"

"Store-bought?" the king of the vampires nearly shrieked. I had the feeling he would have said *"Abstinence?"* in the same horrified tone. "Factory-churned dreck with peanut shells and corncobs as filler? Never! Never while I live!"

"Technically you're not ali—quit that." Tired of waiting for her snack, Fur had abandoned her bowl and jumped up on my legs. She had sharp claws to go with her sharp baby teeth—those puppies had mouths full of sewing needles. "Stop it!"

"My darling, my own," Sinclair crooned as he set the canister down and came to me. He put his lovely strong hands on my shoulders and pulled me in for what I hoped would be some heavy kitchen smoochin'. Maybe we'd shoo everyone out and nail each other on the butcher block. Hmm, no, we made our smoothies there; the others would throw a fit. The puppy counter? *I'd* throw a fit. It was no coincidence that the kitchen was one of the few rooms in this monstrosity we hadn't christened by defilement. "I need you at my side."

"Back atcha, big guy."

"Let us bake love."

"Oooh, I've been waiting all day for—what?"

"Bake love." Was he . . . ? He was! Eric Sinclair was reaching past me and grabbing an apron, which he dropped over his head and then tied behind his back. "That is how you show love to your pets," he went on as if this was a serious topic of conversation and not further evidence of clinical insanity. "You *bake* love. I shall begin with a batch of Apple Crunch Pupcakes."

"Please lose the apron," I begged while Tina sloooowly backed out of the room. "I can psychologically block most of this if you just lose the apron. I can blitz the whole day, just please lose the apron!" Oh God, God, why wouldn't he lose the apron?

"It will not stand! We may have run out of homemade dog biscuits but my precious darlings will never be forced to choke down—"

"Forced? So you've never once noticed how they eat? Because they are not forced. Ever."

"—repulsive store-brand dog treats loaded with by-product meal and chicken heads. Now where . . ." He stood still for a moment, thinking. ". . . where is my mixing bowl?"

I fled the horror.

CHAPTER
FIVE

I like living with a cop. They have the best stories, it's really, *really* hard to knock them out of their equilibrium, they're in and out at all hours, which makes them perfect roomies for the undead, and it's nice hearing stories that don't start with *I stirred from my corpse-nap ravenous for the taste of human blood, and also needed to do some Christmas shopping, so I went trolling for rapists in the Mall of America parking lots.* On the rare occasions I pull my head out of my ass and take a frank look at my living conditions, living with a cop never hits the disad side.

Police work is greedy, though; it's always hungry. Some asshole is always making trouble somewhere and some cop(s) will get stuck trying to fix it, and whether they do or don't, another asshole is always coming along. I was touched and horrified to realize that Nick/Dick saw life in our mansion o' monsters as a respite, a place where he could relax and let his guard down. In a mansion full of the undead. This sort of thing relaxes him. Yeah, weird, right? Poor guy.

If I hadn't known Dick/Nick didn't need the job, I'd have felt a lot worse. But he didn't, so I didn't. Detective Berry was also a Deere, as in John Deere, as in seven-figure trust fund. That brought the number of millionaires in our household to five. (Tina *had* to be rich. She was too smart not to be, dressed far too well—those hand-tailored plaid skirts weren't cheap—taught Sinclair everything *he* knew about finance, had her claws in too many undead pies and, my God, that's such shitty imagery . . . claws and pies? What was I thinking?)

Minnesota was an equitable distribution state, so Sinclair being rich meant I was, too. (I learned more than I ever wanted about equitable distribution vs. community property when the Ant torpedoed my mother's marriage.)

It bugged me sometimes; it was like living in a Richie Rich cartoon as written by Wile E. Coyote: hard to believe, often illogical, always mystifying. How many people were on intimate terms with millionaires? Hardly any, right? And there lies my *problema grande*: I was afraid of becoming the monster Ancient Me had been, and I knew the best way to avoid that hideous future was to stay grounded.

Except I was a vampire. And a queen. And rich. And lived in a mansion. With millionaires. Grounded? Shit . . . not even when I was alive, sharing a duplex with Jessica and brown-bagging it so I could scoop up some Marc Jacobs Caprice sandals. I was always the ordinary one surrounded by interesting weirdos. It only got worse after I died. And despite their claims, I was *still* the ordinary one surrounded by interesting weirdos.

(Also, how sad is it that I could start talking about living with a cop and turn it around to not wanting to be evil? No matter what the topic—the economy, *30 Rock*'s final season, killing the devil, hiring minstrels—it always came back to me not wanting to grow up to be me.)

All that to say I liked living with the new and improved Nick/Dick Berry. He was something else I'd accidentally changed; he was my proof that I didn't have to become the bad guy. Plus, the benefits for me were super cool. Along with not turning evil and not writing the Book of the Dead on Sinclair's skin, Nick's personality change, in my arrogant opinion, was in the win column.

The old Nick: not a Betsy fan. Well, he was in the way that deer hunters are deer fans. Nick-Not-Dick had pulled a gun on me more than once, and not in a sexy role-playing way, either. But that was fair, because Sinclair and I had forced ourselves into his mind without much thought to

how he'd feel about it. He never got over it—why should
he have? We'd violated him; that's the whole thing right
there, there's no way to make it not awful: we raped his
brain to save ourselves.

Ah! But in the new timeline we hadn't done that. My
blundering through the past led to me chomping on the
Antichrist instead of him. And Laura was already fucked
up (see above: Antichrist). So Dick-Not-Nick never had any
vampire-related trauma to work through; he thought we were
all swell. He liked living in Vamp Central. He loved that he
was going to be a dad. He got off on life: he liked the controlled insanity of his day job and the uncontrolled insanity
of life at the mansion.

Case in point: he'd just gotten home from being on shift,
a day of seeing the worst people can do to each other, and
instead of heading for the kitchen to sneak some of Tina's
vodka or for his room to go fetal for half an hour or to take
a hot shower to scald away man's ickiness to man, I could
hear him bounding up the steps to the third floor, where
I was once again trying to figure out which dreadful velvet
clogs to donate and which to burn. And which to (ugh!)
keep.

"Hey! Is my favorite vampire queen in there?" A polite
rap-rap at my bedroom door. "One preferably not having
sex with my favorite vampire king? What am I saying; of

course you're not exercising your marital privileges all over each other. I can't hear a bed breaking or a window shattering."

I rolled my eyes. Break two beds in the same week and people make all sorts of assumptions about your bedroom antics. "Will you come in already?"

"Which brings me back to my first question," he shouted cheerfully through the door. "Is there a vampire queen in there? I just need to talk to someone in charge. But I guess you'll do. Ha!"

"Blow me," I called back, which he knew was Betsy-ish for *Come right in, dear friend.* "And I'm getting more in charge every week. Probably."

"And again I say ha." He grinned at me from the doorway. He was wearing his usual off-to-fight-crime ensemble: tan dress shirt, dark gray slacks, matching jacket, and special-order cop shoes—they looked spiffy, but he could run in them. Except for the shoes it was all off-the-rack, but he was exactly my height (six feet even) and lanky like a swimmer, so he could wear just about anything and look good.

Dick-Not-Nick was not a label whore, but with those shoulders, he didn't have to be. He could throw a gunnysack over his shoulders like a cape and I'd be all, hmm, that looks pretty good, maybe I'll get a gunnysack for Sinclair.

"Ye gods, Betsy." He looked around the room at the dozens of shoe boxes, the closet door yawning open and me sitting in the middle of the floor taking notes and pics with my camera, looking not unlike something my closet had spit up. "Are you still bemoaning the whole clog thing?"

"*Velvet* clogs." I sulked. "And yes. Bemoaning? Really? That's how you think people talk in real life?" But just seeing him was cheering me up. I'd changed the timeline so recently, it was still a huge lift to be in a room with my best friend's lover and know he wasn't terrified of me. I liked Dick-Not-Nick for himself but I wouldn't lie. I also liked him for what he symbolized: I occasionally got it right, and not all accidents are bad.

Knowing the new Not-Nick liked me just fine would have been satisfying enough (I'm vain, but at least I own it). But he *loved* Jessica and he was excited about their baby. Sometimes too excited, because the baby was forcing their relationship to evolve; Not-Nick was feeling the pressure to change lives, and not just his own.

For the better, we all thought. Unfortunately, Jess disagreed. And that, I suspected, was why he'd really come to find me in my room at a time he knew Jess would probably be napping/digesting, Tina would be in her office crunching numbers or talking to a mermaid (yeah, mermaids—they existed, and who knew? I left all that to Tina, having enough vampires on my plate o' drama without adding a side of mermaids), Marc would be engrossed in Web Sudoko, and Sinclair would be scampering about the countryside with Fur and Burr.

No-Longer-Nick was looking over the stacks of shoes I had all over the room. "How come you don't do this stuff?" he asked, moving a few shoe boxes off my fainting couch and sitting down.

"Sorry, what? And be ready to move in an instant if I feel faint. You know that thing is supposed to be used mostly for fainting. I was gonna put up a sign, 'For Emergency Swoons Only,' but Sinclair wouldn't let me, that tightass." I'd had to buy the stupid Bordeaux couch because that was literally what it was: a fainting couch. Back in the day, it was something for the lady of the house to swoon onto, usually upholstered in dark velvet, with a raised back on one end, and the whole thing supported by gorgeous dark wood.

Not that I swooned, but I blacked out now and again, usually when I was about to get killed again, or just after I'd been killed again. And if I ever almost got killed in my bedroom again, I had a lavender couch to swoon onto. Progress, baby. The Boy Scouts had nothing on me, bless their little homophobic hearts. "Half an instant."

"Yeah, sure. You love this stuff so much," Nick-No-More said, gesturing to the many shoe boxes. "Which is strange to me and always has been. They're shoes, for God's sake.

You stick 'em on your feet and out you go. You come back, you take them off, you're done. That's it. That's all it is."

I smiled at him. Not to go all "you're just a guy you don't get it" on the guy, but he was just a guy and he didn't get it. "That's not all it is. Not even close. As a species we've been stomping around in footgear for close to ten thousand years. We had to; the foot's got more bones in it than any other body part. We had to think up ways to protect all those teeny tiny bones, and if today shoes are more about status than need, back then it was one of the ways we tried not to get killed in our prime—so, when we were fourteen or fifteen. Man, it must have sucked to be considered elderly when you still had acne and had barely started to grow boobs."

"Um . . . I think you're getting off course."

"Shows what you know. Listen: the hunters with foot coverings could hunt longer and better, so those families ate better so they lived to make babies and the babies were better fed because they had good hunters, right? The circle of life, blah-blah, but what it means is that shoes are about us evolving through design, *not* heredity. Isn't that fascinating?"

"Um . . ." His eyes tipped up; I figured he was trying to think of a nice way to answer before giving it up: "Nope."

"You're just—"

"—a guy and I don't get it, but what about the guys who design the shoes?"

"I didn't say *all* guys don't get it. Just *a* guy. My friend's guy." I smiled to ease the sting. I didn't care for being marginalized, even by friends; I should try harder not to do unto others what pissed me off when it was done unto me.

"Okay, that's—" He shook his head as if trying to clear a mosquito whining in his ear. I often had that effect on people, and it was wrong that I took pride in that. "Never mind. And when I said the guys who design them, I mean, why can't you?"

Why did the me from the other timeline ever think I needed four pairs of purple velvet clogs? "Why can't I what?" *Velvet's flammable, right?* "Besides make sense of this madness."

"No. Design them yourself."

I stared at him.

"Right?"

I stared more.

"Are you okay?" He leaned toward me and waved a hand in front of my face. "Are you in there still? Helloooo?"

I waved his hand away. "Quit. And I'm not like them. I'm not an artistic genius whose creative outlet would vastly benefit all mankind."

"Okay, um, first I think you've maybe got shoe designers up on a pedestal."

"Do not. They *are* artists, some of the finest in the history of human events."

"My point. And second, why not give it a try? I don't

know anyone who knows more about this stuff than you do. Shit, you reeled off the bio of that guy you accidentally made not exist, that Chris what's-his-name."

"Christian Louboutin." I could barely force my facial muscles, lips, and tongue to form the magic syllables. Gone, all gone, all his glorious works gone and worse than gone: never existed. Never will exist. Because of stupid, stupid me.

"Right, that guy. Have you considered trying to fill his shoes? So to speak?"

"Never," I replied, shocked. "Not once. I couldn't ever do it and it'd be awful to try. It'd be lying, I think, to try."

"Or a tribute to his work! Like cover bands who play Nirvana."

I shook my head again. "No." On several levels. Nirvana, ugh. "My role, it's totally different. I buy them and wear them. I don't make them. Or help them get made. That's not for someone like me, oh *hell* no. I can't."

"Okay, maybe." He seemed taken aback at my vehemence. I told myself to dial it down. Hmm, *oh* hell *no . . . dial it down . . .* next I'd be saying things were "off the chain," because, surprise! We were back in 2010. "But you've never even tried, right?"

I just looked at him. Of course I'd never tried. Penguins don't try to do physics, marmosets don't try to tap-dance, and I don't try to design shoes. The world was enough of a madhouse.

MaryJanice Davidson

"So maybe you should! Try, I mean." He sat back, his blue eyes almost twinkling with confidence. In himself as a persuader or in me as a designer, I didn't know. His dimples—did Other Nick even *have* dimples?—appeared; he was nearly shaking with "you can do it" vibes. "Look, just think about it, okay? I bet you could do it. If nothing else you know exactly what you like and exactly what you hate. You know the styles you like and the colors and the materials."

"I know what kinds of cars I like, too, but I've got no plans to swing by Ford and drop off my résumé."

"Still." He leaned forward, resting his forearms on his knees. "But that's not why I wanted to talk to you."

"Nuts." I went back to sorting. "What's up, No-Longer-Nick?"

He groaned. "Come *on*. Stop it. Dick, okay, just Dick. I'm just Dick. When you see me, just remind yourself it's all about Dick. *No*." He jabbed a finger in my direction before I could get a snicker going. "Bad vampire queen! Keep your eensy brain out of the gutter."

I won't deny it: I did have an eensy brain, and I got off on messing with I'm-Not-Nick on the subject of his new-except-not-really name. Partly because I'm an immature asshat, but also I think I was testing him a little. Because nothing says friendship like immature mind games.

Like I said, in this timeline we were pals; I was curious

to see how far that went. It probably wasn't anything that would have occurred to me to do before I died, which would make me sad if I dared spend longer than two seconds thinking about. So natch, I didn't. There were lots of other sad things I could think about.

The short version: the old timeline Detective Berry went by Nick; this one went by Dick. I disliked change, even when it was for my benefit. Thus the name flogging. My inner asshat must be fed. Constantly.

"Fine, fine. Dick-Not-Nick, why'd you come into my room and dare me to design shoes?"

"Because I came into your room to get your advice on getting Jess to marry me."

Ah. That was something else that might be fun to chat about, but would never happen in real life. Jess loved Nick-No-Longer Dick more than she'd ever loved anyone, I was almost positive. So she'd never marry him. And not even the queen of the vampires could change that, any more than I could change a Louboutin-less world.

Poor bastard.

CHAPTER
SIX

(It's wrong that I was flattered he'd come to me with this. And I knew that. And yet I was taking a couple of seconds to bask in my pride in the wrongness. And now, to business.)

"Prob'ly you should be talking to Jessica about this," I tried, knowing it was lame and that it wouldn't work. I was suddenly super interested in the moss green velvet clogs I'd mentally assigned to Goodwill.

"Prob'ly that hasn't done any good and you damn well know it."

"Prob'ly that sounds about right." My! These hideous green shoes certainly were fascinating. "Uh, you know it's not personal, right?"

Nick-No-More threw up his hands, accidentally tumbling

two shoe boxes off my fainting couch. "Right. Of course. Because her refusal to marry me isn't at all personal."

"Well." I crawled over to the tipped boxes, righted them, then crawled back to my corner. "It isn't."

Like a lot of us, Jessica spent her adolescence observing marriage: her parents', and her best friend's parents'. To say she came away unimpressed is like saying I disliked buying pumps at Payless. Because I really, really dislike it. And the marriages she was ringside for were awful.

I tried a new one: "It's not you, it's her?"

He was rubbing the bridge of his nose the way my mom and my husband did when I was accidentally driving them to a migraine. "I know you're trying to help . . ."

"Oh, I am!" Sorta. I could bend a sympathetic ear, if that was the phrase. I could commiserate. I could get Jessica alone (ambush her on the way to the kitchen, maybe?) and talk Nick-Now-Dick up. He's a great guy, he'd be a good dad, you know he doesn't love you for your money, I didn't rape him in this timeline so his thoughts and impulses are his own, oh my God are you really having another spaghetti squash it's four a.m. for Christ's sake. It was all true and it wouldn't make any difference. Jessica wouldn't marry Call-Me-Dick-Dammit *because* she loved him, not because she didn't.

"I've been thinking about this for a while, and I think I've got a way that you can actually help me."

I glanced up, startled. I'd planned on more *There, there, girls are stupid, you didn't really want to get married anyway, right?*—not an actual plan. "Yeah? Great! Shoot. Uh, not literally."

"Talk her into it."

I blinked. (Which was weird. Like gasping and sighing, I don't think I had to blink. I didn't have to pee, or menstruate, or sweat. Was I blinking out of force of habit? Note to self: ask Marc.) "Yeah, I sorta have been. She's not going for it."

"No, I mean *talk* her *into* it. Just . . . you know." He wiggled his fingers at me. "Use your vampire thing and make her want to marry me."

For a few seconds I didn't know what to say. So I just sat there in the middle of a litter of shoes, staring at him and blinking on purpose, because I was pretty sure I didn't have to blink as a biological function. There was a tangle of responses in my brain.

1) You pig! That's a terrible idea, dumb shit. What the hell is wrong with you? Bad enough to think it, but then cough it up out loud? Are you really asking your girlfriend's best friend to rape her brain until she marries you? Have you lost your fucking mind? Huh? Have you?

2) Y'know, you don't remember this, but you *hated* me in the old timeline for using my "vampire thing" on you. So the irony here . . . it's so huge.

3) You pig! That's a terrible idea, dumb shit. What the hell is wrong with you? Bad enough to think it, but then cough it up out loud? Are you really asking your girlfriend's best friend to rape her brain until she marries you? Have you lost your fucking mind? Huh? Have you?

"I'm not going to do that" is what I settled on. He shivered and I wasn't surprised; I could almost feel the temp in the room drop as I spoke.

He was nodding before I'd gotten *going* out of my mouth. "Yeah, stupid idea."

"Really stupid."

"Awful."

"So, so stupid."

"Don't know what I was thinking."

"I don't think you *were* thinking. And we're gonna pretend you weren't thinking it. And that you didn't think it and then talk to me about doing it."

"Doing what?"

I pointed at him and smiled. "Exactly." Time to ease up. I couldn't take the good of the changed timeline, like Dick-Not-Nick liking me and wanting to live with us, and then blast him because even though he didn't remember the bad, I sure did. "Look, I'll talk to her again, but in—" My phone did the Stewie ringtone from *Family Guy* ("Mom. Mom. Mom. Mommy. Mommy. Mommy. Mama! Mama! Mama! Ma! Ma! Ma! Ma! Mum! Mum! Mum! Mum!

Mummy! Mummy!") and I shoved a shoe box aside and picked it up. Nick had waved and was already heading out the door so I answered. "Hi, Mom. What's up?"

"Your husband," she breathed. "He's here! And it's daytime!"

"Yeah, uh, I need to bring you up to speed again." To her credit, my mom didn't sound terrified. But then, she had no idea how deeply insane my husband now was.

My mother was clever and loving and open-minded beyond belief. She hadn't given a tin shit that I'd been turned into a vampire, she was just relieved she didn't have to see me dead and buried. And I tried to keep her in the loop, because one thing the TV and movie vampires do that drives me nuts (more than one, but there isn't time to go into all of it) is, they kept their loved ones in the dark to "protect" them. And it never works out for them. At all. Not even once. Not ever. Once I realized I was a vampire and likely to be one for centuries, I decided to keep loved ones in the loop. If bad things happened, it wasn't going to be because of some silly contrived Big Misunderstanding That Caused the Whole Disaster and Could Have Been So Easily Avoided, Oh Well.

Still, there was only so much of the "so anyway, I killed the devil and the Antichrist is sulking and also, Sinclair can bear the light now and that's pretty much all the news until the next disaster looms" story I could tell her. Open-minded was one thing, but I didn't want to terrify her. More, I mean.

"You did say so," she agreed. She was practically giggling into the phone. Mom was not a giggler. A chuckler, a guffawer (when the mood was right), a laugher, a chortler. No giggling. "But hearing it and seeing it . . . he brought your puppies over! To play with BabyJon!"

"They're not my puppies!"

"You should see them all playing in the yard. Clive's here, too, and they're just having the best time. It's so cute!"

"Okay, that's *it*. This has gone far enough." I was on my feet before I realized I'd moved. "I'm on my way, Mom. Just hold on until I get there."

"Why? What's the matter?"

"Stay alive, no matter what occurs. I will find you!" I hit End and shoved my feet into the nearest shoes.

Time for the madness to end.

CHAPTER
SEVEN

I made it from Summit to Cow Town in forty minutes. It was a twenty-mile drive, but as usual I had a raging thirst and required a Caribou Coffee mixer (half white chocolate hot chocolate, half milk chocolate hot chocolate, double whipped cream) to suck down so I wouldn't snap from the pressure to eat Mom's neighbor(s). So when I hopped out of my hybrid (yeah, I went green when I could, what are you doing for the environment?) SUV (it was a small one, a Ford Escape, so back off and, also, sometimes vampires needed to haul things) I was clutching my keys in one hand and my hot chocolate in the other.

Which was why I almost spilled scalding liquid all over myself, because my mom was right: Sinclair *had* brought

Fur and Burr over and they *were* playing with BabyJon and Mom's boyfriend, Cliiiiiive, *was* joining in the fun and it looked like a beer commercial, except with a baby and two puppies.

Gah.

My mom had seen me hurtle around the corner (any faster and I'd have been up on two wheels, like an undead cast member of *The Dukes of Hazzard*), so she'd gotten out of her lawn chair (lawn chairs, outside, in December: a tremendous idea if you're actively seeking frostbite) and came to meet me as I tromped down the icy sidewalk. She hugged me, which I half returned, juggling a bit so as not to spill hot milk down her back, then she whispered, "I never thought I'd say this about your forbidding husband, but he's adorable!"

I groaned.

"What?" She broke the hug and pulled back to look at me. "You don't like it?"

I made a rage-sigh-grumble noise.

"Well." Mom glanced at the vampire, the puppies, the toddler, and Clive Lively. "I know you're not a dog girl, but you must love seeing Eric so—so—" She groped for the word.

"Un-vampire-king-like?"

"Exactly. You and I could never know him in life, but

I think perhaps this is how he was. Oh." She squeezed my arms and gave me a "buck up, li'l buckeroo!" shake. "I admit it's not what you're used to, but I think it's lovely."

And you will, I thought but didn't say, *right up until something awful happens and we'll need a ruthless badass to fix it and he'll be at a Puppies 'n' Me class.*

"He should have called before barging—"

"He did, and it isn't barging. He's my son-in-law, probably the only one I'll ever have—"

I raised my eyebrows. "Probably?"

"—and he's family." A light breeze kicked up, ruffling my mom's silvery white curls. She was young—she'd gotten knocked up with me a month after high school—but she'd had white hair since her teens. She and I had occasionally been mistaken for sisters, which she loved and I loathed. Nothing against my cute mom, but hearing "Hey, you two, wanna help me with my sex sandwich?" was enough to put me off sandwiches for six months. The fact that my mom laughed so hard she would have stumbled into traffic if I hadn't grabbed her arm made it all the more surreal.

Here was another contradiction: my mom had little old lady hair and the smiling, unlined face of a moisturizer model, bright blue eyes, and a soft-spoken manner, and she'd had to kick plenty of men out of her way. She'd wrestled a PhD from academia stiffs while raising me almost on her own (even before my dad left her, he'd been a big fan of long business trips). She'd kept the acrimony out of her divorce for my sake as much as she could, while also refusing to go back to her maiden name. "It's mine," she'd sweetly explained to the judge. "Even if the man no longer is, the name still belongs to me and will always belong to me. I decline to return to my maiden name, sir."

Yep. She'd put it everywhere: Dr. Taylor; Professor Taylor; Ms. Elise Taylor, PhD. Business cards, personal and business correspondence, PowerPoint presentations, articles for *The Civil War Monitor*, lectures, journal articles: Dr. Elise Taylor. Due to the force of her will and my stepmother's cowardice when it came to face-to-face confrontation, most people referred to my father's second wife as exactly that: "Antonia Taylor . . . you know, the second Mrs. Taylor."

Heh.

(Yes, I could be a vindictive jerkass, but I came by it honestly. Also, the Ant had it coming. All of it. And plenty more that she didn't get. But that's a piss-and-moan session for another day.)

All that to say my mom was not one to be fucked with. So I chose my next words carefully (for me).

"I like seeing him happy, but it makes me nervous. I don't know why. It's not the dogs. I don't think it's the dogs."

"You're supposed to be the embarrassing partner in need of rescue," my mother pointed out with terrifying accuracy. "It's the king's job to be strong in the face of all calamity, to keep control, to be ruthless when the situation warrants. Not . . ." She pointed at the side yard, where Sinclair was lining up Fur and Burr for some sort of relay race involving rawhide bones for batons. "That."

I shook my head. "No, that's not it."

"No?"

"No, because that makes me the opposite of a feminist and also comes off as needy and insecure."

"Which is a problem because . . ."

"No one can know how needy and insecure I am."

"Ah." Her smile broadened and I laughed; I couldn't help it. "There, now." She leaned in and dropped a kiss to my cheek, smelling like fabric softener and Jergens. "There's my very own girl."

"Oh, hey! Betsy! Hi!"

Blech. Clive Lively was hailing me. This will sound awful but here it is: my two biggest regrets of the changed timeline were no more Christian Louboutin, and my mom had a boyfriend now. You know how the birds-and-bees talk with your parents can suck for every party involved? Try the "maybe you should dump him since the only reason you have a boyfriend is because I mucked with the timeline and hasn't enough damage been done?" talk.

"Hi, Mr. Lively."

"Please." He huffed a little as he jogged over to us. "It's Clive. Mr. Lively is my long-dead alcoholic father."

How could I forget? Cliiiiiive. I managed a chilly smile and faked a cough so I wouldn't have to shake his hand. Never think I wasn't aware of my gross pettiness. I was, but I was also aware I had no choice. He couldn't help being batshit nutball. Same with me.

"The lovely day lacked only your presence, my own." Sinclair had scooped up Burr and Fur before they could try to climb me. Clive had trotted over with BabyJon in tow, who smiled to see me, which showed his four teeth. (Baby-Jon's, not Clive's. Clive had a full set of choppers as far as I could tell.)

When you saw them together, it was a little hilarious since Clive looked like a giant baby. He had cut his wispy brown hair into a monk's fringe and had the soft body men in their fifties sometimes grow into. He was puffy, not fat, with pale, watery eyes and the kind of mouth that turned up even when he wasn't smiling. He looked as threatening as a row of lettuce. Which pissed me off, and I know that doesn't make sense. I dunno; I could count on one hand how many men Mom had dated since the divorce. She seemed to like Cliiiiiive more than the others put together. That also pissed me off, and I knew that also didn't make sense.

"It sure was nice meeting your husband," Cliiiiiive said, handing over BabyJon, who'd begun to reach for me. I took my brother/son/whatever and hugged him, and he honked my nose for my pains, shaking with baby giggles. "We've been having a fine old time."

A fine old time? Sinclair accurately read my mood, as he jumped in with, "Yes, your mother has been a wonderful hostess." He turned to her. "I must thank you again for not holding my unannounced visit against me."

Mom waved it away. "I would have been mad if I'd heard you were in the neighborhood and hadn't stopped by. We've worn out the baby so much he'll sleep for twenty hours."

Really? I eyed Cliiiiiive, who certainly looked well rested. Maybe he took a lot of naps. Oh—she meant the *little* baby. That was good, too.

"But I thought you couldn't get him until tomorrow," Mom continued.

"Yeah, but my schedule cleared up . . ." And my husband went insane. ". . . so I figured I'd surprise you." You and the giant baby you're dating. "And here I am." So like it or lump it, jerks.

BabyJon shrieked in my ear and kicked, his solid little pork-chop-with-toes feet swinging into my belly. Mom had him warmly dressed in a li'l turtleneck, li'l sweatpants, li'l coat, and li'l socks and shoes. His black hair was sticking up all over, looking like wind-mussed feathers, and that, plus his darting movements and cute caw-caw laugh made him look and sound like a crow in diapers. His eyes, a round perfect Gerber Baby blue, met mine and then crinkled as he crowed another giggle.

BabyJon was one of those insidious babies who trick childless couples into having kids. They'd be around him and notice his sunny mood, how he never turned down a bottle or three, and his deep sweet sleeps, and tell themselves, *how hard can it be?*

I had a soft spot for him; he was the only child I would ever have. Here's the pesky thing about biology: if you don't menstruate, you don't ovulate; if you don't ovulate, you don't get pregnant. I'd gone to my grave the first time thinking I had years to settle down, and accepting the fact that I would never be a natural mother was almost as hard as accepting there would be no more prime rib dinners for me, either.

"You sure can tell you're his mom," Cliiiiiive was yakking. "Look at the resemblance."

A) I'm not his mother. B) But I *am* an inarticulate fatty with messy hair who shits in my pants when I'm not drooling all over myself? (Actually that perfectly describes me at Homecoming my freshman year at the U . . . after that night I was never able to stand ginger ale, vermouth, and chocolate milk.)

"You have the exact same smile!"

Was I smiling? Revolted, I put my hand over my mouth even as I glowed a little at the compliment. Cliiiiiive was a clever bastard, defeating me with my own vanity. It was a huge weapon! Like, nuclear huge.

"And he sure likes you, huh?"

Why couldn't he be evil? It was actually pretty selfish of him to not be evil. "Oh, well . . ." I decided to smile and then remembered I was smiling. Oh, he was a clever prick! "We're sibs. I'm not his mom, except legally kind of." Long story. The recap is incomprehensible and weird: cursed engagement ring, garbage truck, double funeral, *viola*! It's a boy. But I didn't feel like telling Cliiiiive the whole story. It was none of his business, for one thing. Also, it was none of his business.

"Ah, my boy." Sinclair reached for his half-brother-in-law/ stepson, but BabyJon was having none of it. "Plehhh!" he said, or something like it.

Not at all put out, Sinclair extended his hand and Cliiiiiive shook it. "I have imposed on you long enough. I thank you again for your hospitality. And my apologies for the, er, deposits the puppies made for you."

Depos—? Oh. Gross.

"Have you heard from Laura?"

"Yeah!" My mood instantly brightened. "She came over to yell."

Mom closed one eye, thinking. "Singing telegram?"

"Balloon bouquet."

"Ah. A lucky thing I didn't bet on the outcome. I've seen her. She was here a couple of days ago."

"Laura comes here? To visit you?" Okay, that was a little odd, but it's not like I *owned* my mom or anything. (*My* mommy! Laura's got her own—oh. Right.) Now that I thought about it, it made sense. Laura had a soft spot for moms; she was always looking for one who wasn't pure evil (Satan) or generally inclined toward evil (the Ant). Still, Mom was . . . well . . . mine, dammit.

Oh, sure. Because this is the perfect time to get possessive about something so silly.

My inner voice was such a bitch sometimes.

Mom's next words were blowing my theory: "Not to see me. To see BabyJon." She took in the look on my face and added gently, "He's her brother, too, Betsy. And she—ah—she's not quite—"

"She doesn't want to see him if it means seeing me."

"That's right," she said simply. Not one to try for polish when straight truth suited all parties. "She doesn't."

"Fine, but then she should stay away from my mommy!" I heard myself and scrambled for damage control. "Because you're busy with your own stuff. Journal articles and baby-sitting and of course you've got Clive here, you've got a demanding social life. It's pretty selfish of her to barge in on that. Clive is your everything!"

"Good God," my mom snapped. Then, at once: "I'm sorry, Eric."

Not even my mom spraying him with verbal acid by saying "God" could put a damper on his day. "Not at all, Dr. Taylor. My Elizabeth does it with terrifying frequency."

"That's not the only thing I'll do to you with terrifying frequency," I mumbled to the frosted grass. At least Clive wasn't getting an earful. I don't know what story Mom told him (maybe that Sinclair was born again—wouldn't *that* be hilarious!), but he didn't blink. Okay, he did, but it wasn't a meaningful blink. He was just lubricating his eyeballs.

Mom was making her tsk-tsk face. "So when it suits your purpose you embrace Clive."

"'Embrace' might not be the right word." I eyed Cliiiiiive out of the corner of my eye and was surprised to see he was eyeing me, too. And: eww. "'Embrace' is definitely not the right word. But between Mr. Lively and

(his fervid sexual demands on my poor frail mother)

BabyJon, you're pretty busy. That's all I was trying to say."

"Sure it was. Speaking of babies, when are you throwing the baby shower?"

"Huh?" I'd always hated that phrase. It made me think it was actually showering babies.

"Jessica. She's due any day, right?"

"Oh, heck no." Just like my mom to start bugging me to plan stuff way ahead of time.

"She has several months to go," Sinclair agreed.

My mom's smile faded and she looked from me to Sinclair to me again. "You're kidding, right? Teasing me? She's got to be due any day—I was a little surprised you let it go this long."

"Due any—" I shook my head. "Mom, she's maybe six weeks along."

"Or twenty months," Sinclair added.

"Right." I shrugged. "Either way, nothing we need to worry about right this minute."

There was a long silence, broken by BabyJon's crowed, "Yaarrgg mehn ma!"

"All right," I told him. "We're going already." I tried to take a mental inventory of the nursery. Plenty of diapers, yep. Wipes, uh-huh. Jars of creamed crap, check. Huh. Even though I wasn't supposed to get him back until tomorrow, I could actually take him today. It was almost like I was a real mom and everything.

"Betsy—Eric—" My mom cut herself off and for a few seconds her mouth opened and closed to no avail. BabyJon, sensing her mood, put his arms out to her so quickly he nearly toppled out of my grip. She took him at once and he chuckled at her and grabbed a fistful of white curls. "I think you—I think there's something wrong."

"No, it's okay. There's plenty of diapers at the mansion." For the moment, BabyJon had forgotten all about me, engrossed as he was in trying to ease my mom's weird distress.

I wouldn't lie to myself: it hurt to see BabyJon so happy with her. But I'd eat my own tongue before saying anything. For one thing, I should be glad my li'l bro had someone in his life who loved him and cared for him. For another, the whole thing was my fault, anyway. If I wasn't always dumping him on Mom, he'd love me, too. This was my only real chance to be a mom . . . and I was blowing off the work.

To be fair, there was often a disaster du jour that demanded I drop everything and dart off into the night; vampire queens weren't built for maternal crises. And it had started as asking my mom for baby-sitting favors I knew she was reluctant to take on. BabyJon was a living symbol of the shipwreck that was her marriage. But she'd known there was nothing to be done about it unless we wanted to have a chat with Social Services. The mere thought would have given me night terrors if I still dreamed. *"Excuse me, but according to this paperwork you're dead. The State of Minnesota frowns on dead people for guardians. Also, your status as a corpse brings up a few other questions, so why don't you have a seat?"*

So it had started as an annoying chore, but BabyJon's pretty irresistible, and after a while she was offering to take him for a day here or an overnight there before I asked. Since I altered the timeline, she liked having BabyJon over for his own sweet self, not to do any favors. I wondered if she felt the way I did—that maybe this was her only chance to be a grandmother, however strange the circumstances, so she went from grudging to resigned to loving.

For the first time in a long time, I thought about my late father and wondered what he'd think about his son by his new wife being essentially raised by his ex.

His new wife. Brrrr. Now was not the time to think about the Ant, she of the pineapple hair (color *and* texture) and utter lack of class. And when someone like me is commenting on someone else's lack of class, that's how you know it's really, really bad.

I gave myself a brisk internal shake. "Listen, we'll get out of your hair. We've got to—"

"You know what?" My mom cut me off. "Could I keep him one more night, as planned? Then I'll drop him off tomorrow. I'd like to see Jessica for myse—I'd like to visit for a while. If that's convenient."

Not only that, but courageous.

I glanced at Sinclair; his thought had come through loud and clear. Once upon a time, I couldn't read minds. Then I could read Sinclair's, but only during sex. Then I could read him at other times. Then he could read mine. We chalked it up to being an undead monarch thing. We could nearly always hear each other if one or both of us was thinking really hard. But I'd caught that stray thought with no trouble; it was like a bubble had popped up out of nowhere. You're surprised it's there, but you know why it's there, so it's okay.

Considering that the last time she visited she was faced with Zombie Marc and Ancient Me, yeah, courageous is the word.

Aloud: "Sure, Mom; like I said, we didn't mean to mess with your plans or anything. And Jess would love to see you. And we could talk—" I looked at Cliiiiiive. "We can catch up."

So we agreed and said our good-byes and BabyJon was thrilled to be staying and hardly fussed when we left, and all the time my mom had this strange, distracted smile on her face, a smile that never climbed behind her eyes.

Well. Dating Cliiiiiive would probably distract me, too. The important thing was, I was there for her. And stood ready to beat him to death the minute he, I dunno, did something I didn't like.

Prob'ly wouldn't be long.

CHAPTER
EIGHT

"Listen," my mom said again. "Something is very wrong here. None of you seem to know when Jess got pregnant—"

"Gross," I commented. "Didn't ever want or need the details."

"None of their damned business!" Jess agreed, lightly spraying my mother with toast crumbs.

"—or when she's due—"

"Next summer, isn't it?" Marc asked vaguely. He was seated at one of the islands, flipping through the January 2007 ish of *Martha Stewart Living*. He frequently reread the "How to Keep a Sharp Mind" article. Was it ironic that he needed to *re*read an article about staying sharp? "Around the Fourth? Hmm, says here anagrams are a way to go."

"Is that like a word jumble?"

"No, it's like when you rearrange all the letters of a word to form new words. Like . . ." He glanced at my mom's coffee cup and his eyes went milky as he thought. ". . . caribou for cuba rio. Or . . . uh . . . permission. For . . . impression? Yeah, impression."

"Sounds hard." I had no gift for puzzles of any kind. No gift, and no love for doing them. If someone whipped out their new crossword puzzle app, I gave serious thought to faking a heart attack.

"Yeah." He smiled and circled the relevant paragraph. "It does. And—what were we talking about?"

"We were saying Jess is due at the end of the month."

"No, no," the lady herself said. "First day of spring. Or something."

"No, that doesn't sound right."

"Of course it doesn't," Sinclair said, filching a piece of toast from Jessica's plate and sneaking it to Fur and Burr. "Autumn."

"Or a New Year's baby." I drained the remnants of my smoothie. "It's . . . you know. Whenever."

"But it's sure nice of you to take an interest, Dr. Taylor," Not-Nick piped up. He'd slipped his toast to Jessica's plate, probably saving Sinclair's life in the process. "We registered at Cracker Barrel if you want to know what to get for the baby."

I gasped at his Freudian slip. "*Crate* and Barrel," I corrected. "Cracker Barrel's the restaurant." Did Crate and Barrel even have baby stuff? I thought it was all yuppie furniture and kitchen accessories. Translation: I'd never set foot in the place and never would. Shit, maybe she really did register at the restaurant.

We were gathered in the mansion's kitchen, our unofficial conference room. Come to think of it, maybe it was official. We sure had enough meetings there. Mom had brought BabyJon over as she'd threatened, and I'd told the others she wanted to come by and say hello and catch up on all our doings. ("Marc's a zombie but Ancient Me won't ever be back, Jessica's still pregnant, and No-Longer-Nick still doesn't hate me. We don't have a cat but Sinclair has two dumb dogs, and the Antichrist hasn't been around much. We're out of milk.")

My mom, embracer of all things bizarre (especially since her only child walked out of an embalming room after dying the first time), was so kind to Marc I almost couldn't watch. He'd been hanging back a bit, knowing he was different, knowing my mom knew he was different, but not knowing how my mom would react to the changes. I could have told him, but why spoil the surprise? Her reaction was the same as it was to my return from the grave: thank God, thank God, thank God.

"Now we won't worry about you so much," she told him, holding both of his hands in hers like he was a child instead of a grown man who towered over her. "Now you can take care of yourself and Betsy even better than before."

"I didn't do such a good job with either," he said with a rueful grin, but his face was lit with relief to be so easily accepted, and he paid close attention to everything my mom said. When she excused herself to use the bathroom, he started to follow her before he caught himself. I failed to hold back my snicker.

He tried to wither me with a faux glare, but even actual glares don't always work. Then he dropped the act and leaned down to whisper (which was dumb, since almost everyone in the house had superhearing), "She didn't even mind that I feel different! Like this." He held out his hands, cool and pale. "And . . ." He gestured to his long-sleeved T-shirt and jeans. He couldn't bear to wear scrubs anymore.

I grabbed his with my own clammy paws. "So you're permanently chilly now, and you dress better. Welcome to our horrible, horrible club. Four words, Marc, four words that will change your unlife: knee-high fuzzy socks. And also those little hand-warmer dealies the deer hunters use, the ones you keep in your pockets."

He nodded and actually wrote it down; he kept a cell phone on him nearly always and a small notebook and pen in one of his back pockets. One of the many ways he kept himself engaged.

"Write down 'the fuzzier the better—my manliness is

not as important as being warm so bring on the pink.' And then write down 'nothing I buy is too good for Betsy.'"

He snorted but didn't look up from his scribbling. "I'm sticking with 'little hand-warmer dealies.' You should have gone into advertising."

"And miss all this?" I said dryly, gesturing to the controlled chaos of the kitchen. Except there wasn't anything controlled about it. Jessica was turning toast into cinnamon toast and then eating it, turning it into fuel for her brand o' crazy; Not-Nick was showing her something on his cell (it must have been pretty cool, because he was also doing jazz hands); the puppies were frisking around everyone's ankles . . . for such a big kitchen, it didn't take many of us to fill it. "Say it ain't so!"

"You love it, so quit that. You love"—he gestured to the not-controlled chaos—"all of this stuff. At first you didn't, or pretended you didn't, but we all grew on you."

I nodded. "Like lichen. Icky, smelly lichen. Lichen found all over the world, in places you'd think lichen would never be able to flourish. The symbiotic lichen." At his raised eyebrows, I added, "Eighth grade science report. Isn't it strange, the stuff you can't ever get out of your head?"

"Fine, we're lichen. Point is—these days?—the 'oh, it's so awful here with all the weird people and weird stuff going on in our mansion of weird' is strictly pretending."

"Nuh-uh!" Blast! Was my cover blown?

"Yuh-huh! The roommates, being queen, being eternally hot and strong and rich, most people in your life liking having you around, the puppies, Sinclair's mood swing—"

"Mood *swing*? That's a mood hurricane."

Ever see a zombie roll his eyes? It's terrifying. "Jeez, Betsy, sometimes I think if you didn't have something to bitch about you'd leave town *looking* for something to bitch about."

Ack! My secret was out! "Tell no one," I threatened, my fingers sinking into his forearms. "Not unless you want me to blab the major spoiler in *A Storm of Swords*."

He yelped and pulled his arm free. "Just sayin'. You know you love this shit."

"Maybe 'love' is a little strong . . ." I was super glad he hadn't called my bluff. Have you seen any one of the *GoT* books? Doorstops. Who has the time? Besides, HBO was doing a pretty good job. More giant books should be made into TV shows and movies. Big time-saver.

"It's not," Marc retorted, then went back to his magazine article.

I looked around the restaurant-sized kitchen. Butcher blocks everywhere, dozens of cabinets, multiple fridges and freezers, multiple blenders (we were all hard-core smoothie addicts), multiple drawers, multiple pantries. Every gadget you could think of. Any dish you wanted to make you could whip up right there. It was always warm and bright here;

we always felt safe. Well. Safe-ish. "Yeah, well. Keep it to yourself, will ya?"

He gave me a look I translated as *You're not fooling any of us*, but since it wasn't out loud I could let it go and keep my pride. Because that's what it's all about! Me keeping my pride in the face of everything, all the time.

Ugh, did I really just think that?

CHAPTER
NINE

Before I could wallow further in the black hole of my vanity and pride, Mom and Tina came into the kitchen. They would have collided but Tina saw it coming and courteously stepped back. Mom, I was sure, had no idea Tina was anywhere near. Certainly not right behind her, as in *Look out! The vampire is right behind you! Also, the call is coming from inside the house!*

"All right." She took a breath, like she was bracing herself to tackle something tricky. Were we out of toilet paper in one of the guest bathrooms? "I want to try to talk to all of you about this again." She'd shoved open the swinging door (I awaited the day somebody would get smacked with it—swinging kitchen doors always led to smacking hilarity according to every TV show about swinging kitchen doors ever made), then came forward enough for it to swing shut behind her. It didn't, though; Tina had caught it and held it, waiting for my mother to notice and step further in.

"I knew something was wrong yesterday. And now that I've talked to Jessica and Marc—and you, too, dear—" Dick-Not-Nick beamed, always happy to be included. A smoothie vote, faithful "forward this to everyone you love so they know how much you love them!" FB follower, the occasional bar brawl: this timeline's version of Nick was a joiner. "—and I think, yes, I think you may be in real trouble. Something is very—yeek!"

Mom's sluggish senses had finally tipped her to Tina's presence. Not for the first time I thought it was amazing and a little scary how quickly you got used to superkeen senses. I'd heard Tina while she was still upstairs. Heck, I practically heard her before she got up that night. At any point up to her arrival in the kitchen I could have told you exactly what part of the house she was in. I knew she was almost out of fabric softener and had switched shampoos. I knew she hadn't cracked open one of her treasured flavored vodkas today, and that she'd spent some time in the attic, likely chatting with Marc (she'd gotten protective after he came back a zombie).

Not bad, right? Then there's this: I knew those things without thinking about them. Without trying to listen, without walking over to her and sniffing her, without keeping an eye out for her. I just knew them. Just like I could shut all that stuff out if I wanted. I tried to think of a non-vamp parallel and the best I could come up with was when you're in an airport headed to your gate, there are dozens, maybe hundreds, of people around you all the time. They're all having conversations and eating and working and using bathrooms and you know all that's going on, the stream of life just flows all over and past you and maybe even through you, but you don't have to pay attention to any of it. You just know it's all happening. And if you're looking for something specific, you can filter through the stream and come up with just what you want.

That was the best I could do and as analogies went, it sucked. Still, I wondered—

"Good God, Tina, you scared the hell out of me!" Followed immediately by, "Oh, I'm so sorry!"

Tina, who'd flinched at "God," managed a smile. "Quite all right, Dr. Taylor."

"Yes, the other Taylor girl breaks the third commandment several times daily," Sinclair teased. He was dressed casually: a Joseph Abboud suit in gray wool he'd had for years, my husband's version of blue jeans and a sweatshirt. He'd been sneaking toast to the puppies, who, now bulging with toast, had abruptly decided, as babies do, that they were going to nap *right now.* Clunk. Snore. "Yet we soldier on."

"I thought the third one was to not have other gods

before the big guy," Marc said, at once interested in a new puzzle. "Right?"

"No, that's the first one. A lot of people think it's the most important, but I think it's just the most important to the big guy." Hearing *God* out loud was like ground glass in their ears, to vampires. Don't get me started on what Christmas carols did. This whole month Tina likely wouldn't go near a retail store of any kind. Thus our *big guy* euphemism. "Put me down for number six. I think the 'thou shalt not murder' is the most important." I caught some of their stares. "What? Sunday school. I occasionally remember something useful. Sometimes more than once a day!"

Sinclair was leaning toward my mom, his body language radiating "solicitous." "Are you all right, Dr. Taylor? You seem distressed."

"Distressed! Yes!" Mom ran her fingers through her curls and made fists, then winced and let go of her hair. "I've been trying to tell all of you that something's wrong with Jessica's baby, and all you want to do is talk about Laura and—"

"Speaking of Ms. Goodman," Tina said, waving her phone at me, "she called."

No, she was waving *my* phone at me. Now where did I leave it that Tina could—oh. I dared not look at Sinclair. It was possible that when we'd come home the night before, BabyJon-less, we had badly wanted some fun. So much fun that we couldn't wait to get started with the fun, and our bedroom was too far away for instant fun, so we'd ducked into the first unoccupied room for our fun, which was Tina's office.

This part would not be fun.

"Yes. Well. Here it is, Majesty." She handed it over. I took it silently. Still didn't dare a peek at Sinclair. "In your, ah, anxiety, you must have dropped it."

"Don't feel bad." Marc gave her a comforting pat on the shoulder. "They've left things where I've stumbled across them, too. Terrible things."

"I would not have minded so much if they had let me leave before starting."

"Wait, you were still in the room?" Huh. Strange how our keen vamp senses hadn't picked up on that. Horniness apparently correlated with dulling senses. Or Tina turning invisible?

Sinclair lost it and started to laugh, which got me going, too. Tina just stood there, emanating Disapproving Elder, which didn't work. I knew she was old and brilliant, but today she looked too much like a cheerleader for me to be cowed. *"Give me a Q! Give me a U! Give me an I! Give me a T! Quit banging in my office, yeeeaaah!"* Cue waving pompoms and her hair in pigtails.

"As I was saying," she said, raking us once more with a glare and then giving up like a sensible brilliant vamp,

"Laura called you. I saw her name come up and snatched it; I pray you will pardon my familiarity with your equipment, and with the Antichrist."

"Sure, sure, no prob." I waved all that away. I wasn't sure if I was thrilled or terrified that she'd called so soon after visiting. "What'd she say?"

"That she is free to join you for Thanksgiving, if you can do it tomorrow. December fifth," she added, in case none of us knew what *tomorrow* meant.

I was so startled I almost dropped my phone. "Wha—? But that's so great!" I turned to the gang, delighted. "Isn't that so great?"

"What's so great about having to buy another turkey at the last—hmm. Turkey. And stuffing and mashed potatoes and cranb—I'll help you shop." Jessica was looking sadly at her (now) empty plate. "Let's go right now."

"Hell yes right now!" I was halfway to the door. "I can't believe it! I thought she'd hold out for weeks!"

"Betsy, please." Mom had stepped in front of me, her hands up, palms out, like she was being arrested. "We haven't settled—"

"Mom, I know, and I promise we'll go over whatever it is later, but I've got to head to the grocery store. C'mon, Jess, I'll drive. We can stop at Dairy Queen on the way." Jess loved eating ice cream (or whatever Dairy Queen claimed that stuff was) when it was cold. She liked her insides to match her outside. "Okay, so." I gave Mom a quick kiss. "We'll talk later, I promise."

"But—"

"Dr. Taylor, as long as you're here, I have been in touch with an old friend. She has agreed to allow me to show you original letters to Clara Barton for the Friends of the Missing Men of the United States Army."

Mom, still pissy about whatever was bugging her, whipped her head around to look at Tina so fast I heard tendons creak. "What? No. What?"

Tina, who could be pretty literal, began again: "I have been in touch with an old friend. She has agreed to show—"

"That's so kind, Tina, but I've seen them. The archives—"

Tina smiled her "I look like a cheerleader but I've been to the rodeo a few times" smile. "No one has seen these except Miss Barton and my friend, who found her brother on her own and thus had no need of Miss Barton's services." (Tina never said *Ms.* She was old-fashioned.) "My friend took her letter back along with a few other things you may find of interest."

Whoa.

"Whoa." My mom disappeared in a puff of Civil War gunpowder and Dr. Taylor took her place. Long before she made her living teaching the Civil War, Mom put the *buff* in *Civil War buff.* For her sixteenth birthday my grandpa gave her some Civil War canister shot, which looked exactly like big dirty rocks, and she cried. Not for the reason I would have cried; apparently certified authentic dirty rocks are a sweet gift. So natch, Tina had been almost a literal gold mine of info. Sometimes I had the idea Mom wanted BabyJon *and* Tina in her house all the time.

Too bad! They're mine! But hey, Mom was distracted and thus off my back, so all was well. Also: they're mine!

On that possessive note, we left.

CHAPTER
TEN

"Dammit! I can't remember if the Antichrist likes terrible cranberry sauce or real cranberry sauce."

"We went through this last time we shopped," Jess reminded me.

And wouldn't need to shop again, or go through this again, if you didn't devour . . . steady, steady. Creating life, she's creating life. Or something.

I gulped down the sarcasm and forced a smile. "I just don't want to get off on the wrong foot when we're close to reconciling." Say it twice. I'd almost dreaded opening my eyes this afternoon, unsure if the new day would bring reconciliation or horror, or reconciled horror.

"Good point," Marc agreed, looking up from Foster's *With Friends Like These.* "Killing her mom . . . that was a huge faux pas. You definitely don't want to make things worse by feeding her canned cranberries. There's only so much a person can take."

"Exactly." I held a sack of cranberries in one hand and a can in the other. We were in the kitchen again, starting to prep the big family meal while fighting the vague feeling we should have gotten started hours earlier.

But it wasn't my fault. This one thing, at least, probably wasn't my fault maybe. What with sipping supper with my husband (okay, *from* my husband), dropping off over a dozen pairs of shoes at the Fairview Avenue Goodwill branch, faking admiration for the wallpaper swatches Jess had picked out for the nursery (*that* afternoon), faking admiration for the way Fur and Burr would scamper outside to poop after eating (Sinclair swore this was a trick he and he alone had taught them), faking interest while Marc explained all the reasons why Daenerys was the queen foretold to usurp Cersei (if HBO hadn't shown it, I didn't want to hear about it), and returning Fred the mermaid's bitchy e-mail #7 (long story), the afternoon had vanished. Along with the morning and the previous week and, also, the previous month and two years. Why did my life speed up after I died?

"Enough mistakes have been made," I decided, still weighing the bag against the can. "Even though killing Satan wasn't a mistake."

"That's probably something you want to keep to yourself," Jess suggested while Marc nodded in agreement so hard I thought he was going to topple out of his chair.

"Duh, and thanks. But that still leaves the question: terrible cranberries or real ones?"

I wasn't so dim I couldn't see fretting over the meal was a little hilarious; most of us wouldn't be able to eat any of it. Not without the help of Mr. Food Processor. Still, Jess was eating for nineteen, Not-Nick always had thirds, Marc liked to smell the food, Laura ate like a twenty-year-old who didn't have to cut calories or work out to look hot and assumed it would always be that way, my mom would take a bunch of the bird home for sandwiches to bring to the U, and Fur and Burr would stand ready to snarf down scraps. I didn't foresee a lot of leftovers cluttering up the mansion fridge(s).

Jess glanced at the horrible clock (it was one of those creepy ones with a black cat whose eyeballs clicked back and forth, and it had followed us from my dorm room to our duplex to the mansion). "What time's dinner?"

I shrugged. Ina Garten I was not. In life my most valued kitchen tool had been the microwave, my mom still cooked like I was living at home and often dropped off leftovers, and if I had extra money I put it in the shoe fund, never toward the food budget. In undeath I couldn't keep solid food down; I was doomed to centuries (at least!) of smoothies and blood. There'd never been much point in learning to cook.

But I wasn't the only one who lived here, and I'd tried to take advantage of that. When I'd explained to Marc that, as our resident gay zombie, he should sort of just know things about entertaining and cooking and such, I got a lot of backtalk about how stereotypes aren't just hurtful, they're lazy. Then he threw his *Gray's Anatomy* at me, which is how I discovered how heavy the unabridged version is. Then I halfheartedly apologized (he could have broken my nose, so it was like I was a victim, too). Then *The Physiology Coloring Book*, which was much lighter, followed *Gray's Anatomy.* He was out of books but within clutching distance of a one-hundred-count box of markers, so I upgraded my apology. Then I changed the subject. Lesson learned.

"I've never done this before," I said, hoping for a few brownie points from the zombie who had unerring aim, "but the important thing is we are going to do it together and not hide behind hurtful stereotypes while wrongly expecting one person to do all the—"

"It's already past four," Jess pointed out, as if I'd lost my ability to tell time along with my ability to have any sort of control over anything in my life. "Turkey'll take at least three hours. It has to be cooked all the way, Betsy; I can't eat undercooked poultry—that might hurt the baby whose due date I never remember."

"That's okay," I soothed. "If it comes out not cooked enough, I'm a creative genius with the microwave."

"That's true!" Jess brightened. She was super pretty anyway, but when she beamed like that she could be on magazine covers. "You found so many things to blow up. It was incredible; I've—*still!*—never seen anything like it."

"Oh, Christ," Marc muttered to his book.

"I got the idea when we bought all those Peeps for half off—remember? It was just before I started my last SDJ (Stupid Day Job), and we were gonna throw that Peep-themed party but had to cancel to hit the sample sale. Soooo many Peeps. So many ways to destroy them. Before I died it was the closest I'd been to being a Bond villain: *"No, Mr. Peep, I want you to* die." I'd sort of impressed myself; at the time I had no idea an evil genius sometimes skulked under my lowlights.

Marc was shaking his head and refusing to look up from Foster.

"Anyway, I'll zap any turkey you think is underdone, just to be safe. And if it takes a long time to cook, that's not so bad. It'll give Laura and me more time to talk. That's all we need, you know—clear communication. I can explain some stuff and she can vent and then we'll gorge on tryptophan and sink into food comas. And God bless us," I added, waving the can like a crutch, "every one!"

"You won't, though." Marc finally dragged himself away

from *With Friends Like These.* "It's a myth. There's trypto-phan in all poultry, not just turkey, and really not much more than what's in lots of other meat. People get tired because of all the carbs they wolf down *with* the turkey, and the legend spreads. Isn't that great?"

Not especially, but I nodded. Oh—he probably meant it was great that he'd remembered that. And it was. "Keep the useless food trivia coming, big guy, some of it might come in handy. Meanwhile, I'll add all the turkey I want to my T-day smoothie. Which reminds me, where *is* the food processor? I'm not gonna drink this dinner alone."

"It broke when Sinclair was grinding up—"

"Please don't finish." Probably a handful of diamonds he would sprinkle into Fur and Burr's coats to make them shiny *and* durable. Nothing was too good for those two fluffballs.

"And your mom's on her way." Jess plunked into one of the director's chairs Tina had ordered. That had come about after Jessica hopped up on one of the bar stools only to lose her balance and take out almost the entire group as she plunged, shrieking, to the floor. She was the bowling ball; we'd nearly been the pins. After that, the bar stools went bye-bye, replaced by comfy red director's chairs (Jessica had declined the offer of a seat belt attachment for hers). "Did you leave your cell in your room again? Anyway, she called mine and started to bug me about whatever the hell's been up her butt lately—I was making monkey tails so I wasn't paying much attention."

"Do I even want to—"

"Chocolate-covered frozen bananas," I told him. Delish! I enjoyed them in life and death. Reminder: buy another food processor. And possibly more blenders.

"I've got to admit, I was surprised. That's not like your mom. In fact it's one of the reasons I love your mom: if something's up her butt, she doesn't let the entire world hear about it ad nauseam. She works through her shit and doesn't drag anybody else into it."

"Betsy, I had no idea you were adopted," Marc said in feigned (I think) astonishment.

"Blow me," was all I had for a witty rejoinder. "You're right, though. Something's been on her mind lately."

"Maybe she and Clive are getting—"

"If you finish that sentence I'll buy your kid a drum set for his fifth birthday. And his sixth. And . . . you get it, right?"

Jess obeyed but, to prove she was uncowed, didn't stifle the snicker. That was fine; one battle at a time. "Okay, well, once we get the Antichrist cooled out, maybe I can sit down with Mom or take her out for supper or something, let her get whatever it is off her chest. I can't imagine what—" I'd dropped the can and bag o' berries on the island, then turned and opened the fridge and was reaching for the turkey when I realized what it was. "Ohmigod. Oh, you guys. We are dead. This is a fresh turkey."

"We had *that* talk last time we were planning Thanksgiving, too." Jessica let out a long-suffering sigh. "How can you concentrate when you've got déjà vu all the time?"

"This is a fresh, organic, heritage turkey." Words could not express the horror. I yanked the thing off the shelf and turned to Jess, clutching it like it was the One Ring made of turkey (and tryptophan, but not enough to make anyone sleepy).

"So? What's the—"

"This thing . . ." I shook the turkey at her. "It was alive, alive! What, two days ago? At most? You ordered it fresh! Or they had one in whatever Rich Girl Supermarket you decided to shop at. This is a Royal Red or a Midget Palm or something." At Marc's blank look I almost screamed, "This was never a Butterball turkey genetically manipulated and raised in squalor then abused and killed and then trapped in a grocery store freezer for weeks on end! And somehow *my mom found out*!"

For a moment Jessica sat, frozen, and I figured I'd have to refresh her memory on a few facts of life regarding Dr. Elise Taylor. But I'd mistaken her immobility for incomprehension instead of dawning terror. She slid off the chair and was on her way out the door in one smooth movement that I admired even as I cursed her for leaving me alone to face Mom's wrath.

"What?" Marc was looking around, probably expecting an assassination attempt. "What's wrong? What's your mom going to do? Wait, is that an adrenaline surge?" He paused and got the strangest look on his face, like he was listening for something inside himself. "It is! Woo-hoo!"

I listened, too, because I knew time was running out and, yep, there was a car pulling in. Since it wasn't being driven with the care of an eighty-year-old woman plagued with vertigo, that ruled Laura out. It could only be my mom, BabyJon (she'd insisted on taking him back to her house *again* last night), and (may God help us in our darkest hour) Cliiiiiive.

"Flee," I advised my friend, who looked equal parts startled, intrigued, and frightened. "Save yourself."

"I don't under—"

"No, really. Get the fuck out of here." Marc read my face, then bolted to his feet and did the zombie shuffle right the hell out.

Sadly, I knew I must face the horror alone. And in socks, no less—there wasn't time to grab a pair of power heels. It was difficult to feign indifferent cool in my sock monkey socks, but I'd have to manage.

CHAPTER ELEVEN

Tina showed my mom in, then went off to do something Tina-ish. I gave serious thought to ditching the turkey and pretending that the plan all along had been to make pumpkin pie smoothies as the main dish—what turkey? what expensive yuppified organic turkey?—but that was chickenshit, and I figured it'd be better to stand my ground, tell the truth, and accept the horrific nightmare guaranteed to follow.

Besides, how do you ditch a seventeen-pound turkey in under ten seconds? Toss it in the yard and pray the puppies (who have bladders the size of dimes and are in the yard twice an hour) don't stumble across it? Fling open the door to the nearest bathroom, toss it into the sink, and pray none of the guests have to use the guest bathroom? ("Sorry again about killing your mom, but—don't go in there! You can't use our bathroom. Get away!") Yank open the basement door, fling the turkey into darkness, and pray no one smelled it or tripped over it? No: better to suck it up.

I. Hate. Thanksgiving.

"Jessica screwed up!" I cried the second I saw my mom. "It's her fault, not mine!" *Hmm. In my head, that sounded courageous, not panicked and whiny.*

Startled, my mom froze in the doorway for a second. "I'm sure there's more to it than that." She was holding BabyJon, who was dressed in a dark green fleece jacket, matching pants, and drool. A diaper bag the size of a couch was slung over her other shoulder. She liked to tease that lugging the extra weight was good practice for the coming osteoporosis. And hunchbacks ran in her family, she'd (cheerfully!) reminded me, just when I dared think there was no way for the horror to continue. "There might be plenty of blame to go around. In fact, I'm sure of it."

"But none for me, right?"

"Of course on you; you're best friends, aren't you?" Mom got that little wrinkle between her eyes when she felt frown-ey but her mouth didn't turn down. She could glare just with her *eyes.* It's as terrifying as it sounds. "I don't think this would be happening if you were a normal person. And honey, I love you, but you weren't normal when you weren't a vampire."

"Thank you?"

"And I think you're going to have to be the one to fix it, because I've got no idea how and I don't think Jessica is even capable of acknowledging there's a problem."

"I don't think that's right." Did I tell Miss Gestates-a-Lot to buy a fresh organic turkey? No. Did I tell her to unhinge her jaw and devour the *last* turkey we'd had in the fridge? No. "Or fair."

Mom raised her eyebrows and I noticed the dark smudges beneath her eyes. A drawback to having light hair and fair skin is it's much harder to cover fatigue, pox (either small or cow), or hangover-induced pallor. She hadn't been sleeping well and I tried to squash the guilt. "Fair? Betsy. You're in your thirties."

"Technically I'm thirty forever."

"And old enough to know about *fair*. It's a word for children."

"Okay, that's fair." *Argh!* "I mean, you make a good point. But the thing is, I really was the victim this time. By the time I found out it was too late to do anything. So really, this is all on Jess."

"Then you should be ashamed," my mom replied with simplicity that stunned me. She wasn't teasing and she wasn't mock-complaining the way parents do when they're pretending their kid is annoying when secretly, they love the annoying kid in question in particular when they're doing the thing the parent pretends to find so annoying. "You must have decided that attitude was acceptable from somewhere, and I can't blame everything on your late father. So I'm shamed, too."

"Don't . . . Mom, don't say that." I couldn't remember the last time I'd been so startled and hurt. I went to her and held out my arms, and BabyJon came to me at once with a wiggle and a "Glaarrgg!" I hugged him to me for a second, knowing I was using the baby for pure animal comfort, and too upset to much care. He was dry and—maybe it was the kitchen lighting?—looked a little jaundiced, and smelled like baby lotion and carrots. Ah! Not jaundice. One load off my mind. What do you even do for a jaundiced baby? Beta-smoothies in their bottles? Stick him under a heat lamp like those roasted chickens at the supermarket? *"Hmm, I like the look of that brunet fourteen-pounder . . . wrap him up, please. And some potato salad on the side."*

I stopped distracting myself with my brother, who was happy to sit on my hip and goggle at the two of us. I faced my mom, who still hadn't moved from the doorway. "I'm sorry you're upset, but it's just a turkey. Jessica and I didn't grow up the way you did and that's not a judgment. I think you triumphed and overcame a lot, starting with your father and ending with mine. But the stuff that bothers you doesn't always bother me, and hasn't for years."

"Betsy—"

I raised my voice. *Please let the humans not hear and the vampires be hesitant to interrupt, and for Laura to be late for the first time in her life.* "I didn't mean for the turkey to come across as this horrible insensitive thing I did to you. But I think we're going to have to agree to disagree on this one because, honestly, I promise we weren't even thinking about you when we got the stupid bird." Wait. That was kind of the definition of insensitive, wasn't it?

The thing about my mom: she grew up on a farm that, in a good year, was only decimated by *one* tornado or lost only *one* crop to drought. Living on a working farm was, outside the pages of a Martha Stewart magazine, hard, brutal work. Unrelenting work, too: the crops don't give a shit about Easter or your Thanksgiving plans or your birthday or your hangover; farms don't offer paid holidays and don't apologize for long hours. Neither do the animals who live on it. Business hours do not and have never existed on a farm.

That's not even touching on her father, who spent my mother's childhood annoyed that his wife hadn't given him a son. This was so stupid in so many ways that, decades later, I still get dizzy if I think about it.

I tried to give Gramps the "hey, dimwad, the *guy* determines the baby's sex, so how about you drop it before the womenfolk rise up and smite your dumb ass?" talk when

I was a teen, and it hadn't gone well. ("Shut up or I'll get the gun again.") And when Grandpa wasn't bemoaning his lack of sons (and, I assume, a seventh grader's grasp of biology), he was explaining to the future Dr. Elise Taylor, Instructor of the Year, John Tate Award winner, and Morse Alumni Award winner, that college was wasted on a girl and she should just shut up and join the army already.

Fast-forward through the "disco will never die" '70s and the shoulder pad power suits (for men *and* women) of the '80s, and Mom couldn't believe it when it became trendy to frequent U-pick orchards.

"They're paying," she'd tell me, dumbfounded, staring at giddy yuppies slaving under a July sun and posing for pictures doing same, "*paying* for the privilege of indulging in backbreaking work. As if paying to ride in a splinter-riddled cart on top of itchy pointy straw behind a steaming horse butt wasn't ridiculous enough."

She had assumed it was a phase, something that sounded cool to the idiots doing it at the time but that they would admit was an embarrassing waste of time and money years later, like velour tracksuits and gold grills. Excuse me: grillz.

It wasn't a phase.

That part of it, the U-pick orchards and pumpkin patches and Saw-Yer-Own-Xmas-Tree lots ("Staggering through snow-choked woods in subzero weather to saw down a tree and drag it back is exhausting and *not at all*

98

fun!"), had been incomprehensible enough, but when the "working" bed-and-breakfasts started popping up she *really* lost her shit. ("Gather the eggs? Feed the pigs, *the pigs?* Look! Look at the brochure: 'Book early enough and we just might let you help with chores.' Oh my dear God, the world has gone mad.") She despised it when the upper-middles played at what had been soul-searing drudgery for her family.

So of course when she found out about the organic turkey (I'd have to find out who ratted), she lost her shit all over again. Because I think, in her mind, organic turkey farms and U-slave orchards and winery grape-stomping and taking out the garbage at the lighthouse you're dropping $350 a night to sleep in—all that turns what she endured into a punch line and makes what she overcame something that was no big deal.

"What's worse?" she'd asked, staring in horror at *Travel and Leisure.* "That these farms have the audacity to charge guests for working? Or that the guests pay?" It got so bad, in fact, that she hated pretty much all parts of the organic-is-expensive-and-thus-awesome! movement. U-pick berries, organic turkeys, honey from the coop farmer down the street . . . it all fell under the umbrella of awful as far as my mom was concerned.

So her being upset was understandable, but (oh, there's my insensitivity: it's baaaack!) we had bigger problems.

What? We did.

"What are you going to do about this?" she cried and, seeing BabyJon's expression crumple, changed her tone. "You had better come up with something, young lady," she added in her sweetest, kindest tone, "or you will regret it always."

I threw up my hands. I mean hand (I was holding Baby-Jon on my hip with the other). "Got any ideas?" I replied in as soothing a tone as I could manage. "Because I've got no friggin' idea, no, I don't." I nuzzled the baby's nose. "No, I sure don't!"

"Coming through!" The kitchen door swung back and then Jessica was framed in the doorway in all her belly-licious glory. Mom came forward so she could come in the rest of the way. "I can't let you do it, Betsy. Elise, this is all my fault. Betsy didn't do anything, I promise. She's covering for me and at first I figured she was running a fever but now I realize it's not right to let her take the hit."

"Yes, well, that's the problem," Mom muttered. "She's not doing anything." To me: "Do you get feverish?"

"Irrelevant! I'm the one who said, 'Drop dead, Butterball Corporation, I've got a hankering for a Bourbon Red so you can suck it' and then wham! The deed was done." She hung her head. "And I am shamed."

"Thanks," I said, the gratitude in my voice cutting through the baby talk.

She shrugged and indulged in Jess-code: "Whatter friends."

Mom slid the diaper bag off her shoulder and plopped it on the counter with a clunk. A clunk? What the hell did she have in there? "What do booze and the color red have to do with you being under a spell?"

"Nothing," we admitted in unison. Bourbon. I hated the smell and taste of it, but I wouldn't deny a bourbon smoothie was sounding pretty good, one with extra bourbon and bourbon on the side. (Side note: I loved the part in *Kill Bill: Vol. 2* where Budd made himself and Elle a booze smoothie minutes before the mamba opened a can of whup-ass all over his face: alcohol + ice + blender = booze smoothie.)

"Then why? Why are we talking about it?"

"We're confessing."

"*She's* confessing," I quickly pointed out. "I don't actually have anything to confess this time. I'm as pure as newborn snow or whatever."

"I am not talking about bourbon! I have not been talking about bourbon even once! Not today, not yesterday, not the day before—I have been talking about Jessica's pregnancy being unnatural!"

"Oh jeez! That!" I sat in a director's chair before I could swoon. Ahhh, sweet relief. The turkey had not been my downfall. I'm sure I will eventually have a downfall, but downfall by turkey sounds too stupid. So *that* was a relief.

"Of course her pregnancy is unnatural. It's okay; we're aware."

"We thought you—I thought it was something else. This?" Jessica gestured to her belly. "Don't worry about this. It's gonna work out fine."

There was no relief on Mom's face, none. Which was fine; Jess and I were relieved enough for all of us. "There it is again. Nobody knows when Jessica's due, how long she's been pregnant . . ." She turned to me. "When I called her earlier, she told me she hasn't been to *any* doctor, never mind an OB. Not once. How does someone who can buy her own hospital—"

"Waste of money," Jess commented.

"—not be under the best medical care in the nation? How did she find out she was pregnant? Why didn't she find an OB? Why doesn't she know her due date? Something is very wrong."

"You're telling me; you should see the food bill."

"Betsy."

"She just needs to update her calendar."

"It's true," Jess piped up. "I hate using iCloud. I think desk blotters are going to make a comeback and I'll be there when they do. After I get all that coordinated you'll see all kinds of stuff go up."

"*Elizabeth.*"

"What?" I asked, honestly puzzled.

Tina answered before my mom could; she pushed open the swinging door with tented fingers and said in a low voice that nevertheless carried, "Your sister's here."

Oh boy. "Here we go," I muttered. "Mom, we'll finish this later, okay?"

"No," my mother replied sadly. "We won't." To my astonishment a lone tear trickled from her left eye, and BabyJon wiggled so hard to go to her I nearly dropped him.

"Here, take him, that'll cheer you up. It's okay. I'll make it right with Laura, you won't have to worry about . . ." My mind on my sister, I was already walking out of the room. "About whatever."

There! That should cheer her up. I didn't know what was wrong with her, but couldn't worry about it now. Once Laura and I were all right again, I'd go back and fix . . . whatever.

First things first and, since she was the one who taught me to prioritize, Mom of all people would understand.

CHAPTER
TWELVE

"Why'd you decide to come? I—" *assumed I'd have to torment you for another six months at least, since you're so frigging stubborn. I am, too, but you got both barrels: Dad's stubbornness and the Ant's. But I only got Dad and—okay, never mind, I guess* my *mom's stubborn, too. Sometimes.*

No, no, no.

"Why'd you decide to come? I—" *really feel like you're not seeing my side of the story here. I get that she was your mom— one of your moms—but come on. She was* Satan*! I bet the planet is stuffed—stuffed!—with people who'd line up to shake my hand.*

Argh, even worse.

"Why'd you decide to come? I—" *could have used more than a few hours' notice that we'd be expected to produce—*

ta-dah!—*a Thanksgiving meal for, what, ten? Plus, even before you got here it turned into an emotional showdown because my mom hated growing up on a farm.*

The Antichrist was giving me a strange look. Nothing I wasn't used to. "You've asked me that three times. Then you cut yourself off and kind of stare into space. Then you ask the question again."

"Just . . . um . . . trying to be a good hostess." Gah, did I look that dim when I was thinking? Who knew my fate was to be the undead John Dorian, MD? "So did you have any trouble finding the place?"

"Are you all right?"

"I'm a little on edge," I admitted.

"Is that why we're in the backyard where your puppies poop?"

"They're not my puppies so *back off.*" I caught myself. *Steady, moron. How can you be this bad at postfuckup playing nice when you've had to do it a zillion times?* "And yes. We can go in if you want."

"Are you hiding?"

"No."

She looked—maybe I was reading into it, but for a second she went from startled to sad. "Are you hiding me?"

"No." I wanted to reach out and give her sleeve a "buck up, li'l camper!" tug and restrained myself. "*Hide* you? Hide *you*? Jeez, not ever. Well, maybe if we were both at the same wedding trying to look hot for the same groomsmen. I might hide you then."

(I would definitely hide her then.)

She let a few moments go by while she studied my face and, I figured, tried to decide if I was lying. So now I was the one who was a little sad. We'd gone from strangers to tentative friends to not-so-tentative enemies to a working relationship to no relationship. Now Laura was likely stuck as Satan 2.0, and we were gonna make nice over turkey smoothies. A little sad? Yeah. Like a little pregnant. I guess we were just sad.

At last she said, "We can stay outside if you want," and I actually staggered a little in relief. And also because in my hurry to get outside, I'd grabbed my Kurt Geiger red velvet platforms, which did not go with my blaze orange parka. They were roomy enough to wear with thick socks, though, so I was once again faced with a question mankind has long tried to solve: comfort or class? At least they weren't clogs. Though platforms were close . . .

"BabyJon's getting another tooth."

"Yeah, Mom told me." I winced. This was my legal ward, my brother/son, and I hardly saw him. Worse, I felt bad that I didn't feel worse about hardly seeing him.

"I come to see him at your mom's sometimes. She's nice," Laura added thoughtfully.

"The best. Not a lot of people her age would appreciate being a de facto surrogate mother." I wondered if that had been a genuine compliment or a dig ("Your mother, who you haven't murdered, is nice. You're lucky to have such a nice mom. My mom's dead, did I mention?") and that was the worst of the whole thing. That I truly wasn't sure if she was being nice or not. Once upon a time, there'd never been a question.

We picked through the half inch of snow that had fallen the night before. The oak tree where I'd buried my cat (twice) loomed in the far left corner of the yard. I'd been (and was) a city girl whose idea of camping had been the Minneapolis Hyatt and roughing it meant Red Lobster, so I could never get over the juxtaposition of a street crammed with ancient homes (by Minnesota standards) that also had sizeable yards. In a time and place where people often had to choose ("Big house or big yard, can't have both, so sorry, you should have moved here two hundred years ago.") I knew I was lucky to have both. Lucky in everything, if I was honest with myself.

The back kitchen door popped open, crashed against the outside of the house, then rebounded closed . . . but not before Fur and Burr made their daring flight for freedom. They made straight for me, like fuzzy incontinent cruise missiles, proving me wrong, reminding me I was lucky in *almost* everything.

"Ooooooooooooooooooh!" Laura oohed. "Oh they're so cuuuuuuute they're adorable and sooooooo cuuuuuuuuute, come give me kisses!"

"Stop that," I said, but I was smiling. The dogs, stupid, the *dogs*. The Antichrist was kind to children and small animals. Why hadn't I brought them out right away as an icebreaker?

They both piled to a halt at my feet and Fur instantly clamped down on my velvet-clad toes.

Oh, right. That was why.

"Ooooooooooooh so cute so cute so cuuuuuute."

"Stop it or I'll need an insulin shot." I gently nudged Fur off my toes. *Well played, tiny missile with teeth. Perhaps I shall spare your life.* "They can be appealing, I'll give 'em that."

Laura had knelt and scooped up Burr and was nuzzling noses with her, so: ew. "Do you know where she puts that thing?"

"How can you be so cold?"

I jerked a thumb at my chest. "Undead."

She ignored my lameness. "They're irresistible. I'd think after Giselle died, you'd want another—"

"Cat," I finished. "Not dogs, plural. Here's the problem: dogs try too hard. All the time. And it's kind of flattering for a *very* little bit and then it's just sad. Dogs are the awkward kid in high school who wants *so* much to fit in, who tries *so* hard to pull off cool and just can't. And then you have to pretend you didn't notice that they've been trying too hard, and that makes it awkward. Pretty soon you feel sorry for them, which is annoying. You don't want to feel sorry for them. You kind of wish they'd give up on the cool thing and go home. But they don't ever. And so you're stuck. Because who's going to have the courage to tell them, 'You're not cool and the more you try the less cool you get, it's like an equation that way'? Nobody."

"And . . . ?" She'd tucked the puppy under her arm like a football and stood.

"And . . . oh, right, my analogy: that's why I prefer cats. Because cats *are* the cool kids, and they don't give a shit. And the less they care, the cooler they get. That's also like an equation."

"You were like this before you died, weren't you?"

"Yeah," I admitted, and her lips twitched upward for half a sec. A tiny smile or the onset of a seizure? "Oh, and I forgot—way more apartments will let you have a cat but hardly any let you have dogs. And you can actually leave town for more than eight or nine hours if you have a cat, but dogs, in addition to being super needy, need near-constant supervision. It's like hanging around a toddler who isn't yours, who can't talk and isn't toilet trained and freaks when you leave and almost knocks you down when you come back. Yeah, a nonverbal randomly pooping toddler who you didn't give birth to but are still trapped with."

Since she was looking more and more appalled, I tried to get off the dog thing. "You could have a cat at your place, right?"

She glanced away. "I'm not there anymore. I moved out a few days ago."

"Oh." Huh. Not a peep to me, and vampires could lift a *lot*; we were invaluable as movers. But that was understandable. It hurt but I understood. It burned like fire but I understood. The sting of betrayal was like acid on my eyeballs but I understood. "You left the Dinkytown apartment?"

"Yes. I had t—yes."

"I'm sorry." I meant it. Dinkytown was a stretch of Minneapolis near the East Bank, a neighborhood that had been around since the 1940s but was always trendy. Unlike McMansions and bomb shelters, Dinkytown had never gone out of fashion; it was a town within a town, crammed with bookstores and bike shops and quick-but-good restaurants. Laura's apartment had been in the Historic, which (also like Dinkytown) had always been cool. The building had been built in the late 1800s and had recently gone through a massive update, so the place was classically historic on the outside, but had Wi-Fi and flat-screen TVs on the inside. I knew she'd loved it, not just because we all love our first apartment when we escape—uh, move out of our parents' house—but for its own schizophrenic self.

"A kid lived there," Laura was saying, "and I'm not a kid anymore."

Oh-ho. Behold the signs we are enduring the rise of the Antichrist: for nation shall rise against nation, many false prophets shall arise, and the most terrible sign, the Beast shall giveth up her cooleth Dinkytown digs.

Beware.

Time for another subtle subject change. "So how about this weather! Also, thanks for coming over. Everybody's really glad you came."

"Why?"

God, this is torture. "Why wouldn't they be? We're sisters, BabyJon's our brother, this is our family now."

"Your family." She set the puppy down just in time; she walked about four feet, then squatted and peed. The dog, not the Antichrist. "Not mine. You killed mine."

"*No.*" All at once I was super pissed at her. Partly because the "woe, woe" thing was aging faster than yogurt, and partly out of my own guilt. "You still have your mom and dad, your *real*—"

She cut me off. "Our father and Little Horn were my real parents."

Little . . . wait, what? Never mind.

"Nope. Not at all, not for half a second. Your real parents took you in and loved you and fed you and sat up with you when you had the flu so bad you were barfing in your sleep—"

"Who told you about that?"

"The vampire queen sees all." Nope, she wasn't buying it. When was I going to consistently remember she not only wasn't impressed by vampire powers, she thought they were inherently evil? "It was my mom because you told *her*. And while your parents were doing all that stuff they also saved up to send you to college and did everything they could to be all-around awesome parents and when Satan popped in and played 'This is your life' they *still* loved you and you were still *their* daughter.

"Your dad's a minister and your mom's a nurse; they've spent their lives helping people and bringing you up— because you're their *daughter*—to do the same, and you can't get much more white knight than that." One of the perks of being a bad person is being able to spot the good ones. "They know you're the spawn of Satan and they don't give a shit. That's why they're *real*."

Laura just shook her head in denial and went on being gorgeous. Hard to say which one was more annoy—oh, who did I think I was fooling, the gorgeous thing was more annoying. In faded jeans—not artfully or artificially faded, but wore-them-to-tons-of-soup-kitchens faded, with a long-sleeved U of M crimson T-shirt under an unzipped dirty-brown jacket she'd had for years, hair loose and messy, her big blue eyes rimmed in red like she'd been crying or was about to start, her nose red for the same reason.

So annoying! Fuck it. No more screwing around. No more long awkward pauses or pretending things were almost okay when they were very damned far from being okay, nope, enough, it was time to grab the Antichrist by the horns.

"D'you want to know what your mother said when I killed her?"

Her (lipstickless yet perfectly red) lips parted but she said nothing. And for a second I could almost feel the air crackle between us. This could be interesting. And by interesting I meant fatally gory.

But the crackling quit because the door again popped open, rebounded, and would have smacked Sinclair if he hadn't caught it, stepped into the yard, and carefully let it close behind him.

"There you two are, you bad little bitches! You were very bad to run away and I have been just *sick* about it."

"I'm sor—"

"He's talking to the dogs." I sighed, rubbing my eyes. Could vampires get a fatal aneurysm? Please God, let them be vulnerable to fatal aneurysms.

"Yes indeed," Sinclair said, bounding over to us. He was in another dark suit, not cheap enough for casual wear but not expensive enough for a family dinner. "I could never refer to the two of you as bad bitches. I am certain I would dislike getting staked in the chest."

"My God," Laura said, and Sinclair politely inclined his head. "Ah . . . sorry about that. I've never—I knew Betsy had done something but I didn't—" She stopped in confusion for a second. "I've never seen you outside in the daytime."

"I understand your confusion."

"He knows he looks scrumptious with the sun bouncing off his cheekbones," I added. "Don't hate him because he's dazzling."

Do not indeed and by the by, my own, are you all right?

I was new to the telepathy thing; Sinclair was, too. In the movies and comics people who can read someone's mind have entire conversations in surround sound: the one in their head and the one out loud. Not this girl. I had *no* chance of following both at the same time. Half the time I had no chance of following the only conversation happening. Even when I was one of the participants. I prayed she wouldn't babble something I should be listening to.

It was tense, I thought at him. Or would that be *to* him? *But she's still here and she's still blond. When you came busting out your timing was perfect and do* not *say "That's what she said."*

Sinclair's snobbery came through our link loud and clear. *Certainly not.*

(Note to self: find "That's what she said" bumper stickers and slap 'em on everything he owns.)

Whew! Laura's lips were still moving. She had no idea I hadn't been—

"Right? Don't you think?"

"Yep. I think exactly that. About what you just said."

"What *did* I just say, Betsy?" Her eyes were squinty with bitchiness, or because she was facing west.

Before Sinclair could cover for me with a bluff, prompt me with what she'd said, or stab my sister so I could get away, I tried: "What you've *been* saying, Laura. And not just since you got here today. It's like you keep bringing it up because you think I've forgotten about it."

"Yes, well, my sister's murder of my mother tends to prey on my mind. I'll drop it," she said grudgingly, almost but not quite apologizing. "For now at least. No reason the rest of your guests should have to endure our—"

"Family problem?" I prompted.

"—insipid power struggle."

Hmmm.

"I'm sure we can be civil for one meal," she decided.

Her confidence was inspiring, since I wasn't sure at all. Also: "your guests"? Cold, cold. But that was a worry for half an hour from now. Right now I was exulting in the "I guessed right!" moment, which felt as good as "wait, the test results were negative?" and "I'm getting how much back for my tax refund?"

Laughter in my head: *Well played, my love!*

Damn right!

And so self-effacing, it's quite fetching. Out loud: "We're pleased you could join us today, Laura."

"Thanks. I wanted to see my brother anyway."

"How's your drive now? You know, since you're running over to my mom's these days."

No need for envy, darling. You know your mommy loves you best of all.

Shut. Up. Aloud: "Laura moved out of her Dinkytown place."

He politely arched dark brows. "Oh?"

"She said it was a kid's apartment and as of a couple of weeks ago she wasn't a kid anymore."

Sinclair's expression remained politely inquiring, but the corner of his mouth twitched and I didn't need a pipeline to his thoughts to know why. My husband was old. Not "isn't it adorable how when you were born I was excited about starting middle school" old or "when I was your age they hadn't invented computers yet" old. He had decades on me (I was vague on purpose about how many), so by definition he looked at the world in ways Laura and I couldn't. Thus, her whole "a few days ago I was a kid but now I'm *totally* an adult so, like, just be aware that I'm officially a grown-up 'n' stuff" thing was hilarious to him. Luckily he wasn't a rude jerk like me. Most of the time he wasn't a rude jerk like me.

"We should love to see your new home," he was saying.

"Even if it's Hell?"

Sinclair didn't pause. "Yes indeed."

Yeah, sure. Spoken like someone who hasn't been there.

Laura came up with an insincere smile and a "sure, *that's* gonna happen" shrug.

"Is Hell rent-controlled? Wait, if Hell was real estate would it be Manhattan prices or Memphis?" I'd been there (Hell, not Manhattan, though I'd also been to Manhattan) and it was like being stuck in a beehive. The beehive . . . *from Hell*! Lots of little chambers, lots going on . . . *in Hell*! My stepmother worked for Satan; she was the assistant . . . *from Hell*!

"Whenever you wish," the classy half of our partnership continued.

"And what kind of housewarming gift do you bring to Hell? A plant's out of the question. Candles, too, I bet. Maybe a gift card? But to where . . . hmm . . . IKEA? That would just suck. Did you know IKEA designed their entrance like a cow chute to the slaughterhouse on purpose? Machiavellian bastards."

Sinclair was still doggedly pretending we were two parts of a civilized and intelligent couple. "Truly, Laura, we would be delighted to see you anytime. We are glad you're here with us now."

"And let us know what you want for a housewarming

present. Are you having a party or just casually mentioning to people that you're registered at whatever place you would register at?"

"It doesn't matter," she murmured, and I caught the context on that one (I almost never do, so I try to mark the occasion). *There's no point in answering your question since you're not invited to my new place, big sis, and even if you were, why would you think a Galleria gift card changes one single thing?*

Sinclair's sympathy came through loud and clear. *Be patient, my own. I have every confidence your shrill charm will wear her down.*

Thanks, asshat.

"After you, Laura." He stepped back so she could walk past him and into the kitchen, and I kicked him in the back of his right knee when her back was to us. His surprised yelp was followed by my sinister giggle, and he'd chased me through the kitchen and into the main hall before remembering to go back for the puppies.

CHAPTER
THIRTEEN

My mom didn't hesitate to **carpe** *the* **diem**. *She walked right* up to Laura and gave her a hug. "We haven't really talked about it, hon," she said, putting an arm around Laura's shoulders and walking her toward the dining room. Laura was several inches taller, so my mom had to either tip her head back or rise on tiptoes to make eye contact. Since she was wearing her comfortable-but-no-support Freudian Slippers, I figured it'd be the former. "But I've been meaning to tell you I'm so sorry about your mother."

"Why?" For the first time that day Laura sounded honestly curious, not bitter.

"Because it's terrible to lose a mother," she replied simply. "No matter who she is."

Jessica had been following them, of course; they were

headed toward the dining room. But when she heard *that* nugget she turned her head away, so I caught up to her and slung my bony arm around her pointy shoulders.

"It *is* always terrible to lose a mother. Except when it's not." I got a small smile for that and was glad.

"Hon?" Not-Nick's voice floated in from the kitchen. "Do you want milk or Coke or a V8?"

"Yes," she called back.

"Just promise me you won't mix them," I begged.

"There's also ginger ale."

"Yes. And an orange. And some Newtons. You can put the gravy boat right on my plate. *Two* oranges."

I could hear Tina coming down the stairs—Thanksgiving dinner 2.0 was served. We'd skipped the organic turkey for a few reasons: the time factor (nobody wanted to watch or listen to Laura and me making awkward small talk for hours), the practicality factor (hardly any of us would eat the thing), and the 'tis-the-season factor (Laura agreed to bring the turkey to a food shelter, simultaneously relieving my mom of something to be annoyed about as well as speeding up the dinner hour).

Our dining room was huge and unused. We were all on different schedules; living in the mansion was a lot like living in a dorm. Somebody's always asleep, somebody's always awake, somebody's always in the kitchen looking for a snack. When we did congregate for a formal meal, it was always in the kitchen, unless a bunch of us were on our way somewhere (like the Princess Diana exhibit at the Mall of America), in which case we'd eat in Tina's yellow minivan with black runners. (She was starting some sort of bee thing, but it was none of my business.)

All that aside, the dining room was too big and too old and too fancy for most of us to feel comfortable using it for everyday meals.

The dark wood (was it walnut? I could never remember . . . something the Founding Fathers chopped down with their own hands, by which I mean their slaves' hands) on the walls and under our feet did nothing but increase the gloom, not just in the room but through the whole mansion. The houses on Summit are old, huge, and a challenge for their designers due to the lack of light for the location. Which is why there were more solariums than bathrooms in a four-mile radius.

The room had built-in shelves and hutches that, back in the day, held lots of china and . . . I dunno, other stuff designed for storage within china hutches. We kept it full of two sets of china, several sets of paper plates, cups, and napkins, and for reasons I'm not interested in discussing, Monopoly (Tina was a goddamned cutthroat), Chutes and Ladders (I hate that goddamned cheap spinner), and Candy Land (I hate that goddamned Molasses Swamp).

The hot-tub-sized chandelier, which looked like it would

creak if it ever moved, and kill thirty people if it fell, loomed over the dining room table (also dark and creaky), which, best guess, could seat seventy or eighty people or two hundred people . . . I dunno, I wasn't a caterer. It was big.

Last was the fireplace, also big. So big that even with the flue closed the wind would come whistling down the chimney. *Hmm, the wind appears to be coming out of the south-west today.* You know how some people say a fireplace is "big enough to roast an ox!"? This one wasn't that big; it would, at most, roast a small cow.

I'd question the sanity of anyone describing the room as cozy, intimate, warm, or board game free. And I wasn't the only one . . . like I said, we tended to eat in the kitchen.

The whir of the blender chopped through my thoughts as efficiently as it was chopping through cranberry jelly. Which meant . . . yes! Here came my dinner now.

"Is it a spell?"

I was surprised my mom had asked such a question straight out like that until I realized she hadn't. She and Laura were whispering together and had forgotten I could now hear a cricket fart when I applied myself. Especially since the blender had just quit.

"I have some ideas . . . let me do some research, Dr. Taylor."

"Really?" My mom sounded almost tearfully grateful.

"I'd be so grateful, Laura. I can't get any of them to admit what's going on, never mind care. Thank you so much."

The Antichrist ducked her head and smiled. I figured she'd scuff the floor with her toe and murmur, "Aw, shucks, ma'am, twarn't nothin'," in another few seconds, which I looked forward to since it would be hilarious.

What could Mom be bugging Laura about? *Please, please, let it not be some kind of sex question.* Not that an unholy virgin would be much help. I sometimes pitied the poor nameless bastard who was destined to punch the Antichrist's V-card.

"You mustn't be so hard on yourself, Dr. Taylor. Betsy couldn't see something if it knocked her down the stairs. Which Jessica's belly could actually do."

"Hey! Knock it off, you guys."

"No one's talking to you," was the frosty retort.

"You're talking by me! Or near me." By now we'd assembled in the dining room, save for BabyJon; Mom and I had put him down for a nap.

Put down . . . heh. I always think of the *Ghostbusters II* scene where Sigourney Weaver tells Bill Murray to put the baby down, and Bill goes, "You're short, your belly button sticks out too far, and you're a terrible burden on your poor mother." All I could come up with for BabyJon was, "You are a drooling machine," and, "Also, you're *still* incontinent."

Tina had slipped in behind me, setting the spreadsheets and stock stuff and whatever else she did aside for the day.

"How's it going with Laura?" she whispered, which was polite of her since she probably heard everything.

"She's definitely gonna murder me in my sleep," I murmured back.

"No worries, my queen. We would never let her do such a thing."

"Thanks."

"And if for some reason we did, we would spend the rest of our lives avenging you."

"That's not as comforting as the first thing you said."

Laura's voice cut through Tina's response. "And Betsy must always, always be comforted."

"It's true," I said gratefully, "and thanks for understanding."

She sighed. "I was being sarcastic."

Nuts. "Is this what it's going to be like for the next few hours?"

"Is my angst about my murdered mom bringing you down?"

"One: yes. Two, duh." I held out my hands like a traffic cop. A traffic cop trying to direct the Antichrist to a safe lane. "Look, if it's gonna be like this, fine. You've got every right to be pissy—"

"Pissy!"

"—but it's not fair to everyone else. So if the plan is for

you to needle me every chance you can grab, can we at least do it where our friends and family—"

"Stop calling them that."

"—don't have to sit through it, too?"

"I don't know," Marc said thoughtfully. He had the watching-the-coolest-tennis-game-ever look on his face. "I'm caught up on everything in the DVR. This is the closest I'll get to new drama until *Sons of Anarchy* starts up again."

"Come on, ladies." Not-Nick sighed, pulling out Jessica's chair for her. He'd already set several drinks at her place. No oranges, though. "Play nice. It's Thanksgiving."

"It's *not.*"

"Oh, picky picky," I snapped. "The holiday's not about calendar dates, except when every company and school and government office in America needs to know what day to close." I knew, *knew* I should be taking the moral high ground (I hardly ever got the chance), but after careful consideration of the parties involved and the setting, the best I could do was *fuck this shit.* "You've got cause, we're all in agreement that you have cause, and it's a lie anyway. You're not a bit mad that the artist formerly known as Lena Olin said hello to my sword with her neck."

"What did you say to me?"

"Proof!" I cried, pointing at her. "You're not mad! You just wanted to come over and mope because you're a blonde."

Uh. Prob'ly should rephrase so it didn't sound like a blonde joke. *How do you know when the blond Antichrist isn't mad? When she's the blond Antichrist!*

"Nice 'N Silky #43," was the terse reply. "Shimmering Wheat."

"But that's awful!" I couldn't hide my horror. "That stuff is so caustic—don't you listen to your color technician's advice? If your local salon doesn't have one—but they will, what is this—1955?—you can always use the Web, or call one of their 800 numbers. What were you thinking going in blind like that, you reckless fool? That stuff will ruin your ends and the roots will show; it'll soak up the dye, but unevenly because it damages the follicle, too, but that's not even the worst of it—"

"Please focus on the real problem instead of seizing on the part of the problem you think you can get a handle on!" This in a yowl. Also, I loved how the Antichrist could almost always work in a *please* even when she was near-foaming with rage.

Jessica had taken the seat Not-Nick had held out for her; he'd sat down, too. They both had identical expressions of exhaustion on their faces. Marc was sitting across from them, hand under his chin as he watched. Sinclair, Tina, and my mom were just standing there. Funny how I knew that three very different people were having more or less the same thought: *the two of them have got to work this out, so let them.*

I was still scoping the Antichrist's deceitful coloring. "So those are contact lenses, huh? Okay, that's annoying— lots of people *have* to wear them. You, you only had a pair made so you could stick it to me. Not cool, Laura. Your mother was the Lord of Lies and now you are, too."

"This isn't about who is—"

"Me. It's me."

"—or isn't—"

"It's you."

"—cool!"

"You're right," I agreed. "Your tacky dry ends and blond roots and the coming eyeball infection are all your own problem. You're not a victim here, you know. You *chose* to dye your hair, and I'm sorry I wasn't there for you when you made that decision, but now you have to live with the consequences."

"Live with the—" Wow. She was spitting while she raved and not even apologizing. Most unusual in someone who would apologize if someone stepped on *her* foot. "Con- sequences! You?" Again with the spittle spray. Not even an *excuse me, I know that's gross, sorry, I'm upset.* I don't ask for a lot from the Antichrist; why couldn't she meet me halfway? "You don't know what the word means."

"I do, though! I can spell it, too; once in seventh grade I beat Jessica *so* bad in the spelling bee and as a *consequence* I won a Dairy Queen Blizzard. C-o-n-s-a-q-u-e-n-c-e."

Tina opened her mouth, then closed it quick when Sinclair moved his head in a teeny tiny head shake. At the same time, Jessica did a spit-take and shrieked, V8 running down her chin, "Oh, you liar! It was a tie and you know it!"

"It was not! You choked when you had to spell *euthanasia*."

With the Herculean strength only moms with babies trapped under cars and hormonal pregnant women were capable of, she stood so quickly she almost flipped the table with her thighs of rage. Not-Nick let out a yelp and managed, barely, to stop any of her glasses from tipping. Meanwhile, Jessica was on her feet and jabbing an unpolished finger (apparently the baby could accidentally suck the nail polish into itself through its shared bloodstream and *why* was I sad I'd never be pregnant?) at me. "And then *you* choked when you had to spell *quarantine*. And they didn't have time to do a sudden death spell-off because that's when Jeff Perryman pulled the fire alarm and we had to evacuate the gym and so it was never decided so we both won!"

"But when we were in the parking lot waiting for the fire trucks, you had a chance to—"

"Shut up shut up SHUT UP SHUT UP **SHUT UP SHUT UP!**"

The room practically shook in the backwash (literally) of her rage seizure. I've been out in thunderstorms that weren't that loud. I wiped the spray off my cheek. "If you're gonna do that, could you not stand so close to me? I might have killed your mom but at least I say it and don't spray it."

Her mouth was moving, but all that came out was a high-pitched gurgle. Until that moment I hadn't known gurgles could even *be* high-pitched.

"Did you know that *consequence* is a neutral term?" Marc was tapping his iPhone, which did lots to keep his brain busy. "There can be a good consequence or a bad one; it's more like another word for outcome. Jessica is pregnant and as a consequence has assorted food cravings. It's not good and it's not bad, see?"

"And that's how I know you've never seen her dip sweet pickles in mayonnaise," Dick-Nick said, earning an elbow in the side from his pickle-dippin' sweetie, whose rage-gasm seemed to have passed; hormone-inspired rage-gasms were as quick and dirty as regular orgasms, and thank goodness.

Great. Now orgasms are gonna be in my head the rest of the afternoon.

Probably I should, what's the word . . . ah, got it. Focus.

"Right!" I was relieved for all kinds of reasons. "Okay, a little off topic, but there, see? Not only can I spell the word—Tina, you can have your turn in a minute—"

"She doesn't need a turn," Sinclair said quickly, the first thing he'd said since walking into the room.

"Plus, I've got the definition from the Wiki Man. So yeah, I know what consequences are."

"No. You don't." Laura's contact be-lensed eyes narrowed. "But you will."

"That sounds bad," I said, about half a second before she yanked me out of the world, fury her only fuel.

CHAPTER
FOURTEEN

"One day," I said without opening my eyes. "One day I'm actually gonna see this sort of thing coming. I'm going to learn from past fuckups and be proactive and actually *see this shit coming.* Dammit!"

"Yes, well. Not today."

Laura's voice. Double dammit. I was in no hurry to open my eyes, as I knew where we were, but lying on the ground with my eyes closed was, at most, a temporary reprieve. And I guess a vampire queen shouldn't be found in a fetal position while whimpering in fear and telling herself it wasn't cool to suck her thumb.

I opened my eyes. "Most people—when they throw tantrums?—maybe break a vase. You, though. You drag people to Hell."

"It's not a tantrum," Tantrumey McTantrum snapped. "I just got really furious with you and acted without thinking regardless of the *consequences*."

"Okay, I'll give you that one. Here it comes, all official: zing!" I blinked and sat up. I knew my focus should be on an irked Antichrist but I was distracted by Hell being weird(er).

When I'd been here before, Hell was a waiting room (with all the horror that entails) and a beehive (ditto). The devil had explained, in as bitchy and condescending a manner as possible, that my puny brain couldn't grasp the complexities of another dimension. Because that was what Hell was: something entirely apart from the world, a place that was shaped by Satan's will and determination. Normal rules didn't apply.

My puny brain had wrestled with the sanity-eroding idea of another dimension by coughing up a waiting room, which was perfect. Terrifying, yet relatable, a place shaped by the whims of a power-tripping dermatologist and his only-work-hard-enough-to-not-get-fired staff. Hell had the receptionist desk, thin cheap carpeting, flickering fluorescents, and the out-of-date cooking magazines with all the really good recipes torn out by hostile patients. And several doors that led only to a fire escape and a broken vending machine (dermatologist) or any place in Hell the devil wanted you to see (Hell, obviously).

My puny brain showed me one of the doors led straight into the heart of Hell, an area where you could see everything happening all the time. There were chambers everywhere, thousands of them, so many that even if you couldn't make them out you knew something awful was taking place in each one . . . which made it a thousand times scarier. It hurt my brain to attempt even a rough count. And even though my puny brain was being shown something relatable, it was still disorienting and scary.

Good try, puny brain. I know you did your best.

That was then. This is now (apologies to S. E. Hinton). No waiting room, no stacks upon stacks of cells. Instead we were in the middle of what felt like a great gray mist, something that enveloped us and only hinted at things we couldn't . . . quite . . . see.

Hell wasn't just different. It was gone.

CHAPTER
FIFTEEN

"This is bad," I observed. I was pacing in a small circle around Laura while the mist whirled and swirled around us in a sinister and off-putting manner. I was trying not to think about *The Mist*, *The Fog*, or any horror movie where the villain was the weather. "Really very bad."

"Oh, you get it now."

"Of course I get it," I snapped back. "I'm not *that* dim." I was almost positive. "The devil told me this is a dimension that she, being an angel—"

"I know."

"—could come to anytime, could use as a doorway from here to the real world anytime, something ordinary people just can't—"

"I know all this."

"—and not only could she come and go from here, like an interdimensional South Station, her will actually shaped the reality around here, again, something regular people can't do—"

"Betsy, I get it!"

"—but you can because you're half angel."

"Why are you expositioning stuff I already know? This isn't a comic book. *I know all this.*"

"It helps me to think about it again and hear it out loud and, jeez, are you ever going to quit complaining?"

"That's rich, coming from you."

I let that pass because I was determined to be the bigger person, and also, she had a point. "When the devil died, so did her version of Hell. So this"—I gestured to the fog—"is a limbo-type thing. I wonder where everybody is?" The second I asked, I saw the answer. "Probably keeping out of the way while the managerial hierarchy shakes itself out. It's like when you're working at a Hollywood studio and a new boss replaces the old one, all the little fish keep under the radar until they figure out the deal with the new boss." Hmm, Hell and Hollywood in the same analogy. No one's ever done *that* before.

"This is what you've stuck me with." I couldn't tell from her tone if Laura was accusatory or pissed or scared or a combo. "All this. Hell's literally smoke and mirrors right now and I've got no idea what to do."

"Well, hell, neither do I. Plus, I'm dealing with all this in sock feet." We both looked at my feet. When we'd come in from the yard with the puppies, I'd kicked off my shoes and stolen a pair of Tina's purple fuzzy socks, warm out of the dryer. Ah, the sensual thrill of warm clean fuzzy socks that weren't your own . . .

I'd been annoyed at the puppies and Sinclair, and—

Sinclair!

No, wait. Like this: *Sinclair!*

Nothing. Not an answering peep.

Sinclair! Where are you? Why aren't you bugging me from the inside of my brain?

I couldn't hear him. He wasn't there. Oh, Christ, did that mean he couldn't hear me? Was I just a bald patch in his brain, too?

"This is what I had to show you." Laura was whining as if I gave a *tin shit* about her problems right now. And yeah, that attitude was probably why I was in Hell in stolen socks. I wasn't unaware. Just unimpressed. "I figured the only way you'd get it is if you saw it. So here it is."

Since Laura had never liked my husband, this probably wasn't the time for *ahh, God, without my man inside my brain I cannot function in society!* Plus, as a card-carrying fembot I probably couldn't say it without cracking up. But I had to say something. And as much as I didn't want to show throat, the Antichrist had a point.

"I'm sorry. I've got no idea what to tell you. If you wanted me to feel bad, I do, but I'm still not going to apologize for not letting your mother murder me. And as long as we're talking about your mom *again*, where are your wings?" Laura had inherited her mom's wings. (Yeah. Angels really do have wings. Listen up, Mormons: you're wrong about *that*, too.) Apparently they were always there, but in the other dimension that was Hell, you could see them. The way Satan 1.0 had explained it, her wings were always there and so were her hellfire weapons. But they could only be seen at just the right times. Laura could *make* them visible if she was upset enough, but that didn't mean she was making them appear. She was just making use of them.

Hers were like big sparrow feathers, an unromantic mixture of dappled browns. When you could see them, anyway. Her mom's had been those of a huge evil crow (like there were any other kind).

"I don't want them," she replied sharply. "I haven't decided if that's who I am yet."

I did an internal eye roll at the absurdity, but managed to keep it off my face. My eyes, actually. "And you never answered my question."

Laura had wandered a few feet away and I could barely see her in the gloom. It was a little like being inside the Gopher Hole in a dense fog. You knew there were eighty thousand seats in the stands and you knew people were in

CHAPTER
SIXTEEN

Yes! We were in Hell!

(This was what my life was. I was glad to fall through a hole in the world and plop into Hell, where my sister was temping for the devil. Oh, and the devil was trying to goad me into killing her. Unless I'd guessed wrong, in which case the devil was gonna squash me like a grape.)

"Tricky tricky," she panted, easily dodging my fist. And then my kick. But my other kick landed—ha! A perfect day to wear my pointiest leather boots. Take that, Satan! And that! And—

"Ow!" She was pretty fast for someone at least five billion years old. What had I been thinking?

I remembered my theory. I remembered my utterly insane idea that this wouldn't be a fair fight . . . and why that was actually *good for me. Why it could be the saving of me . . . and him. And maybe even the future.*

Because time is a wheel.

"You think . . . He loves you?"

"Really? We're gonna chat about God while we're trying to kill each other?" My ears weren't ringing so much as booming. And it was suddenly almost impossible to see out of my left eye. Was that my blood or hers making everything look pinkish red? Probably mine.

"It's the last . . . conversation . . . I plan to have . . . with you. So answer."

"Yeah, then. He does. Sure He does."

"And me?"

"Of course . . . He still loves you . . . moron! That was never the issue . . . moron! You big stupid moron!" Normally I didn't have to think of what to call people I was pissed at. Asshat, dumbshit, shitstain, fuckface, jizzbucket, fucktard, dickweed, cockknocker, jizzhole . . . it all usually came tripping off my tongue in a glorious rain of obscenity.

Had to work for the insults now, though. It was hard to think, what with all the red stuff in my eyes and the booming in my ears, which I was pretty sure were also bleeding.

I felt her hot little hands close around my neck and start to squeeze. I punched. Punched. Punched—nothing. Should have found the time to take a martial arts course. Yoga couldn't help me now.

It was tough work, bitching at the devil while being throttled, but I was up for the challenge. "How come . . . older you get . . . dumber y'get?"

"Yes, He does," Satan replied, a thoughtful look on her bloody face. "I suppose He does. He must, you know. It's one of His rules. I think I . . ."

"Gggsssshat!"

"I think I want . . . I'd like . . . to go home."

"Stop it!" It was Laura, yelling from a galaxy far, far away. "Stop it—don't—you're killing her—stop killing her!"

No idea. No idea who she was talking to. Her mom? Her sister? A player to be named later? Wow, look at all the blood coming out of me! Almost as much as a live person! Weird!

"Don't! Don't! What are you doing? Let go!"

It was good that Laura was here. Was almost here. What was keeping her, anyway? I needed her here. My plan wouldn't work without her here. Oh, Laura, I'm so sorry you're here.

Satan grinned at me through bloody teeth. Her hair had been yanked from its neat coiffure and she looked kind of Medusa-esque. With luck she'd need a deep-conditioning treatment after she'd beaten me to death. "Uh-oh."

"My thought . . . xxxactly," I gurgled.

"You'll have to do it in front of her."

". . . kkk . . ."

"You'll have to steal her future while she watches."

". . . nnn . . ."

"Him or her, Betsy? Now's when we see."

". . . favor . . ."

"What?" I had actually landed a good one—splat!—in the middle of her narrow Lena Olin face. Finally, I'd surprised her. Really surprised her. Not the fake stuff she usually showed me. Had been showing me all along. "What, stupid girl?"

". . . want one . . . favor . . . a wish . . . want it . . ."

It was probably all the skull fractures, but her eyes, usually brown, and recently dead black like a night sky without stars, seemed to burn. Eyes on fire, that was what they looked like—and it wasn't quite right. She wasn't human, this was an angel, I was killing an angel and she was killing me and she was a creature I did not understand, could never have understood, asking for an explanation had been a waste of time and had only increased her contempt and her eyes were like nothing I'd ever seen, her eyes her eyes oh God oh please help me now God her terrible terrible eyes . . .

"Yes! One! For what you'll do. Now do it! Your worst, vampire queen, show me your worst and choose!"

I almost didn't. Almost couldn't. I had never been so frightened, never. In the end it was my essential stubborn nature

(fuck you Lena Olin you're scary but you're gonna die or I'm gonna and I'm fine with dying again because time is a wheel)

that allowed me to reach for nothing

"Stop! Stop! Stop!"

and grasp the Antichrist's hellfire sword

"Don't! Betsy! Motherrrrr! Don't!"

which only Laura or one of her blood could wield

"Let go of me! What are you—let go!"

and shoved it in the devil's heart. Or where the devil's heart would have been, had she ever had one.

Laura's last shriek cut off like someone had thrown a switch. Maybe someone had.

Shocked, Satan looked down at the piece of light sticking out of her chest. I have to admit, I was surprised, too, though I was pretty sure this had been what she wanted, what she had been planning from the minute Laura was born, the minute I'd come back from the dead.

But knowing wasn't the same as doing. Astonished together, we looked at the chunk of Laura's soul, the pieces of her self she made into weapons that could kill angels and vampires, and then at each other. Neither of us knew what to do.

So I shoved the sword in harder. I dunno . . . it just seemed like the thing to do. So I went with it.

"Finally," said Satan, and she died.

I wasn't falling for it, though. I mean, probably she was dead.

But because Dr. Taylor didn't raise no fools, I took off her head with the backswing. "I chose," I told her head as it bounced past me. "Happy now?"

CHAPTER
SEVENTEEN

"Well, last word, singular." There was a long pause while I observed Laura wasn't a) leaving, b) shrieking at me to shut up already, or c) killing me. "'Finally.' That's what she said when she knew her plan to make me have a plan was going to work."

"You can't tell me the Lord of Lies actually wanted—"

"I don't *know* what she actually wanted. I barely know what I want half the time. I just know she wasn't sorry to die. I think . . ." It took a couple of seconds before I could articulate what I knew was true. "I think she was very tired. And tired of being tired." Awesome cover by Jane's Addiction aside (*much* better than Jagger's take), I really did have sympathy for the devil. Not a lot. But yeah, some. Even when I was afraid she was killing me, some. "I think she knew there wasn't anything she hadn't seen a million billion times. I think when life can't offer up any surprises, ever again, what's the point in staying around?"

"That doesn't make anything right."

"No."

"Not any of it." Laura had shoved her hands in her pockets and turned her back to me. "Not one thing."

"I know." I swallowed a smile at the Antichrist's double take when she spun back around to face me. "No, really, I know. It was a crap thing to do to you. I knew you'd be the one stuck with the bag." I shrugged. "I knew and I did it anyway. Plus, I half-assed it and it shouldn't have worked at all. I'm the one who should be dead."

Silence. Hey, she didn't rush to agree! That was something. The balloon bouquets had definitely softened her up. Thanks again, 1-800-FLOWERS. Is there any squabble you can't heal?

"And since I'm coughing up all kinds of details where I come off like a sock-clad sociopath, I'll tell you I wasn't smart enough to think of anything else. And she was tired. That's why Satan is dead." Oh, and because I had a choice: Laura's future or Sinclair's. And I chose Sinclair's. But there was a limit to the amount of truth I thought she could handle.

No. That was a lie. There was a limit to the amount of truth I was willing to share with a volatile Antichrist with the powers of a god in Hell.

Laura sighed. "You can't get out of this by playing the genius ditz card."

Okay, time and place, time and place, but I couldn't help being absurdly flattered. Genius ditz! That was me all over, except she was only half right.

"I'm not trying to get out of anything. I'm telling you straight out, it was a shitty thing to do." I spread my hands. "I'm owning it, okay? I still suck at it, but I'm getting better. You should have seen me when I was twenty."

Which I didn't say lightly, because Laura *could* see me when I was twenty. Not only could she use Hell to travel through space, she could also travel through time. At first, she could only do that with "strong physical contact," the devil's euphemism for "smacking the shit out of the vampire queen." But in almost no time, in a scary amount of no time, Laura had gone from zero knowledge and control to pretty decent knowledge and better control. In this case, *no time* meant less than a year. And she didn't have to touch me to do it. I was starting to wonder if Satan had pulled that whole "contact with one of your blood" thing out of her ass.

"It's nice you're telling me this," Laura was saying, so I pasted on my politely attentive expression. The eyebrows were crucial for that: raised *slightly*. Too far and you looked like a bad improv actor; too little and you looked like you didn't give a tin shit. Like so many things in life, a fake "I'm listening" look was all about the middle ground. "But words don't change anything. 'Sorry' doesn't fix anything."

"No," I agreed, "but not saying it is kind of a douche-bag move."

She almost smiled. "I'm still stuck with"—she gestured to the nothing again—"this. I still have no idea what to do and I'm *stuck* with it. How can I turn my back on this? But how can I take it on?"

"Sorry." I hated to even think it, but the girl who'd informed me she was a grown-up was going round and round a *lot* with the "it's not fair!" bleating. A) She was right, and b) it didn't matter. Sure, it wasn't fair and, sure, I'd wronged her. And anytime you drop by a playground, you'll hear a lot of the "it's not fair" battle cry, because things started being not fair pretty much the day you're born. Kids had to cry about it; grown-ups had to deal.

It was probably too soon to point this out.

"Sorry," I said again. "I don't know how to fix this. And I'm pretty sure I'd be out of my league to even try."

"Yeah," Laura said sadly. "Me, too. So: see how it feels."

And like that, the gray fog swallowed her and I heard the muffled *pop* of air rushing into the space she and her boo-hoo 'tude had just occupied.

The Antichrist had dragged me to Hell, heard my apology, and then coldly left me there.

It was just me. Me and the fog and Tina's fuzzy purple socks.

"Yeah?" I cried, shaking a fist at . . . uh, nothing. "Well, I take it all back, how about that? Your mom was horrible and I'm glad she's in pieces, how about that? You can leave me here to rot and she'll still be dead! How about that? And you sound like a fucking baby with all the 'it's not fair,' how about *that?*"

Then I remembered the nature of the fog. That there were a billion souls out there somewhere, and any one of them could be hearing this.

I shut the hell up.

CHAPTER
EIGHTEEN

My wife and my sister-in-law fell off the world and I could not stop them.

To my shame, I did not try. I stood like a weakling child and watched. And then I went away inside myself because, at my core, in my essential self, there was always the weakling child who could not prevent the deaths of those he loved, and who lacked the courage to follow them on their journey.

I spent decades not following them; I expected to spend centuries. And for the first time since I met my queen, I realized anew that immortality could be a curse to the cowardly.

". . . my king? Sir? Sir?" A familiar voice, one I had loved long. "Eric? *Eric?*" Ah. This is where I am. This is what we are doing. Following her foray into familiarity, Christina Caresse Chavelle would now bite her lip and do something she hated. I was comforted by a routine that had begun when I was four and recovering from rubella. The uproar over the consequence

(ah . . . consequence . . . such a familiar word today . . . my queen would say it is the word of the week)

of my illness had hit my parents hard. I did not know it at the time, but the stress caused me to sleepwalk. If not for Tina's timely slap, I should have blundered into one of the ponds and drowned. She woke me, she comforted me, and the next day she began teaching me to swim. It would not be the first time, or the last, I was saved by a quick-thinking woman who loved me.

Father, you thought my rubella-rendered sterility would put an end to the Sinclair name; you thought having no grandchildren by your son was the worst thing that could happen to our family. You made us believe it with you. Oh, my father, you were correct in many things; why not this one?

I caught Tina's hand an inch from my face. "I am fine," I said distinctly. "You may restrain yourself, however tempting your impulse."

She gifted me with the ghost of a smile, gone so quickly it might never have been on her sweet face at all. Beyond hers was a ring of others, all wide-eyed and fretful.

I stood

(when did I lie down?)

and apologized. I noted the dining room table had been shoved across the room and there was a sizeable mess of broken plates and spilled drinks everywhere.

I apologized again.

"That's okay," Jessica said at once. From behind Detective Berry, I could not help but note. At some point in the last— I glanced at my watch—four minutes, he had seized her elbow and tugged her behind him. This was wise, if ultimately useless. "Listen, it'll be okay. You know we'll get her back."

I did not.

"I think she'll have to get herself back." My mother-in-law reached for my hand. "But she can, I'm sure. And if not, you'll think of something. Just—don't worry. Okay? You'll figure it out. Ah—we'll all figure it out." Her small warm hand squeezed mine even as her expression told me the former was truer than the latter.

I appreciated the sentiments, but had no time for them. "Words are wind," as Mr. Martin had written many times. (I had read and reread the Song of Ice and Fire books because Elizabeth refused; they were delightful and astonishing. But I refused to watch the televised series, no offense meant to *Mssrs*. Bean and Dinklage.)

Words, in fact, were worthless; wind could at least be channeled for power. For I had no idea how Elizabeth would "get herself back." Nor did I know how I could go to her. And that only if she—I gritted my teeth and forced the thought to its logical conclusion—only if my dear one was yet alive.

I could not feel her within me. Our fragile telepathic bond, so new, had quickly become invaluable, something we wondered how we had ever done without. As luscious in body and charming in mind as Elizabeth was, it was as humbling as it was arousing to show a woman the most dreadful places in your mind, and have her embrace when all others would shrink back. The loss of our priceless link was nothing less than devastating. Priceless as the dictionary defined it: "of inestimable worth." There was nothing; probing for her spark was like feeling the bloody hole left behind when a tooth was yanked.

"We must go to Laura's new home."

Tina nodded, her furrowed brow smoothing.

"New home?" Dr. Spangler asked. He had kept back; he had not rushed to comfort me when I was back to myself. I would wager he'd endured my paroxysm by distancing himself until my foolish indulgence had burned itself out. A wise man in death as well as life. "She's moved?"

"Yes, as she is now an *adult*." I could not keep the scorn from my tone; I did not try. "A thwarted, angry child with delusions of maturity and the power of a god." My fingers actually twitched, I wanted them around her neck so, so badly. *Ah, sweet sister-in-law, your mother's well-deserved murder was not the worst thing that could happen to you; no, indeed. I will show you. I will.*

If I could get my hands on her, that is.

"I don't think she'll stay in Hell for long," Tina ventured.

"Nor do I, and so we must be ready."

My oldest friend nodded once again. "We will be, my king." She did not waste words on comfort or predictions she had no way of knowing would come to pass. She never had, and it would be a poor time to begin. Tina knew what the others did not: if the queen was dead, so was the Antichrist. *If I had to burn every vampire on the planet to bring that about, I would. Including myself.*

Tina knew that, too.

CHAPTER
NINETEEN

Stranded = bad. Hell = bad. **Stranded** *in* **Hell** = *very terribly* awfully horribly dreadfully bad. Whew! That was a lot of adverbs. Wait . . . adjectives? Definitely should have paid more attention in Miss Wilson's English class. At least I wasn't trying to distract myself by pondering a past regret.

"Don't panic," I gasped aloud. Regardless of the damned who may or may not have been lurking just beyond the mist, I had to think out loud or go crazy. It wouldn't take much for me to lose my shit. So I embraced the urge to yak-yak-yak. "It's not as bad as it seems. It's not! It'll be fine. It will! You're a badass shoe shopper with an utter lack of conscience at sample sales. And also, you're a vampire. The queen of them, even. So take it easy. And you should probably stop talking out loud."

Okay. Good pep talk, good advice. Or at least not terrible life-ending advice. So I was marooned in the hellfog for who knew how long. Stay put or walk?

I know all the survivor show guys (they're always guys, for some reason) say if you're lost you should stay put so the rescue team can find you. Except *I* was the rescue team. Laura was the only one who could go back and forth from hellfog to earth to hellfog; her mother could, too, but (whoops!) I'd killed her.

But if I had to just loiter in one spot until Laura (maybe) returned to (possibly) 'port me back, I'd (see above) lose my shit. So against everything Bear Grylls had tried to teach me (also, I'd rather succumb to dehydration before wrapping a urine-soaked shirt around my head), I started to walk.

And walk.

And walk.

This might not have been my best idea. I had the feeling I could walk for a long time and never find a Starbucks. Which would be, of course, the coffee shop . . . *from hellfog*!

I managed a giggle, which didn't lighten my mood because it was swallowed by hellfog and just sounded sad. I could occasionally make out other shapes through the fog, but they never seemed to get closer and that was A-OK with *this* girl. In fact, after about half an hour I started to declench. I was still abandoned, still stuck, still wishing I hadn't thought about Starbucks because I wanted a hot chocolate with a side of O negative in the worst way, but nobody seemed to be sneaking up on me or even approaching me. I'd think my rep was preceding me, but even my vanity wasn't that all-encompassing. I figured the damned were as lost in the fog as I was; they were trying to keep their heads down until they could think of what to do next, as I was.

Heck, if I was one of them, I'd be fine with the "head down until further notice" plan. I'd definitely be doing my best to avoid notice, though it went against most of my instincts. Ha! That made me think of my late stepmother, the Ant, someone who'd be unable to keep her head down. Even when she tried for subtle and unassuming, she put off obvious and overdone. Every damn time. So I needed to get back to counting my blessings.

There were worse things, I reminded myself, than being abandoned on a strange spiritual plane with piles of bad guys (they had to be bad; they were in Hell, right?) who were damned.

"Oh, hell."

I went cold(er). That voice. There *were* worse things and I had been stupid to forget it for even one-half of one second. My hackles were trying to rise so hard I was nearly on tiptoe. I knew that voice; oh, yeah. The voice of my shattered family, the voice I hated beyond all others, the voice that was my own personal Vietnam.

Think of the devil, and her *assistant* appears.

I whirled to confront the most fiendish denizen of Hell in the history of humanity: my stepmother.

CHAPTER
TWENTY

I had tasked myself with many errands, most of which I forgot when I turned and beheld my queen.

"Ohhhh boy," was how she greeted her king and liege lord. "I don't even have the words for how scary you look."

"My trousers," I replied with the dignity I had used as shield and weapon ever since my sister's murder, "are at the dry cleaner's."

"Bullshit!" the queen cried gleefully. "You just like letting your knees swing in the breeze. Also, Bermudas? Not your best look."

She was right on both counts, blast it.

"Now, granted, there are lots of ways you could look worse in navy shorts," she conceded, circling me as a tailor would admire her alterations. Ah . . . tailor. I needed to book time at Heimie's Haberdashery, a fine local establishment run by those who knew the most important aspect of a suit was the fit. I had not been looked after so well since the '50s. Though I try not to dwell on it, I was forced to flee my last haberdasher when he expanded his business and hired tailors whose strengths were . . . diverse.

To my dismay, I discovered there were such things as *rodeo tailors* and all that entailed: Pearl snaps. Arrowhead pockets. *Rhinestones.*

Ah, St. Louis IX, patron saint of French haberdashers, if only your benign influence had spread to the Americas.

Elizabeth, who was still prowling around me, stiffened. "Rodeo tailors? Are you seriously thinking about rodeo tailors? Because . . . wow. I've got so many questions if you are. Big number one, what's a rodeo tailor?"

I chuckled and snatched her to me. Her blue-green eyes narrowed in mock annoyance (my Elizabeth functioned in the grip of either of her primary emotions: feigned annoyance and actual annoyance). It was a dreary day, the sun hidden behind scudding clouds slick with rain. If the sun could effect an escape and shine, the stiff breeze from the northeast would keep the air chilled. It was a day made for rereading Dostoyevsky's *The Idiot* while sipping Bowmore in front of the de rigueur crackling fire. A miserable day.

A wonderful day. As were all the days since my queen prevailed upon the devil to give me the sun, and did not see such a thing as extraordinary. All things were possible: Picnics. Golf. Bermuda shorts.

"I can't lie," she said, rubbing her nose against mine. "Your hairy knees are pretty cute."

"As are yours, my love."

"No chance! I shaved my legs the night before I got creamed by that Aztec. I never have to shave them again. Hairy legs on women aren't ever going to be in vogue in this country, right? Because that would heartily suck. Where are we going?"

"Somewhere I can sweep you off your typically well-shod feet." Though technically I already had; as I pressed her against me and walked, her feet swung and kicked in the air. She had found me returning from my newly established routine, and so Summit Lookout Park was across the street.

"Ahhhh, nuts." Elizabeth groaned across my neck as we swiftly crossed. "Sinclair, come *on*. Enough with the al fresco banging. Plus, it's gonna dump buckets on us any minute."

"Your throaty murmurings are, as always, an exciting prelude to our lovemaking."

"Sinclaaaaaair," my queen cried. A less-besotted gentleman might have classified it as a whine. "C'mon, the park *again?*"

"The mere sight of the New York Life Eagle inflames me. I must have you." We were across the street by now, entering the small, lovely park, so I scooped my bride into my arms. You would think, as she was now more comfortable, she would have less to say.

"It's friggin' freezing out here and the eagle statue creeps me out."

But no. "There is no one around," I assured her as we passed the lookout marker.

"Because it's friggin' *freezing* out here and, if you don't remember me mentioning this twenty seconds ago, it's gonna spit freezing rain on us any minute."

"If my lust was not already inflamed by cradling your supple limbs, your siren's voice would have done so."

"Look, I get it, okay?" she was saying and saying and saying while I looked for a secluded spot. "You haven't been able to bang outside for a hundred years or whatever—"

Was it possible she did not know how old I was?

"—and now you can, so you're getting back to your farm-boy roots and stuff, but you'll still be able to do this when it's, say, July. July? Doesn't that sound nice? Fireworks and picnics and lemonade? And *then* sex? Because I thinkmmmmmmm."

I silenced my love in a way that was efficient yet pleasurable. For all her aired grievances, her lips were warm and yielding. When I set her down at the base of some trees that, despite the season, offered some cover, she clung to my neck all the way down.

"Far be it from me to argue with your penis," she grumbled

as she unbuttoned her red and black checked coat. I slid my hands beneath her emerald cashmere sweater (a sensible birthday gift from Tina) and she gasped as I found her lovely deep breasts.

Have I mentioned you have the figure of a Victorian courtesan? Catherine Walters would envy you.

Could you maybe not think other women's names while we're doing it? Hmm?

I laughed in her mouth and she playfully nipped my lower lip. Her long pale fingers were busy at my waist, my belt, my zipper. Now it was my turn to suck in breath (odd how habits born of necessity are the last to leave us) as she found me, grasped me. Wondrous insanity: in my Elizabeth's embrace I was an inexperienced teenage boy, greedy for love and made clumsy by that greed.

Well . . . since we're resigned . . . could you please fuck me hard and a lot? Right now?

I laughed and tweaked a pert nipple, then followed her curves with my hands until I was stroking her sweet center.

"I think something is happening," I murmured against her lips.

"Yeah, to me, too." She was wriggling beneath me, inviting access even as she kept most of herself modestly covered. Impressive! "Can you move now? A lot? And really hard and f—"

Something beyond the sun, I thought, lost in her body's sweet welcome. *Something beyond the light.*

Mmmm . . . the love talk is terrific, but to paraphrase Julia Roberts's prostitute (a prostitute who only banged one guy), "I'm a sure thing." So: move now. A lot.

Chuckling, I obliged, to our mutual satisfaction.

"My king?"

I looked around. We were in the kitchen. An untouched smoothie was at my right. I had been lost in my thoughts; I had been indulging in memories while my beloved had been taken from me.

Unacceptable.

"I

What is happening to me?

apologize."

"You destroyed the dining room and then laid out part of a plan and then mysteriously disappeared, presumably to sleep the sleep of the deeply pissed. You were saying you could help us during the day," Dr. Spangler prompted. "Because you can bear sunlight now."

Something beyond the sun. Something beyond the light. "Yes," I allowed. "That is so."

"Just say what you need, chief," Detective Berry said. It

was at times difficult to remember he was an authority figure, an investigator with years of study and training to call upon. Detective Berry had the build and coloring of a fresh-faced farmer's boy (having been one myself, I recognized the look), perhaps even the youngest boy. But not for the first time, I was grateful we had someone with such a background in our home. "We'll see if we can't get it done."

"Thank you, Detective."

He rolled his eyes at Jessica at my formality, which I affected not to notice as Dr. Spangler edged the smoothie closer. "Tina and I went shopping late last night and we got lots of fresh fruit. It's your favorite," he said, wide-eyed and hopeful. "Double raspberry."

I looked at the drink and felt nothing. I picked it up and sipped. Nothing. "My thanks, Doctor. I doubt I have ever been prescribed a smoothie before."

"Yeah, well. First time for et cetera." He waved a hand and sat down in the seat across from me. "I was wondering, with Betsy gone, how long are you gonna—uh—" He looked at my mouth. In particular, my teeth. "Is that gonna be a problem?"

"That is not—" I began coldly, but stopped myself. Because these people were not roommates and they were not coworkers. And in all fairness, it *was* their concern. "That is not anything you need worry about. I would never harm any of you, nor by inaction allow harm."

"Oh, jeez!" Jessica shifted in her seat almost violently. I watched her with attentive wariness; at no time was a pregnant woman to be underestimated. My mother had been pregnant with twins; my father, years later, still shuddered when recalling some of the famed irritability. Elizabeth referred to them as rage-gasms. "That! Nobody's worried you're gonna pull a Count Chocula on one of us. Mmm, Count Chocula. But you and Betsy mostly feed on each other, right? And we don't know when we're gonna get her back. Are *you* gonna be okay, is what we're wondering."

I looked at these people, my people. Jessica, great in her body, and Marc, great in his mind. Nick-No-More (I should use his true name, rather than let Elizabeth's ramblings sink in and take root in my brain), who stood for the law in our home, and Tina, who did not. Tina was my link to my old family and the new; she was the bridge. And Elizabeth . . .

My Elizabeth had brought me my new family; I had not had *any* family for decades and, foolishly, assumed I never would again. I can only see my parents and my dear sister in my memory's eye; I see my new family every day. I guarded the dead with my mind; I would guard the living with everything else. Woe to those who pondered harm to any one of them.

Or, as my delightful queen would declare: "Which one of you asshats is looking to get punched in the face?"

Succinct woman, my queen. Always to the point. Though I still had no idea what an asshat was.

"It is kind of you to worry," I told the room at large while looking at Jessica. "But perhaps you should stay off your feet for a while. The twins must be making you tired."

"Twins?" Not-Nick asked, easing into the chair beside his sweetheart.

"Twins?" Dr. Spangler repeated, looking the mother-to-be over with a practitioner's eye.

"Twins?" Jessica echoed. She appeared to think about it, absently rubbed her great stomach, then nodded. "Sure. Twins."

"I assumed," I said vaguely. Why had I said such a thing? I had been thinking—ah, yes, my mother's pregnancy. Similar symptoms and of course the lady herself was rather sizeable, all the more startling as Jessica was normally quite slender. Why think of such things now? Doubtless a way for my mind to distract itself from the horrid chasm created by the queen's disappearance.

Disappearance? That made it seem subtle. Elizabeth had been taken, snatched, *ripped* from me.

"Sure, twins," Not-Nick said, nodding. "That makes sense."

"Yes indeed," Tina agreed. "Only . . ." Her pale brow furrowed. "Dr. Taylor seemed a bit perturbed."

"Mmm. Yes." I had a dim memory. My mother-in-law

had concerns about Jessica's pregnancy; I approved and attributed it to her maternal care for Jessica. Jessica, a fine woman and a loyal friend to my queen, had received little maternal care in her own childhood. From what Elizabeth had confided, it was a pity Jessica's parents were not still walking the world. It would have been deeply satisfying to strangle them both and bury the bodies in a thriving piggery.

"Right, so it's twins," Jessica was saying. "Due next month."

"I thought you were due last month," Dr. Spangler commented.

Tina looked up. "My understanding is that you will not deliver before summer."

"Right." The mother-to-be shrugged. "So. It's covered."

"Yes." As all was well, gestationally speaking, I was able to focus on the pressing concern. "We need to find Laura Goodman." *And I need to strangle her and bury her in a—no. Not yet.*

"Yeah, that'd be nice, but we know she's moved." Dr. Spangler glanced around the table and topped off Jessica's smoothie. "And she sure didn't ask any of us to help lug her couch and books and Sunday school medals and Antichrist memorabilia."

Jessica picked up her glass and sipped. Now sporting a charming mustache, she offered, "If she *had* asked, I would have been glad to pay for movers. I've moved without them and it sucks." Seeing my surprise, she elaborated: "When Betsy and I moved to the duplex. She insisted we split everything to do with the duplex; she didn't want me to pay for everything. It was the only way she'd agree to be roommates. And when we drew up the moving budget, she asked me to put the van money toward the next sample sale. It sucked," she summed up, "and the sample sale wasn't too great, either. But I sure as shit gained an appreciation for what movers have to do. It's soooo hard to move a dresser up the stairs! It's heavy if you don't take out the drawers, and awkward if you do, plus you've got to lug in the drawers one by one."

Detective Berry cleared his throat. "I could find out Laura's new address. But . . ."

"Oh, jeez," Dr. Spangler said, then he quickly glanced at me, doubtless assuming *jeez* was less dreadful than *Jesus* to my unholy ears. Which was accurate. "Sorry. But Dick, I don't think you should do something that'd get you in trouble."

"I don't think I'd get in trouble," he began, but I held up a hand.

"No need to take the chance, though you are kind to offer. I know where she lives."

"No shit?"

"How d'you know that?" Jessica asked. "Who told you?"

As one, they all looked at Tina, who gave them her best inscrutable smile and said nothing. She knew, but left the satisfaction of the disclosure to me. Tina was always courteous.

"Man, Betsy's right," Dr. Spangler said. "You've got spies everywhere. That's part of the head vampire thing, I think. And listen. I've been meaning to ask you . . ."

"Yes?" Reticence was unlike the man.

"Did you—when you died and came back, did you know right away what you were going to do? Did you plan on . . ." He looked around the large, inviting kitchen. "Any of this?"

I thought of the depths of my living rage, and my cold despair. Vengeance had not come cheaply and, as Tina had warned, had brought no peace. And then decade after empty decade followed, years of knowing every trite saying

(*money can't buy happiness, you get what you pay for, a bird in the hand is worth two et cetera*)

is true.

"No. And I had no essential urge to rule, or even to be a good man. I wished to be left alone. For long years, it was my only wish." I looked into Marc's deep green eyes, cloudy now as he paid close attention to what I was saying. "It was always difficult. To realize that however long you walk the earth, your loved ones can never return. That no matter what you overcome that particular journey does not end for you. How do you become resigned to something unthinkable? You are forever apart and while the alternative is dreadful to contemplate, you can mourn the man you once were. I mourned. And I moved on, after a fashion. And then I met the queen. Perhaps it will be different for you. But already you have what I did not." I did not say it, but sensed Marc knew—they all knew—what I meant: he was not alone.

A pregnant silence passed, broken by Marc's brisk, "Actually I was more worried about how to keep my licensing current, but all that stuff's been, y'know, preying heavily on my mind, too."

"Then I trust I have set it at ease."

"You bet. But listen—who's getting you intel on Laura? I'm not the spy, and I know Jess isn't the—"

"I am the spy." When they remained unenlightened, I elaborated. "There is a tracer on Laura Goodman's car. I placed the device."

"Betsy *also* said you're a hands-on kind of monarch."

For the first time in a while, I felt like smiling. "More now than I have been, to be sure."

"Is that why you're always on those walks? You're running around placing tracer devices and figuring stuff out and other sneaky stuff?" Dr. Spangler turned to Jessica and Detective Berry. "I thought it was all about the outdoor daylight sex."

For the first time in a while, I groaned.

"Give us *some* credit," Detective Berry said kindly. "You two return all disheveled with your clothes half on and rumpled. In December! And grass stains everywhere . . . what *else* would you be doing?"

"*Who* else would you be doing?" Jessica added with a sly smile.

"I was wrong to discount your deductive skills," I said, unable to keep the chagrin—or the admiration—out of my tone.

"Not mine," Jessica said cheerfully. "I didn't use 'em. Betsy told me. Well. She complained at me. That's like telling, right?"

They observed my deepening discomfiture and laughed. It was a lovely sound; there was no mockery in it. Even though Elizabeth was gone, the family she had brought me was a comfort.

They would do for now.

CHAPTER TWENTY-ONE

"Oh, hell," my dead stepmother, Antonia O'Neill Taylor, said again. Like dying in some car vs. garbage truck nonsense, going to Hell, toiling as Satan's assistant, and then running into me in the hellfog was a terrible thing *for her*. Okay, that actually does sound pretty terrible. But I wasn't having much fun, either. "What are *you* doing here?"

I glared at her, this nightmare of polyester, a bad dye job, and the wrong makeup, the woman who'd driven a bulldozer through my parents' marriage. One of the many strange things about Hell I didn't understand was the . . . citizens, I guess would be the word? Anyway, some of them looked as they had in life; some didn't. Some of them were always in the middle of being tortured. Some just kind of wandered around like they were in an airport but didn't know their flight number. Some seemed happy to be there, some bemused, some horrified, some indifferent.

My stepmother, the Ant, had been somebody in Hell (no one who knew her in life was surprised). She'd been possessed by the devil and had given birth to Laura. She was so awful that she was possessed for *over a year* by the devil and no one noticed. (This! This is what I was up against!) So she was the Antichrist's biological mother. (It's weird. I know. I don't understand it myself, and people have tried to explain it to me. Several times. I'm never going to get it and I'm fine with that.) Then, in Hell, she was kind of Satan's assistant/almost friend. I didn't think it was a coincidence that the first person to approach me, out of what were probably millions of souls, was the Ant.

All this to say she *chose* to perceive herself wearing one of her awful polyester-blouse/miniskirt combos in hot pink and black, her bright, stiff, pineapple-colored hair, and her wobbly, cheap pumps. She looked like this *on purpose.* There were deranged drooling serial killers in Hell who had more self-respect.

"I'm not any happier about being here than you are to see me." I'd been staring in horror so long, I finally remembered to answer her (rude!) question. "Believe me."

"You're not playing the victim today," the Ant told me sternly. "You're the one who made this mess. Serves you right to get dumped in the middle of it."

"So's your face." I was a little rattled. I managed to rally and come back with, "How'd you know I was dumped? Did you sic Laura on me?"

Her glare of dislike was so intense, it nearly knocked me over. Wow, flashbacks to my sweet sixteen party. "I didn't have to. It seemed logical. You wouldn't have come here on your own, and since you're here by yourself, I assume someone brought you. And since you're here by yourself, that same someone dumped you. And since you killed the Boss, that leaves Laura. And serves you right," she sniffed.

"Wonderful." I turned. It had taken me an hour of walking to stumble across the Ant; time to walk in *any other direction*. For as long as it took. Years. Decades. Whatev. "Lovely seeing you, die screaming again, 'bye."

I'd taken about ten steps when I heard, "Well, hold up."

I snorted. "Pass." Who would I run into next? Hitler? Henry VIII? Aileen Wuornos? The Boston Strangler? (Wait. Was he even dead?) Whoever it was, it would be an improvement.

C'mon, Henry! Let's rumble and then work it out over hot chocolate while I explain that it's sperm, not eggs, that determine the sex of the infant and by the way, Anne Boleyn's daughter was five times the ruler you were. Not literally. Because you got really fat at the end. Elizabeth just got wrinkled.

"I said hold up, you horrible bitch."

A *vast* improvement.

I heard her little tripping steps come closer. Hmm. I wasn't making any noise when I walked, but her clop-clopping was as it had been in life: tacky and loud. She expected to make that noise, so she did. Hellfog was weird.

"I suppose you're wondering what the deal is." She had, more's the pity, caught up to me and now gestured vaguely to nothing, highlighting her tacky pointy red nails. Lee Press-On stock had probably taken a hit beginning the month she died. It might not ever rebound. "With everything like this."

"No, not really. Just—" I shut up. This was no time for "I'm lost and I miss my loved ones and I'm scared, bwaaaaah! And also, I'm thirsty." I'd die again before confiding anything like that to the Ant. Also, could I drink blood in Hell? People here were probably thirsty and hungry and couldn't eat or drink, and also couldn't die (again). That was why it was Hell. No, best to keep the confidences to myself. "Just out for a walk. In the middle of a bunch of nothing. For I'm not sure how long."

"The thing is," the Ant said, ignoring my words in hellfog as she did in life, "they're all waiting to see what you girls will do."

We girls? Uh, okay.

"Maybe if you look around a little bit, talk to some people, you might get an idea."

And maybe if you ever really looked in the mirror, you'd

remember that women in their forties should not wear hot pink anything, or miniskirts, unless they are Heather Locklear or Maria Bello and you, Antonia, are no Heather Locklear or Maria Bello, you're—wait, what?

"What? Get an idea?"

"You know." Again with the vague look-at-my-Press-Ons gesture. "Talk to them. See what they're thinking."

"How can I talk to them? And why would they tell me what they're thinking?" I asked, incredulous. I figured the Ant would be mean and bitchy, but not insane. Clinically, anyway. "I can't see anything and they're all out there hiding in all this . . . *this.*"

"Look. Not to sound *Matrix*-ey, but this isn't really fog, you know. And we're not really walking. Well, you might be." She stopped and looked at me thoughtfully. "I'm dead and technically you are, too, but my spirit is here. Not yours, though; you're here in the flesh. But Hell doesn't distinguish, I guess." Another thoughtful glance in the distance. "Not unless someone tells it to. Remember the werewolf you picked up?"

"Hell isn't the dog pound, and yeah, I remember." Antonia, a former roommate, had died saving my unworthy neck, been buried, and then I'd found her in Hell and brought her back to the mansion. In her body. Which was also still in the cemetery. (None of us had a clue. We were just glad to have her back.) Then she and her boyfriend moved out. I'd gotten a Christmas card from them just a couple of days ago. The warm inscription ("We're in California and all the blondes are as dim as you") had almost brought tears to my eyes.

"Yeah, thanks for the *Matrix* analogy. Remarkably helpful. And you're the worst Morpheus I've ever seen."

"You shut your mouth! I'm not black!" she snapped. "That stuff about my grandma was *made up.*"

Whoa. "Simmer," I told her. Jesus-please-us. If ever race mattered less than—than anything, I'd think, it'd be in hellfog. When stumbling around in a never-ending hellfog, were people honestly judging their fellow stumblers by the amount of melanin in their skin cells?

(Of course they were. It was hellfog!)

"Look, I don't even know for sure who's here and who isn't . . . how would I? Satan might have kept attendance records, but I don't. Laura probably doesn't even know. Maybe you don't, either." With the murder of her boss, the Ant was high and dry. I squashed the teensy amount of sympathy I'd felt for half a second. "It'd be one thing if I was looking for—for—I dunno, Jessica's parents?" With Jessica's endless-yet-brief pregnancy, her useless mother and father had been on my mind lately, mostly because they were on *her* mind. I could count on one hand how many times she'd mentioned them in the last fifteen years. I'd need both hands and a foot and a half to count how often she'd brought them up in the last month. "But how would I even know how to find them, if I ever went completely batshit insane and decided to talk to them, ever, about anything?"

"Oh, jeez! Lookit this! Lacey, look who it is!"

No, it wasn't. It sure wasn't. It absolutely wasn't—

"It's our girl's little friend! That Betsy girl!"

I turned. Not because I was in any rush to see Jessica's parents, but because the sooner I did this, the sooner I could get the fuck away from them.

And to think, I thought the worst I could run across was the Ant.

Hellfog *sucked.*

CHAPTER
TWENTY-TWO

"I must apologize again," I explained to Dr. Taylor as I handed her my squirming ward. "Truly, Elizabeth and I wish to be more tactile with BabyJon."

"Tactile?" Dr. Taylor snorted, an unlovely sound. "It's stuff like that that's preventing you from being any kind of parent. It's being a mom and being a dad. And that's it. It's not chopper parenting or tactile parenting or attachment parenting or being a martyr mom or slow parenting. She is the Mommy. You are the Daddy. The end."

Somewhat taken aback at the good doctor's vehemence (which, in truth, Elizabeth and I both deserved), I could only attempt to finish explaining. "Our good intentions, however, keep getting tossed with every *crise de la semaine.*

I was wrong to let our baby remain at the mansion last night." In truth, leaving my boy had been close to a prayer . . . or an offering. Knowing Betsy wanted the infant to spend more time with us, I had been unwilling to let Dr. Taylor take him again. *This will prove I am a worthy husband, a worthy king, a noble father. Karma will take note and return my queen.*

At times I am a stupid man.

"You and your excuses." When she rolled her eyes, my mother-in-law looked remarkably like my wife, so much so that it was a near-physical pain to me. "'I've been kidnapped. My wife is trapped in the future. My wife is trapped in the past. My wife was kidnapped by the Antichrist.' Blah-blah."

"Yes, well." The only son I would ever have was birthed by a woman my wife despised. It was to the queen's credit that she held none of it against the infant, a fine, strong, handsome boy. It was to her mother's credit that this was as close as she had yet come to our deserved scolding. "I am come with another poor excuse for an excuse."

Jessica peeked around me. "Hi, Elise!" She had asked to accompany me and I had acquiesced. I was more than grateful now. I surmised Jessica had wished to reassure my mother-in-law that we were well on the way to retrieving Elizabeth. In truth, my queen's absence left me grateful for any company. What had I become?

Dr. Taylor feigned startlement. "Oh! Jessica, I didn't see you there."

"Yeah, sure, very funny." She stepped to my side, the great curve of her belly preceding her, and stroked one of BabyJon's black curls. He smiled at her and popped a thumb (his own) in his mouth. "He's sooo sweet! Betsy says he's the kind of baby that tricks people into having them."

"She would know, as she was that kind of baby herself," Dr. Taylor said, smiling. "She hardly ever cried. She only minded being hungry. Nothing else could touch her; she slept through an actual tornado once. Literally. A tornado. My ex-husband and I spent the night cowering in our base-ment and our baby only got pissy when I was slow to get her a bottle. It took a while," she added, "what with the kitchen being half gone."

"She still sleeps like that," Jessica commented. "She slept like the dead before she was dead. Listen, d'you mind if I come in to—"

"You know where it is," she replied, stepping aside. Though I had other things on my mind, I could not help wonder: Food? The guest bath? Whatever it was, Jessica indeed knew where it was. "Eric, if I didn't know something was awfully wrong with you, I would now."

"Beg pardon?"

"It's broad daylight . . . sort of," she added, squinting at the cloudy sky. "Lunchtime. This—the sunshine—it's too new to you. You wouldn't flaunt it and you wouldn't be careless about it. And right now, even though you're doing something denied you for decades, you couldn't care less, couldn't you?"

"I have more pressing concerns," I admitted. In truth, there could have been a raging tsunami and I would be indifferent.

"No doubt. Why don't you stay for a bit? I wanted to—oh."

I had heard the car; I had noted the driver had shut off the engine. My phone, tucked snugly into an inside jacket pocket, shook gently. Tina notifying me of Dr. Taylor's guest. Surely it would not be this simple.

Jessica turned to look. "Oh boy."

My sister-in-law climbed out of her car, her fresh loveliness masking her bitter soul. She checked when she saw us standing on the front sidewalk with Dr. Taylor, faltered, then walked toward us.

Mmm. It *was* going to be this simple.

The silence as Laura Goodman approached was profound, almost like a living thing. It would not have surprised me to see her actually pushing through it like a mime. And oh, how I wanted to hurt her. I wanted to strike her and make her bleed and force her to return to me my queen.

I must not do that yet.

Dr. Taylor handed the infant to Jessica, who clutched him to her chest without looking away from the new guest. I recalled what Elizabeth had said about the Antichrist's penchant for all things maternal: *She collects mother figures. Even though she loves her adopted mom, she's known for years her bio mom was out in the world somewhere. Then she met her and yikes, right? So whenever she meets a friendly woman who's the right age, she's kind of drawn to them.*

As she approached, Dr. Taylor greeted her with a calm "Laura, I told you I was sorry about your mother, right?"

"Yes, ma'am."

"Good." I saw what would happen and did not move. In fact, I indulged in an internal smile. Laura's penchant for maternal figures, while understandable—

Crack! Dr. Taylor's palm slammed into the left side of her face.

—might in this case prove fatal.

"Whoa," Jessica said, taking two steps backward, still clutching my infant. In those two seconds I saw something remarkable. Laura's eyes, normally a pure blue, flared poison green and then faded to what I can only describe as banked blue coals.

"I understand why you did that," she said politely, touching her reddened cheek. "Please don't do it again."

"She's my only daughter! What did you think would happen?" If I had not had occasion to make note of this behavior before, I would now. My mother-in-law was a formidable woman on and off the playing fields of academia, and ought not to be fucked with. "How dare you even *think* of coming here without an impressive apology in your mouth? *And* my daughter in your company!"

Laura just looked at her and for a long moment, no one said a word. Not even BabyJon, who merely watched us with a baby's peculiar intensity. Elizabeth referred to it as the "there's a monster sneaking up behind you!" look.

"If I did have an apology," she said at last, "that slap would have smacked it right out of me."

"You come in here right now," Dr. Taylor ordered. "You come in and explain yourself. And also have Rice Krispies bars."

Her face lit up even as Dr. Taylor's handprint deepened. So Elizabeth was correct; her half sister had an inclination for mother symbols, something I could use to my advantage. "All right. Sure, I will."

Dr. Taylor swung the front door open wider and stepped back to let the Antichrist in. She appeared to have forgotten us completely until Jessica, loitering in the hallway, cleared her throat. Then she ran a distracted hand through her white curls and said, "And you guys, too, I s'pose." She turned to follow Laura, leaving the door open for us.

"Wow." Jessica's eyes were so wide they seemed to swallow

her small, pointed face. "That went a *lot* better than I thought it would."

"It could have been worse?"

"It might still get worse. Want some advice about your ma-in-law?"

This woman had cleaved herself to my queen years ago; except for myself, she knew my queen best. I had great respect for her opinion on all things Elizabeth. "You have my full attention."

"It is a bad, *bad* plan to piss off Elise Taylor. Betsy didn't turn out as Betsy all by herself."

"What a simultaneously horrifying and comforting thought."

Jessica laughed as I stepped aside so she might walk ahead of me. My son laughed, too, peeking at me over her shoulder and waving his chubby hand as if to beckon me forward.

Obedient, I followed.

CHAPTER
TWENTY-THREE

So here they came, Jessica's dead parents, shuffling through the hellfog with the artificial smiles that had been their trademark. Of all the hellfogs in all the timelines in all the universe, they had to etc., etc.

"So nice to see you!"

"Thank God you're here."

I raised my eyebrows at the Watsons. The last thing in life he'd said to me was, "Get your fat ass out of my house." The last thing she'd said was, "Don't forget to tell your stepmother I'm coming to her luncheon." Tough call to figure which was more scarring. They were both so horrible in so many ways it was tough to pick just one awful thing to freak out about. I don't even have the words for how amazed I am that Jessica turned out so great. It's one of those things that seem impossible, like getting books back to the libe on time every time.

"Can you believe all this?" Mrs. Watson said in her faux hearty voice. I noticed they looked (chose to look?) exactly as they had in life, him in one of his tangerine plaid sports coats, matching tangerine shirt, white tie, and red slacks, and her in one of her sparkly red cocktail dresses, seamed black stockings, and red Marc Fisher pointy-toed pumps. She was a former showgirl, and her taste for sequins had never worn off. The two of them looked like a) something a pimp would have too much self-respect to be seen in and b) someone a pimp would have too much self-respect to have hanging off his arm.

I noticed the Ant had done that thing where someone wanders a couple of feet away and looks in the opposite direction, the "you know and I know I can hear everything but I still thought it'd be fun to give you the illusion of privacy" thing. Nice of her, I guess.

If I instantly starting jogging away, would the Watsons follow me? What was worse, being cornered in hellfog where I'd have to have a conversation with these shitheads, or being chased in hellfog by these two shitheads and eventually have a conversation?

Ugh. *The Tiger and the Lady* (or whatever the story was called) this wasn't. Also, lamest story *ever.* Who writes a story and doesn't end it? Jerks.

"Betsy?" Mrs. Watson prompted. "Can you believe it?"

"Oh," I replied. This once, I hated being right. "You think we're gonna have a conversation, don't you?" The Watsons were one of my earlier lessons that things could look okay on the outside and be horrible inside. It was a lesson I would have been happy to miss. One I wished Jessica could have missed, too.

"Now, now," Mr. Watson said amiably. "I think you can agree we've been . . . uh . . . adequately punished."

"Oh, I don't know," I replied, smiling. "You're not screaming in agony and you don't appear to have been on fire for the last fifteen years. Eagles don't come and eat your liver and come back to eat it again after it grows back. You're not shoving boulders uphill only to have them run you over—squish!—just so you can start again the next day." My smile made both of theirs dry up and disappear, the first nice thing that had happened in the hellfog. "In fact, you both seem fine to me. Unchanged, even."

"We're not! We *have* changed," Mrs. Watson assured me. "We've been punished and, you know, we've—uh—what's the word?"

I blinked, amazed. "Is the word you can't think of *repented*?"

"That's it," Mr. Watson said. "That's the one."

"I get it!" I said, because I finally did. "You think I'm your way out. You think that because I love your kid I'll help you. You—" I had to laugh and shook my head. "You actually think that."

"We love our kid, too," Mr. Watson snapped.

"And we've been stuck here since we died. Life's gone on without us."

"I'll say. Did you know the president's African American?"

"We know," they replied in dour unison. They had identical "I can't believe I'm missing this!" expressions on their faces.

"Don't remind me," the Ant murmured on the off chance I wanted to deal with three asshats instead of two.

"Reelected," I reminded my stepmother, and got an eye roll for it. Sweeeeet.

"And you! Who do you think you're fooling?" Mrs. Watson jabbed a finger topped with sparkling reddish brown polish, a color that looked a lot like dried blood. Shiny dried blood. At least *her* nails were real. "You were quick enough to suck up to us when you wanted to get in with our crowd."

And you've got no idea all the bigotry she had to overcome to do it, I thought but didn't say. *And what's up with "in with our crowd"? What, the charity circuit is high school cliques, redux?*

Oh, God. What if it *was*? I should warn Jessica. They were always calling her up . . .

"Anytime we were throwing a party for the somebodies

in town, I could count on the second Mrs. Taylor to sniff her way in."

"That's true," the Ant replied. I was intrigued by her demeanor for the first time in . . . ever? She wasn't acting like she was cornered or ashamed or embarrassed. Mostly she was radiating borderline boredom. Like what*ever* she'd done in life wasn't nearly as bad as what *they'd* done, so what was the point in discussing it? "There was a time I would have put up with almost anything to get an invite to your annual Black and White." A thin smile. "No pun intended."

"So what's changed? We're here, you're here. You think you're better because you got to run some errands for the Lady—"

"Sorry, what?" I asked, startled into taking part in the conversation. "The La—oh. Carry on." The Lady? That was the most pleasant euphemism for Satan I'd ever heard. The Malicious Tricky Horrible Jackass Bitch didn't come out so smoothly. The Lady. The Laaaaaaaday.

"—and now you're too good for us?"

"I'm too good for you because I never tried to fuck my kid. I also never found out my husband was trying to fuck my kid and then hit my kid so she wouldn't get the bread-winner locked up."

They glared at her, and the Ant stared them down with another expression I'd never seen: bored to the border of impatience, like when a hapless Girl Scout knocked on the door to hawk Thin Mints. Like they were nothing to her; barely worth getting upset over. Me, I was gaping in amazement at the second Mrs. Taylor, who for the first time ever seemed . . . what was the word . . . awesome? Yep. Awesome. It was overused, sure, but in this case it was the literal dictionary definition of awesome: inspiring awe.

There wasn't much Thing One and Thing Two could say to that, so they turned back to (blech) me. "You'll tell her we're sorry." It was astonishing to me that even in death, Mr. Watson still hadn't picked up basic niceties like *please* and *thank you.*

"I will, huh?" The Ant was doing the "I'm not really here and I'm not hearing any of this" thing again. I envied the pose. It made me wish I wasn't here and wasn't hearing any of this.

"And that it was all just a misunderstanding," his wife added.

"A misunderstanding?" I thought about how, at the end, Jessica had been reduced to waiting for her father behind her bedroom door. I say *waiting* and not *hiding* because she was waiting for him with a baseball bat. Which she used. A lot. "What'd you tell the ER docs? I always wondered." Oh, wait—they were EW docs. For some reason Marc wanted me to keep up-to-date on hospital slang. "You were sneaking into your daughter's room for some post-conference-call rape and fell on her bat? With your head and shoulder and ass? A lot? Because I would have liked to have been there for that." The thought made me gurgle laughter right in his face.

"A misunderstanding," Mrs. Watson repeated firmly. Another trait from life carried over in death. She could will herself to ignore—or unsee—anything. "And we're going to be grandparents."

I made a mental note to ask the Ant how people in Hell found out stuff. Could they spy on us? Did people who had died the day before bring everyone up to speed on current events? Was there a bulletin board somewhere? *Mr. and Mrs. Watson are going to be grandparents. Mr. Miller's daughter won the Citywide Kickball Competition. Madame Drummonde's great-great-great-granddaughter is having a potluck.*

"And those babies are going to be a handful," Mr. Watson said.

Babies? As in more than one? Swell. Which had a double meaning because Jessica's belly was so big! Heh, that was— shit, I should be paying attention. "Oh yeah? Suddenly you're all about the grandparent thing? You sure didn't give a shit about Jess in life."

"We did, too!" said the woman who had bloodied Jess's nose and lip for telling the truth about her husband. "I *told* you, we've *changed.* And because of your timeline tampering, Jessica's babies are very, very special. She'll need help and we're happy to step in."

It took everything I had to keep the disinterested expression on my face, because I had just been walloped with the staggering realization that Jessica's pregnancy was severely fucked up. I'd blown off her pregnancy at first because I didn't know how it had come about. In the old timeline, she wasn't pregnant and Nick had understandably and regrettably vamoosed from her life. Post-timeline-tampering, she was hugely pregnant and Not-Nick was devoted to her with zero plans to relocate. It made sense that I didn't have any of the details. I was just happy she was happy.

But no one else knew the details, either! How? How the fuck had I not realized that *no one* knew how long she'd been pregnant? That no one—including Jess herself—knew her due date? That though it seemed to us like she'd go a gusher any day, we were all sure her delivery was weeks or even months away? She hadn't even seen a doctor, for Christ's sake, and nobody cared! *What was happening in that uterus?* Suddenly I was afraid of Jessica's belly for a reason that had nothing to do with how often turkeys kept disappearing from our fridge.

"Gnnn unn," I managed. I could keep looking unimpressed, could keep from seizing the Watsons and screaming, "What do you know about this, you amoral shitheads?" and then banging their heads together for five or ten minutes, but I couldn't swallow all that rage and shock and fear and verbalize, too. Not yet. "Mrrrgggg."

Luckily the Watsons were focused on their main interest: themselves. (Okay, I was selfish, too, but I wasn't that bad. Usually.)

"Her babies are doing all that shifting," her mom was saying, "and I'll bet they'll do it after they're born, too. She'll need help. And you—you've got influence down here."

"Down here," that was funny. It was another dimension; there wasn't a "down" like there wasn't an "up." But the stuff we're taught about Hell sticks with us, I guess. Even when we're *in* Hell.

"No." Oh, good. I could talk again.

The damned parents looked at each other, then back at me. Mrs. Watson tried a cautious smile. "But we're sorry."

"You're sorry you're in Hell. Not about what you did to get here."

"I didn't even do anything!" she snapped. "It was all him—fucking pervert. I wasn't involved in any of it."

The only thing that kept me from killing her was remembering she was dead and in Hell. "Yeah, that whole mind-set, Mrs. Watson? That's why you're in Hell."

Her worthless husband decided to add his unasked-for opinion. "You could help us if you wanted."

I shrugged. "Maybe." In truth, I had no idea.

"You could. You got that dog bitch out of here. Everybody knows the Lady wanted to stay on your good side.

And she let you kill her. You've got influence. More now than before, too."

Dog bi—oh. Antonia the werewolf. And the Watsons were wrong. I didn't get my roommate out at all; Lena Olin did it for me. It wasn't a card I could play again, even if Satan 1.0 was still alive. Influence? Someone with influence wouldn't have been dumped here, and then stuck here. Watson was wrong all the way across the board. Shocker.

"Yeah, well." And like that, I was tired. It was exhausting being around them and not putting a fist through each of their lying skulls. "I'm not going to help you."

"Who are you to judge us?"

"Exactly," I said. "I'm a terrible person. A bitch and a liar, selfish, and not any kind of a genius. And all that before I died. I'm way more horrible now. And I'm still judging you. Doesn't that tell you anything?"

"That you're not who you were before. And so you can help us."

Listen, you useless harpy, I can't even get myself out of here, you think I'm wasting frequent flier miles on you?

I didn't say that. I said, "She'll never know I saw you. She'll never know you're here. She might wonder, but she won't *know*. And you will never, ever be grandparents to those weird babies. They won't know you. They won't hear stories about you. To them, you'll just be something that happened way before they were born. You'll be as real to them as online banking is to me. Something they'll vaguely hear about and not be very interested in."

"You can't! Jessica would—"

"Don't say her name, you useless twat. I don't want to hear her name come out of your mouth."

"We've changed!" She kept saying it, and I was betting she even believed it. Hilarious and sad. Or just sad and sad. "We know we have."

"You haven't, though. I haven't, either. Which is why you're staying and I'm going." Mr. Watson opened his mouth and I held up a finger. "If either of you says one more thing to me, I'll tear you up. I'll go home with your guts under my fingernails."

At last, I spoke a language they understood. Because they didn't make a peep while I walked away. The Ant fell into step beside me, and after a minute or so I knew that even if I looked back, I wouldn't be able to see them.

I didn't look back. My stepmother didn't, either.

TWENTY-FOUR

I was seated at Dr. Taylor's kitchen table, watching the Antichrist and Jessica split a cereal bar the size of a brick. My mother-in-law lived in a three-bedroom home with two and a half bathrooms (the *and a half* always amused me as a younger man; I would picture a bathroom neatly cut down the middle, with a real estate agent extolling the virtues of a half toilet). Her home was charming—cream and lavender walls, pale blue carpeting—and well kept. Dr. Taylor's various awards and certifications were framed in the living room; pictures of her and my wife were everywhere. When my wife had lived here as a teen, the third bedroom had been devoted to her shoes. Now that room was for my ward, BabyJon, and filled to bursting with infant detritus. Dr. Taylor was an indulgent parent.

On my occasional visits, I enjoyed getting a sense of who my wife had been before she became my queen. One of the pictures was Elizabeth's mug shot. She was glaring at the camera and had the beginning of a black eye. Her hair was quite short, what Tina called a pixie cut. She was not yet out of her teens.

Sheer stubbornness prevented me from asking about that particular photograph. Both women knew I was curious and confidently waited for me to break down and ask. I knew they thought I would break and so I would never ask; I would go to my grave again having no idea what Elizabeth had done to get arrested in downtown Minneapolis. Tina or Not-Nick could have found out for me in less than an hour; still I would not indulge. A mystery for the ages! Assault? Breaking and entering? Grand theft? Kidnapping?

"I'm still pissed at you," Jessica said to Laura with her mouth full, lightly spraying my mother-in-law with cereal crumbs. Dr. Taylor was so used to such treatment (not only from Jessica, alas) she merely blinked and brushed the crumbs away from her eyes. "But my babies come first. Hate you though I must, I've gotta feed them. It's my maternal imperative and stuff. It's the only reason I'm sharing anything with you."

"I understand," Laura said gravely and almost (ah, so close!) kept the smile off her face.

Dr. Taylor rapped the kitchen table, a blond wood piece with a white ceramic tile top, a sharp sound that almost cut through Jessica's crunching. "To the matter at hand. My daughter's safe." I noted it was not phrased as a question.

Laura looked startled, then hurt. Absurd. "Of course she's safe."

"Where?"

"Uh . . ." Incredibly, her gaze flicked to me as if she expected me to spring to her aid. I looked back and said nothing. When I sprang to her, it would not be to help. "Uh . . . nothing you need to—she's safe. She's not hurt."

"Did you dump her in the past?"

"No!" The Antichrist shuddered. "Oh, gosh, never! Never, ever again. Oh, *God*!" Her horror and dismay were understandable. I love the queen. I love the queen. And I would go to my death smiling if it meant she was safe. Those things are true. And the thought of her gaily tripping through history, accidentally stomping a fish as it tentatively flopped on land to breathe and then walk; choosing a man at random in her desperate hunger, draining him, then leaving Paul Revere to sleep off the remainder of April 18, 1775; stumbling through England while accidentally seducing Henry VIII, who would succumb to blood loss before he met Anne Boleyn; inadvertently helping Napoleon escape his St. Helena exile and liberating Central America; finding herself drawn by the smell of blood during William Seward's assassination attempt, but unable to keep the brave admiral from bleeding to death, thus preventing America's purchase of Alaska . . . no, that was too absurd a consequence to contemplate. However, I could foresee any or all of the others happening.

I love the queen. And I could foresee any or all of the others happening.

"Once was enough." The Antichrist was still shaken at the thought of what would happen to the universe had she exiled Elizabeth to the past. As I saw Jessica and my mother-in-law nod in unison, I had not thought there was anything the four of us could agree on, but apparently, this was most definitely it. "For both of us. No, I wouldn't—even if I hated her, dumping her in the past could—could—even if I hated her I wouldn't do that to the universe. And I don't."

"Oh, sure you do," Jessica said easily. She was jouncing BabyJon on her lap and sneaking him tiny bits of her cereal bar. She was so casual about what she was doing and saying she didn't bother to look up. "You hate her almost as much as you want to love her."

"I—what?" Laura shook her head in such adamant denial, her face was obscured by blond waves for a full ten seconds. "No."

"Laura." This in an exasperated tone. "You absolutely do. You liked her at first—no, that's not true, either. You . . ." Her dark gaze shifted to the ceiling while she sought *das richtige Wort*.

"You liked the *idea* of her," she said at last. "Of a big sister. But she wasn't much like the fantasy, huh? Pretty much the opposite, I bet. Especially when you want so badly to be good. It must have been horrifying to find out that big sis was the queen of the undead. There's not much positive spin you can put on that."

I was struggling not to let my jaw unhinge in astonishment. Had I not thought earlier that no one knew Elizabeth better than her dear friend? That had been truer than I knew; I had been a fool to consider it so lightly. Jessica had outstanding insight, and while I was fond of her, and respected the trials she had endured, I had dismissed her as not much more than a trust fund child, someone who was given everything and earned nothing. My embarrassment was only outweighed by my admiration.

"How d'you know that?" Laura asked.

"Hmm?" She looked up from the gurgling infant, who was now drooling cereal. "Which part?"

"That I want so badly to be good."

"Because Betsy knows, you silly cow. And she told me. She wants to be good, too. You guys have lots more in common than either of you'll admit. Yes, you *do*. Yes, you *do*." She fed a chortling BabyJon more cereal.

"I don't hate her," the Antichrist said in a low voice. She would not look at any of us. "I just want her to be better. I want to be better. She says she's scared about turning into—" A glance at my mother-in-law; a glance at me. I moved my head a quarter of an inch to the left and right. "—a bad person," she finished, recalling that Dr. Taylor didn't know much of anything about the woman the queen referred to as Ancient Awful Me. They had met only briefly, and Betsy's destiny had been kept from her mother; the queen had insisted and we had sworn. Elizabeth shared quite a bit of her new life with Dr. Taylor, but (understandably) not everything. "But I don't think she's scared *enough*, you know? Sometimes I think she talks about it because she thinks she's supposed to. It's not so much that I hate her. It's—"

"You fear her," I finished.

"Well. Yeah." Laura's clear gaze swept all of us. "Aren't you guys? I mean, really: aren't you?"

"Of course," I replied, and now it was my turn to receive startled glances. "Anyone who isn't is surely a fool. I am many things, and in the past I *have* been a fool, but not about this, I trust. I fear the queen. How else could I love her and follow her?"

I should have anticipated the uproar that followed. I did not. So perhaps my days of being a fool were not as far behind me as I had assumed.

CHAPTER
TWENTY-FIVE

"That was so sucky, I don't even have the vocab to recount how awful it was. And I've been here—what? An hour? A day? Of all the days not to wear a watch." I cursed the impulse to take off my watch and rings to stuff the turkey no one ate. Why had I ditched the watch? Did I really think I was going in up to the shoulder to stuff the bird? Thanks-giving is horrible.

"Your watch wouldn't work here, anyway," the Ant said. She probably thought I would find that comforting.

"I'm like a dog in this hellfog." At her muffled giggle, I scowled. "No idea how much time is passing, and I kind of want a chew toy to play with." I was thirsty, but I almost always was. This was my usual steady thirst, but at least it wasn't getting worse. "Of all the people to run into!"

"Yeah, but of course you were going to run into them."

"Nightmare. Utter nightmare. The Watsons and—" I closed my mouth. The Ant had actually been kind of cool during the Watson nightmare. This wasn't a movie. We weren't gonna team up to fight crime. We weren't going to learn valuable lessons or gain crucial insight into each other's personalities. I was pretty sure that was fine by both of us. "The Watsons," I said again, pretending that had been the original end of my sentence.

The Ant shrugged. "Well. You know how those people are."

Oh, wonderful. Back to this shit. I rounded on her, if you can round on someone in hellfog. "Is this why you're such a bigoted asshat? Because you're worried there's an African American—"

"They're African *Africans*," Hands-across-America sniffed.

"—in your family tree—"

"There *isn't*. We've been *over* this."

"—and you deal with it by distancing yourself every way you can—including racism? Because, if no one's thought to mention this to you: lame beyond belief. Staggering lameness. Lame to the nth power."

"You shut up," she said, annoyed. Why did most of the people in my life love me without reservation or hate me? Nobody took the middle ground on that one. It might say something about me. Possibly something bad. So I decided to stop pondering. "You've got no idea who I am or what I've gone through. You've never had any idea and you've never cared."

"Yes! Correct! I never and I never." I was in no mood for the "but I'm so misunderstood" wangstfest. "Listen, why don't you track down your grandmother or whoever—I'm sure most of your relatives *also* went to Hell—and ask them."

"They're not here," was the quiet reply, and I was so startled by her tone I couldn't think of anything to say for a minute. "The ones who could answer that question—none of them are here to ask."

I wasn't an idiot. Well, that was a lie, but I knew I was mostly interested in the Ant's family drama because it was a problem that a) I hadn't caused, b) I wasn't expected to fix, and c) had nothing to do with i) vampirism, ii) Hell, or iii) Satan.

"Did you tell my dad any of that stuff? Because he wouldn't have cared," I added when I saw her open her mouth. "Look, fair's fair. I was quick enough to bitch about him when he did stuff I didn't like, it's only fair to give him props. And I'm telling you, he wouldn't have cared. Dad would never have judged someone based on their race when he could judge them based on how much they made after taxes and who they voted for."

She was already shaking her head. "I don't think you've

got any idea what it was like for someone like me to land someone like your dad."

"I assumed you lost a bet."

Nope. She wasn't having it. Clearly not a joking matter. "It was—everything. Being his wife was everything. I wouldn't have done one thing to screw that up. I'd never have dared—how could I tell your father what I wouldn't even admit to myself? No." She shook her head. "I never told him."

"Well, he knows now, right?" I looked around the hell-fog as if expecting him to come strolling toward us.

"He's not here, either," she replied, and that shut me up.

Not for long, though. I could tell the Ant didn't want to discuss it anymore. But there wasn't much else for us to discuss. Our fears for the ozone layer? Whether peep-toe pumps were gonna be huge in the spring? (They weren't.)

"Okay, well, this can be the last note on the wrongness of bigotry and then we can change the subject."

"Goody," she replied sourly.

"Because I kind of want to circle away from your family shame and back to what you said about 'those people.' Jessica's parents don't give African Americans a bad name. They give incestuous enabling asshats a bad name. I mean, they're horrible even for incestuous enabling asshats."

"They are." And she actually smiled at me, a real one. She was really pretty when she didn't try so hard. I was so weirded out by my atypically generous thought, I smiled back.

CHAPTER TWENTY-SIX

"What? What?" I was surrounded by shrill, cawing ravens beating the air with their frantic movements. Ah . . . no. That was unkind. I was surrounded by my mother-in-law, my queen's best friend, and my sister-in-law. I had not realized I could feel so fully surrounded by three women smaller and weaker than I. "This cannot be news. Of course I fear the queen. That is why she is queen."

"Young man, love isn't about—"

"This isn't the nineteenth century, you flapping d—wait. When were you even born?"

"See? See? My Betsy-related ambivalence is entirely justified! The king of the vampires is scared of her!"

I held out my hands in as placating a manner as I could manage. I had no time to deal with a mob mentality. Also, when the mob was women, I feared the mob mentality. "Will it assuage your tension if I tell you I fear her in a loving way?"

"No!" Jessica yelped.

"Actually, that *does* make it better for me," Dr. Taylor admitted.

"Eric Sinclair!" my sister-in-law nearly screamed. She was running her hands through her hair and shaking her head. She looked quite deranged. "You telling me you're scared of the vampire queen is scaring me to death! That does not make me feel better! That makes me want to leave her where she is forever!"

"Ah. About that." I took off my outer coat, folded it in half, and hung it over the back of one of the kitchen chairs. I was not certain what would happen next, but wanted the increased mobility in any case. "I insist you return my queen at once."

"Maybe it's battered spouse syndrome. Sure, she beats on him, but he loves her anyway," Jessica murmured to Dr. Taylor. "Sinclair's got Stockholm syndrome."

I quelled a snort. Laura was still seated at the table, her hands braced against the ceramic tiles, glaring up at me. She looked equal parts angry, cornered, and defensive. "Where is she? And how will you return her to me?"

"Us," Jessica corrected. When we looked at her, she shrugged. "Fine. Him. Whatever."

"I'd think you'd be enjoying the peace and quiet," Laura muttered.

I stared down at her until she met my gaze. "I am, and that is irrelevant. You have taken what I love most. I will not survive without her. You are killing me. Do you understand? You are killing me." I looked at her, this beautiful woman, this terror, this child, this monster, this beauty. "Regardless of the love and care my wife has for you, do not think I will not avenge my own murder."

Laura held my gaze for a few more seconds, then glanced away. Before I could press the issue I heard a most unwelcome sound. For all her power, Laura had weaknesses I could use. Weaknesses I *was* using. I sensed she would bend to me without much more pressure. I did not desire a crowd and, beyond that, could not think why Tina had disregarded my text. "We are getting far afield. Laura, why are you here?"

She opened her mouth. She heard the screech of tires outside and a fury of slamming doors. She closed her mouth. *Dammit. Dammit.*

"Huh." Dr. Taylor frowned. "Clive and I don't have a date. And the book club doesn't meet here this week. We meet—"

"It is open," I called, so Tina would refrain from kicking the door down. Then, to my mother-in-law: "I apologize. It's inappropriate for me to invite others to your home."

"If it keeps my door from getting kicked in, invite away." At my small smile, she added, "It's the only reason you would've been rude."

I rose from the table. "Pardon me, ladies." Alas, not quick enough. The front door opened and there were hurrying footsteps in the hallway. It was a narrow hallway, running parallel to the living room, past the half bath (hee!), and then spilling its guests, in this instance Tina, into the kitchen.

"You!" was how she greeted the Antichrist.

"Stop that," I said mildly. "I received your message. Did you not receive mine?"

"I sensed duress," she lied. That was not one of her powers.

"She's lying!" The hallway had spilled Dr. Spangler into the kitchen right behind her. "She saw where you guys were and wanted to Hulk out all over the Antichrist. Hi, everybody."

"Tina, you can't park like that in the middle of the— hey, move it or lose it, Marc. So both of you have things to move or lose." Detective Berry waved. "Hi."

Tina, meanwhile, was now standing over the Antichrist. She had neglected her winter jacket and was wearing an old pleated skirt, bare legs, a pair of Elizabeth's saddle shoes that had not yet been donated, and a turtleneck several sizes too large. In fact, now that I took a closer look, it was my—

"If I hadn't made her grab that out of the dryer, she'd

be yelling at Laura in her bra," Marc whispered to Detective Berry.

"So you're the one the straight guys are super pissed at? Because show me the harm in Tina yelling at the Antichrist in her bra."

"You hope the yelling will degenerate into pulling hair and then a tickle fight, don't you?"

"I'm not apologizing for that," Berry replied easily.

Tina was oblivious of the turtleneck-, brassiere-, and tickle-fight-related whispers. "How dare you come here without the queen? Did you think to taunt Dr. Taylor? Of all the inappropriate places for you to go! Why are you here?"

"That was about as far as we got before you came in," Dr. Taylor said. "Sit down before you combust."

"It's okay, Tina," Jess assured her. "She didn't dump Betsy into the past. The universe is probably safe for at least the next couple of hours. Also, please note I'm holding an innocent baby. So nobody start any shit."

Sage advice. Yes, this was one of the oddest confrontations I had ever taken part in, involving no less than the Antichrist, the beloved aunt of my childhood, an infant, a Civil War scholar, a billionaire, a homicide detective, and a dead physician.

"If anyone does start some shit, it will be me. The rest

of you will keep your shit under control. I am the only one who should start shit of any sort."

"Everything's fine," Dr. Taylor said, standing to receive her "guests." "We're just talking. But I think it's sweet that you all charged to the rescue."

"I told her she should have stayed out of it," Marc tattled. He wandered up to Jessica and pulled something small and orange out of his jacket pocket. "Here. Drink this. You're low on folic acid and potassium."

She gifted him with one of her dazzling smiles, popped the top, jiggled BabyJon over to her other shoulder, and swigged.

"You told her to stay out of it," Dr. Taylor prompted, "and then followed her?"

"I've watched everything on our DVR," he said, as if that was an explanation, "and Amazon hasn't dropped off my new books yet."

The Antichrist, it gave me great pleasure to note, looked like a cat surrounded by Rottweilers. "You know, I recently lost my mother," she began, and was actually booed by Jessica and Marc. And blllrrppp'd by BabyJon.

"Totally different thing," Marc began.

"Apples and orange juice," Jessica gurgled.

"This isn't about you," Dr. Taylor said with simple severity. "Although, now that I think about it, some of it is."

"Your mother was trying to kill the queen!"

Ah. Tina was cross.

My smallish maiden aunt (I must, I must stop thinking of Christina Caresse as I did in my childhood) towered over the Antichrist (Laura had remained seated). "That seems to be the part of the story you most like to leave out. Your mother and the—that other woman—essentially *destroyed the future.*"

"That's the second time you've danced around something I haven't been told," Dr. Taylor observed. "When Elizabeth does get back, we're having a long talk."

A problem, I surmised, for another day.

"Before the two of them could get started this time around, the queen put an end to it. No one yet understands how that came about, but what we all know to be true is that your mother tried to kill our queen. If Her Majesty hadn't put an end to your mother, *I* would have."

"Okay," the Antichrist said.

When a sword made of hellfire didn't come swinging out of nowhere and remove her head from her shoulders, Tina blinked and we eyed each other for a moment. Old friends, our telepathy had nothing to do with the supernatural.

Well, that went better than I expected.

I am relieved you have not been killed. Also, we'll discuss why you ignored my text to stay away.

"So anyway," Laura continued, "I came over to tell Dr. Taylor what I think is going on with Jessica's pregnancy."

"This isn't how I expected this to go," Marc confessed. He and Detective Berry were in the corner. Detective Berry kept shoving Marc behind him, and Marc kept peeking over his shoulder. "And I'm dead, dammit!" He gave Detective Berry a shove that nearly sent the man sprawling. "What exactly are you saving me from?"

"And I want to hear all about it," Dr. Taylor said. "But if you didn't steal my daughter to punish her, why did you?"

"I kind of had to," she explained. She seemed sincere and remorseful and hurt and angry. To my annoyance, I felt sympathy begin to slide past my anger. "Hell's a mess and I don't know what to do with it. Betsy knew when she killed my mom that I'd probably have to take her place. I just wanted her to really see what she left me with. They're going to be more scared of her than she is of them. I'll get her back pretty soon."

"Oh." Jessica rubbed BabyJon's back; the infant had dozed off around the time Tina was waiting to be decapitated. "That works for me, I guess. It's not like Bets can't take care of herself. It was still kind of a dick move, though."

"Don't say *dick* in front of the baby," Marc scolded. He removed items from another parka pocket. "And eat this," he added, handing her a strawberry yogurt and plastic spoon.

"You've turned yourself into a walking fridge," Detective Berry observed. And it was true. Marc had said more than once that he no longer felt the cold. But his parka—something handed down from his father—was sturdy, the color of crushed green olives, riddled with pockets, smelled of sawdust and feathers, and worked very well as a refrigeration unit.

"Like I was saying, I have some idea about Jessica's pregnancy. But . . ."

"What?" Jessica asked.

"It's just there's not much point telling you about it while they're here." Laura nodded to indicate Jessica, Marc, Tina, Dick, and (eh?) me.

"Oh, I don't agree. You can tell me now because if it's good news they'll be fine, and if it's bad news, they'll be fine, because something is making all of them"—she gestured to our small group—"not care."

"What is this?" I asked sharply. "If there is bad news I insist you tell me at once."

"Because of Betsy's timeline tampering, Jessica's pregnant with any or all of her potential babies at once."

"What the hell are you talking about?" I snapped, and was almost as startled as they were. "Ah . . . my apologies. I am apparently laboring under some stress."

Of all people, the Antichrist smiled at me. "Don't worry. Betsy's fine, and Jessica's fine, too. There's not as much to worry about as you thought."

Absurdly, that comforted me. I had forgotten another thing about family: when you were with them, it was possible to let your guard down. I was out of practice.

CHAPTER TWENTY-SEVEN

"This is gonna sound dumb, but I only just realized something's up with Jessica's pregnancy."

"What's dumb is that you're telling me."

"Granted, granted. Pretend you care, okay? I'm cut off from my support system today." I gestured at the hellfog. "You're my sounding board."

"I didn't do one thing in life to merit this kind of torment," the Ant muttered, but made a "come on, then" gesture.

"Stop praying to the devil; it's creepy. Okay, before Laura and I did our hilarious version of the *Back to the Future* movies minus the cool car and future gadgetry, Jess wasn't pregnant and she and her boyfriend had broken up. I get back and she's out-to-here preggo and the guy who isn't

Nick loves her and lives in the mansion with us. Happily ever after, right?"

"So?"

"So nobody knows when she got pregnant. Nobody knows when she's due. Nick doesn't know; Jess doesn't know. I was fine with me not knowing, but it's definitely odd that Jess is as clueless. She hasn't seen a doctor. She's completely unconcerned about all of it. And none of us thought anything of it, either."

"Until you got here, right?"

"Right!" I grabbed her arm, then loosened my grip when she flinched. "How'd you know that? What's going on with Jess? Is she okay? Are the babies okay?"

"Sure." The Ant picked my fingers off her arm, one by one, like they were leeches. She looked *this* close to shuddering. "The Lady thought this might happen. We even talked about it a bit."

"Good. Now talk to me about it a bit."

"Ah . . . okay. Let's see . . . the best way to break this down for you. And me without my parallel universe mechanics flash cards."

"Oh, man." Stuck in hellfog. A chat with the Watsons. Jessica's scary-ass pregnancy. The Ant as my only route to clarity. *God, never have I feared your wrath more. You're as vengeful as a teenage girl venting breakup rage on Twitter.* "Just break it down."

"You're different since you were killed and ruined the cruise I was supposed to take with your father."

I gritted my teeth. Anything I said would make this take longer. "Yessssss?"

"You can do things you couldn't before."

"Yessssss?"

"Your friends are different, too. Or, rather, things that would have affected them one way before you died affect them in a different way. Because of who you are. Jessica's perfectly ordinary. And given her parents, she should be pretty grateful."

Don't say anything or it'll take longer. Don't say anything or it'll take longer.

"But her babies aren't. They're shifting through parallel universes. In one universe Jessica's only three weeks along; in another universe, Jessica's babies are almost full term. The babies are healthy. But they're going to be different, because Jessica hangs around you."

"Oh."

"Mm-hmm."

"That's so incredibly lame."

The Ant shrugged. "I didn't make any one of these rules. I just sometimes explain them to lost vampires."

I snorted. "Hilarious."

"The trick is going to be figuring out which babies she has. Which parallel universe they'll be from. Or will they

219

do that shifting thing throughout their lives? That could be interesting."

"If by 'interesting' you mean 'terrifying,' then sure. Interesting it is. I'll have to figure out how to break all this to Jess. But you promise they're okay, right?" I hated showing any vulnerability to the Ant, even when she was being nicer than I'd ever known her to be, and certainly more helpful. But I couldn't keep the anxiety from my tone. It'd be hard enough to explain the weird to Jess; how could I explain if something went wrong?

"Yes, she's fine and the babies should be fine. Just different, I promise. For what that's worth to you," she added.

"Today it's worth a lot," I said without thinking, and I was so disappointed in myself I almost groaned aloud. Parallel universes! Timelines! Hellfog! All conspiring to make me not hate the Ant. *Lord, Lord, what are you doing to my sense of how things should be?* I got back to a less off-putting topic. "So what's with nobody noticing she's not showing and then she is showing and doesn't see doctors? How come I didn't realize what was happening until . . ." I trailed off. That one I could maybe answer on my own. The hellfog wasn't earth. The normal rules didn't apply. Or as Marc would say (he spent way too much time on the TV Tropes website), YMMV (Your Mileage May Vary).

"Yeah." The Ant accurately read my expression. "You had to end up in another world to realize what was wrong in yours. As to why none of you noticed—I wonder about my son."

My son. But this wasn't the time for a turf war over BabyJon. Although he was mine, mine, *mine*. "He's special," I agreed. Really special, and not just because he was the sweetest sweetie ever. He was irresistible. He even melted Sinclair's cold, cold heart like an Eskimo Pie dropped on a July sidewalk.

Even better (given where he lived), the kid couldn't be hurt by anything paranormal. He could get run over by a car, but if a vampire tried a chomp or a werewolf tried a slash, he'd shrug it off. I can't tell you how much that baby freaked out the Cape Cod werewolves. It was pretty terrific.

"I think it's something he does unconsciously, and you're all picking up on it. If you were all painting in a closed room, you'd all get headaches, right?"

"Sure." Stray off topic much, Ant? Painting?

"I think because the baby isn't concerned about Jessica's babies, you're all picking up on that, so you're not concerned, either. It's only going to affect people in close proximity."

I stopped walking and snapped my fingers. "My mom! She kept babbling something about the babies during our Thanksgiving Take Two party—"

"You had two Thanksgivings?"

"Focus, Antonia! First painting and now T-day 2? But yeah, we did so Laura would start to forgive me for killing her mom, except she dumped me here instead. Forgiveness may come later; I haven't given up hope and could you at least *try* to hide the delighted grin?"

"Sorry," she said, which was the purest lie I'd ever heard.

"Anyway, my mom, Dr. *Taylor*, would not shut up about Jessica's pregnancy. We all kept blowing her off. I remember being annoyed that she kept bugging me about it." Remembered, hell. It was downright embarrassing to recall my annoyance. Memo to me: when I get back, grovel for Mom for a couple of hours. Make liberal use of the phrases *you were right all along* and *if only I had listened*. Cue repentant gnashing of teeth and pulling of highlights.

"Yes, well. My baby's influence would be cumulative, I think."

"The painting-in-the-closed-room theory." At last it made sense.

"Yes. Your mother baby-sits my son"—I waited in dread, sure the Ant would verbally scald the shit out of me while expressing her displeasure, but (*thanks, God!—at last you cut me a break*) she let it go—"but isn't around him enough to—to—"

"To catch the 'no worries' germs he's putting out," I finished. Okay, it wasn't terribly scientific. It wasn't scientific at all. But it was good enough for this girl, for now. Best of all, Jessica was okay and her weird babies were okay. There were worse things. I made a mental note to keep that in mind *all* the *time*. And I wouldn't deny it was a relief to get actual proof I wasn't the worst mom ever—BabyJon could only "infect" us because he was around us so much. Maybe it was the plane-crash theory. We don't think about the millions of flights that land safely every year, but when the media flogged a crash, you felt like airline disasters happened all the time. When we weren't hunting killers or stuck in Hell, BabyJon was with us. Watching Laura beat a serial killer to death stuck in my mind more than the time BabyJon shampooed with his bowl of Cheerios. "Sure, I get it."

"Oh, goodie. I was sure I'd have to break out the hand puppets."

"You said you and Satan talked about this?"

"Yes."

"Other stuff, too, I bet."

The Ant shrugged.

"You liked her?"

Another shrug. It was like talking to . . . me. I instantly shoved the horrifying thought far, far back into the cobwebby recesses of my mind, never to be heard from again.

"You were her assistant for a while—by the way, that hasn't surprised any of us."

She barked a surprised laugh. "You don't know the half of it, Betsy."

"Why'd you help the devil?" I couldn't help asking; it was something I'd always been curious about. "With anything?"

"She asked me," was the simple reply, and with that I had to be content.

"So how long do you think I'll be stuck here?"

"That's up to you."

"I'm positive that's not true." I thought about it. "Yep. It's not true."

She made an odd sound (sigh/grunt? groan/mutter?) and rubbed her eyes. "Can you please skip to the part where you've learned a valuable lesson and go away, so I can go away, too?"

"Antonia. Look at my face." She looked. I pointed to my chin. "This is my serious face. My 'no, really, I *don't* get it' face."

"If you can't figure it out on your own, I can't help you." She paused and considered. "Won't help you is closer to it."

"Antonia. I didn't pop through the back of a wardrobe and end up here. I didn't pray to a Ouija board. I didn't lose a bet, except possibly with Jesus. I was dragged and dumped here."

"Dim. Dim bulb." She was rubbing her forehead. Cool, I got a getting-a-migraine forehead rub from the Ant! Who, after over a decade, was being upgraded from skank nemesis to worthy foe. "'From hell's heart I stab at thee.'"

"Well, I'm not too keen on you, either. And cribbing from *Star Trek*? Plus, keep it down. All we need is for ten thousand damned *Star Trek* fans to hear you and we'll be stuck in a Picard versus Kirk conversation for five thousand years." Thinking it was bad enough; hearing myself say it out loud was horrifying. "So no more *Tar-say Rek-tay* references."

"It's Melville, you moron. 'For hate's sake I spit my last breath at thee.'"

"Gross."

"There are so many souls here. But you've seen me and you've seen the Watsons."

"Don't remind m—"

"I *am* reminding you, moron! Think! For once, stop your eternal fucking babbling and engage your brain!"

"I'm the vampire queen, you shouldn't talk to me like that," I whined.

She had the 'I'm counting to ten' look on her face. "You did something. Think about it."

If this was the movies and I was a stock Mary Sue character, the Ant would outwardly hate me but inwardly think I was terrific. Her sarcasm would shield her caring; her scolding would only be to help me learn. Tough love.

"I've got no idea."

"Then you're useless and you should be set on fire until you're a big useless pile of ash, you useless dumbass."

It wasn't tough love, it was zero love. And it sure wasn't the movies. Didn't Mary Sues eventually win everyone over? Tell you this: they were aggravating to read about (*"This* archenemy has fallen in love with her, too? It's her sixth archenemy! Not one of her nemeses has a spine!"), but the chance to be a Mary Sue? C'mon, who wouldn't? That was the life.

"Even now, even now I can tell you're not actually thinking about the problem."

"You caught me," I admitted.

"So focus!" she screamed, plunging her hands into her hair and doing a credible Elsa Lanchester impersonation. *She's alive! She's aliiiiiive!* "Abandon your derailed train of thought and stomp your inner ditz."

"Sure, I'll get right on that at half past never. My inner ditz and I have an understanding. And don't forget, I'm a ditz with power."

"Yes! You are! You're the one who keeps forgetting. How did you find me in all this?"

"I didn't. You found me. You came right out of the hellfog and put the cherry on the shit sundae of my day."

"I sure did." Odd (and annoying) that my cherry remark didn't get under her skin. In fact, she sounded almost . . . pleased? *Good dog, you did it!* pleased?

"And then the Watsons fou—and then we found the Watsons." I'd been so busy bemoaning my bad luck about meeting the three people in hellfog I couldn't stand, I hadn't thought about what that meant.

"You were about as happy to see me as I was to see you," I remembered. "Like I was a chore you were assigned. And . . . I *am* a chore you were assigned!"

"One of my worst," she agreed, making me happy.

"Right! Something you had to do, except in this case I was some*one* you had to do and we're not even gonna acknowledge the sex subtext on that one."

She nodded so hard she nearly fell over. "Agreed."

"You said I *wouldn't* come to Hell on my own," I thought out loud. I was essentially thinking about it as I verbalized. "Not *couldn't*. And then when I was bitching—"

"Sorry, can you narrow that down a little?"

"—about meeting the Watsons; give me two seconds to finish the thought, okay? I was all 'of all the people!' and you were all 'you were going to run into them anyway.' Wait. Is that right?" I thought about it. "Yeah. That's basically it. So could I have?"

She stared. "I don't—is that how you think? For real?"

"Now who's not focusing? Could I have come here on my own?" I didn't even need the nod. You know how when you come up with something and you just get that it's right? That was now. "I could have come here on my own," I said slowly. "Which implies . . . that I can leave on my own?"

"Yes. It implies that."

"I was thinking about you and you came. I was thinking about Thing One and Thing Two and *they* came. Can I . . ." This was too easy. This couldn't be the actual answer. "Can I think my way home?"

She nodded. "Yeah. I'm pretty sure you can."

"How? I've been thinking about how much I want to get home from the moment your kid dumped me here. I can't feel my husband, can you get that? The place where he was . . ." I couldn't trickle tears, but that didn't mean I couldn't cry in every other way, and suddenly it was so hard to talk. "It's like a footprint in my brain. He's not there. Just some ghost image of him. If just wanting to be back with my family is what it takes, I'd have been back about two seconds after I landed."

"Maybe you need help."

"Maybe, huh?"

She opened her mouth, and her grin widened. "Naw. Too easy. Like taking a hammer to one of those fat fuzzy caterpillars."

"I have no idea how to respond to that." Never had I said something more true.

"I think you probably need help like Laura needed help the first few times."

"Oooh, yeah! Like that bogus 'you've gotta have physical contact with one of your blood to travel between worlds' rule I am almost *positive* Satan made up just to fuck with me. At first Laura couldn't, and then she could, and then she got better, and now she can do it on her own."

"So . . . ?"

"Practice makes perfect," I finished, glum. The fat fuzzy caterpillar was sad. "Use something until I don't need the tool—or the crutch?—anymore. What, just click my silver shoes together? Lame."

The Ant didn't say anything.

I didn't say anything. But I quickly cracked under the stress of silence and said, louder, "What, just click my silver shoes together? Lame!" Still nothing. "If I look down, there's gonna be a pair of silver shoes at my feet, aren't there?"

She shrugged. "I don't make the—"

"*Please* stop." I looked. Yep. Sparkly silver, cute matching sparkly bows, low wide heels. The way I'd always pictured them as a kid.

I glared at the shiny things. I'd have been delighted any other time, in any other circumstance. But in the hellfog, they just looked childish. A really lame deus ex machina. A *shoe ex machina*. Ha! "Really, Antonia? Silver goddamned shoes?"

She shrugged with a grin. When her mouth wasn't twisted in a snarl, she had a pretty smile. "I don't make the rules. And who makes them here in the future has yet to be seen."

"Swell." I bent, pulled off Tina's socks (trudging through

hellfog in socks—at least I didn't have to worry about leaving my shoes here), slipped them in my pocket, then stepped into the silver shoes. A perfect fit. Of course.

"How come they're not ruby slippers?" the Ant asked, brows arched in curiosity as she stared down at my feet. "That's what they're supposed to represent, right? How Dorothy gets home from Oz?"

"How Toto got home. I never gave a shit about Dorothy; Toto was the protagonist. Dorothy was strictly transportation. He's the only dog I've ever liked. Well . . ." I considered. "Him and Fur and Burr. The dog who played him got paid more than a lot of the actors, so I guess the Munchkins had lousy agents. Did you know that in the books, Toto could talk all along, he just chose not to? Baum had to retcon that one a little."

"You've educated yourself about the strangest, most useless things." Was that admiration I heard in her tone? Nope. Just loathing.

"Anyway, also in the books, they were silver shoes. They made them ruby slippers for the movie because Technicolor was a new thing and they wanted to take advantage. But in the books, the shoes were silver. And the books were a hundred times better than the movie."

"You really know a lot about shoes."

"Yep." I had to admit, they looked terrific on me. Since I

was wearing them barefoot, I hoped they wouldn't shred my feet too much. Yes, I'd heal quickly, but it's never fun to grow blisters. "Okay, so. I'm not ungrateful." I could almost see the Ant physically brace herself. "But this is, among other things, anticlimactic."

"Sure it is." She laughed. "Real life often is."

"Oh boy. You think this is real life?"

"As close as we can get."

"Mmm." I looked down at my absurdly sparkling toes. "All right. So I'm gonna make with the clicking in a few seconds. Listen." I tried to find the exact right words, and couldn't, and tried anyway. "I know you didn't want to help me. Thanks for doing it anyway."

"Why wouldn't I? It was *so* entertaining." Then, at my look: "What? We don't have DVRs here. Watching you blunder from one problem to the next, always making it worse without a clue why, and ultimately a victim again of your own shortsightedness . . . this was better than a movie. A summer movie, even."

"And like that, I hate you again." Click. "Thanks again. Jerk." Click. "Also, there's no place like home. There's no race like foam. There's no laying with gnomes." Click.

"What are you doing now?" she asked incredulously.

"Hey, if it's about my brain more than the physical world, it shouldn't matter what I say, as long as I'm visualizing correctly. Ha!" I crowed as the hellfog started to fade, as my stepmother's shade started to fade. "I was right! It's working! Suck on that, Antonia! And thanks again, I guess."

She opened her mouth but I never heard her comeback. Ha! Thanks a bunch, silver shoes.

TWENTY-EIGHT

"People don't change," the infant Antichrist was informing me while the others were putting on their jackets and preparing to leave *casa* Taylor. "They like to think it, so they say it. But it's just something, uh, some people say."

Tina, Dr. Taylor, and I all picked up the *old people* context. I traded glances with my old friend. *Calm. Be calm.* The surest way to annoy a child is to call attention to the fact that she is, in fact, a ch—

"What nonsense," my mother-in-law said, exasperated. "Laura, I'm sorry, but I can't accept any sort of 'this is how everyone is in the whole wide world' pronouncement from someone who's been voting age for less than three years. I understand that you're more than a pretty girl from

Minnesota, but some things are true no matter what your pedigree is."

"I don't see what pretty has to do with it," she muttered, and I had to agree.

"I understand that you're a paranormal force of extraordinary power, maybe even destruction incarnate. And you've been that for not quite two decades. You can't rent a car yet. So enough of your pronouncements on humanity."

"Then how about not-humanity?" she snapped.

"Sorry, what?"

"Him!" Ah. The moving finger pointeth at me. "Your daughter's husband, the king of the vampires! She's killed the devil and he's here to bully me into bringing her back."

"Not at all," I said helpfully. "Merely to tell you that if you do not return the queen, I shall kill you."

"That's not bullying," Tina agreed. "It's a straightforward if/then proposition." She turned to Jessica, frantically shaking her head; Marc, making slashing motions across his throat; and Detective Berry, who was holding his head in his hands. *"What?"*

"Nothing," they returned in mumbled unison, followed by Jessica's whispered, "Should we go outside and let them thrash it out?"

"DVR's empty," Marc reminded her.

"Screw that," the expectant mother replied.

"Laura, you have never approved of me," I said, "and really, never of the queen, either. Which was irrelevant to me until you snatched her from the world. And it has nothing to do with what we have or have not done. You distrust our very nature. We could present the world with a cure for cancer, and you would explain it away by assuming it was a way to keep our prey healthy."

"That *would* be just like you," she said, startled into agreeing.

"Oh, Laura, really!" Dr. Taylor snapped.

"Because we cannot change. Vampires are predators who feed on humans."

"Yes."

"Evil incarnate, as you are thought to be destruction incarnate."

"Yes." But this time, she could not meet my gaze, and I finally understood.

"Laura." I took her small, warm hand in mine. It trembled like a small animal, a rabbit in a trap. "Laura, if you do not wish to be evil, do not do evil. That's all. That is the big secret. You were not born to destroy worlds. If you do so, that is by choice and not by blood. Really, all this drama because you've read *The Bad Seed* too many times?" I chided her gently.

"If you're even being honest with me, it's not that simple.

Don't you understand?" She took her hand back. "There's no one like me anywhere. So no matter what happens, no matter what I do or what anyone does, I'm stuck."

"Yes." I smiled. "And in that, you and your sister are exactly alike."

"Oooh, now with the trash talk," Jessica commented.

"Not at all. Come with me," I coaxed. "Let me show you something that will make you feel young, as when the world was new."

"Wait," Marc said. "Where have I heard that?"

"Curse your near-perfect recall of all things pop culture," I said, leading Laura to the front door.

"*Wrath of Khan!*" he cried, galloping down the hall after us. "That does not bode well for us! Unless Khan wins in this case!"

"You should all see this," I said. "Now come along."

"Eric, are you sure . . . ?" Tina trailed off, and I knew her startlement was profound by her use of my first name. She knew this was a secret I had guarded jealously. It was still so new to me. I wanted to share it only with the queen. But this was no time to close ranks. Quite the opposite. If we were a family, a true family, it was time to behave as such.

"Stay here with Dr. Taylor until it is full dark," I told her. "Or have Marc take you straight home. We shall all be there shortly. The queen as well, I am sure." Laura wouldn't look at me, but I held to my confidence. "I don't want you to risk further harm. You were foolish to come here at all, which we shall discuss at a later time." That was as severe a reprimand as I could manage, because I knew she was upset and worried for me . . . and for Elizabeth. Tina did not normally risk immolation.

"It's okay," Marc assured me. "I'll run her home right now. She likes my trunk."

"This is the sort of thing that makes people scared of vampires," Laura commented.

"Thank you so much," I replied politely. "I have never once considered that in all my years of being a blood-seeking denizen of the night." *Ah, careful. Careful.*

"Actually, I do like his trunk," Tina said quickly. "It's roomy and he leaves book lights . . ." She mimed turning on the light on a miner's helmet. "And blankets, and books, too. And yesterday he recharged my Kindle and put that in there. It's nice!"

To my surprise, the Antichrist burst out laughing. "Sorry, it's just—the mental image—it's nice that you like it—" She dissolved into giggles. "It's good that you take care of them."

"Oh, yes." Marc smiled at her. "It's a full-time job, you know. It keeps me busy." And I realized he was smiling at all of us.

As they began to file out, I turned to say my farewell to Dr. Taylor, who had left the hallway. "Thank you for—"

"Eric, wait!"

I stopped and stepped back from the door, swinging it almost all the way shut to keep the heat in. The others had filed out, Tina hidden under Marc's parka/refrigerator/ shield. "Yes, Dr. Taylor? What is it?"

"This." She had run to the living room and plucked Elizabeth's booking photograph off the wall. Beaming, she brought it to me. "Here," she said, looking up at me with my wife's eyes. "I know it's your favorite. You keep it until you get her back."

Unspoken: *This is all I can do for you.*

Unspoken: *I know you'll get her back; this is my token.* This meant much to me, because although I was fairly confident Laura would bend to my will—*was* bending to my will— and that Elizabeth had things under control where she was, life and death had taught me nothing if not that things do not always happen as planned.

I took the picture carefully, like it was a baby bird. "Thank you." For one dreadful moment I thought my voice was going to crack. The dreadful moment passed and not a dreadful moment too soon. "I shall keep it for you until."

Until. Vague and hopeful at the same time.

"Thank you." I realized I had already said that. I realized I needed to leave. To my horror, I found I was close to weeping. I vowed I would not break down and sob in front of a woman wearing Jack Skellington slippers. "Thank you, Dr. Taylor."

She nodded and smiled. "You'll get her back. When you do, bring the picture back and I'll tell you all about it."

"There is no need to threaten me," I said dryly and left as quickly as dignity allowed.

CHAPTER
TWENTY-NINE

"This is a bad idea," Detective Berry said as he helped Jessica out of the passenger seat. "But I gotta say, it's nice to see you out in the lack of sunshine."

The sun had been coyly hiding behind clouds for the last couple of days, but it was only midafternoon, and quite bright. (Compared to the deep dark of the some twenty thousand midnights since Tina turned me, it would have to be cloudy indeed for me to think it less than bright.)

We had not driven far from Dr. Taylor's home; we were parked outside the First Presbyterian Church, which had been here since 1855 . . . half again as long as I had. It was an enormous structure, brooding over Vermillion Street with thick walls. The twin towers and white arches gave it a Romanesque look, as if the congregation had plucked their church from medieval Europe and brought it to Minnesota piece by piece. I had long admired it.

Laura had parked her car on Sixth Street, behind mine and Marc's, and walked to my side. Marc had his phone out and was giving Tina, snugly ensconced in his trunk, a tedious moment-by-moment update. "Okay, we're all standing on the street. But it's Hastings, so nobody's getting run over like dogs. Now we're all staring at a huge church that looks like it's gonna be stormed by medieval peasants any second. Now your boss and my roommate are walking up to the doors of the—uh—Eric? I think that's a very bad idea."

"Come with me," I said to Laura, who had fallen into step beside me.

"Are you trying to make me bring Betsy back so you won't kill yourself?" she asked, seeming honestly interested. "Because I have to admit, I'd be torn on the right way to handle that. Not just for me. For all mankind."

"You were explaining to me that people cannot change. Something you learned after your endless twenty years on the planet."

"Now Eric's making fun of Laura's age," Marc dutifully reported. "Did she think she was being subtle in Mama Taylor's kitchen with that 'people don't change, it's just something old people say' stuff? Because I'm only a couple years older than she is, and I still winced. Ooh, now they're approaching the big wooden double doors of the church. I guess he's gonna threaten to burn himself ali—oh, my God! He's opening the door! And he isn't on fire! So far!"

"Come along," I told the Antichrist. "Come pray with me."

"Pray for what?" Laura whispered, following me into the church.

"My wife's safe return," I replied. "And peace on earth for all mankind, I suppose. If you're inclined. I myself am not; how dull that would be!"

She followed me through the fellowship hall; much of the first floor was used for coffee and snacks after the service, potluck suppers, and the occasional reception. To the rear were several smaller rooms used for classes and day care. To the left was a sizeable area for coats and, past that, steps leading to the chapel.

I walked up the steps, leading the Antichrist by the hand.

"The amusing thing is, there was a time when I believed you were right. That we don't change; we cannot change. That people were good or bad or cowardly or brave but, ultimately, not terribly original or interesting. Certainly not inclined to modify behavior or, if they did, never for long.

"And then I met the queen. And through her, all the extraordinary people now in our lives. Including you, I suppose," I added with a smile.

"Now he's taken her into the part of the church where they hear the service!" Marc nearly shrieked into his phone. "And he's still not on fire or anything! But I'll keep you posted on the fire thing! What? I'm shouting? Sorry!" I could hear Detective Berry helping Jessica up the steps. "Hurry up, you guys, you're missing this!"

"Which has been, I admit, a mixed blessing," I finished. "You know I love the queen. But . . . ah . . . yes. Mixed."

Stunned, Laura allowed me to lead her to the altar.

"But I eventually learned that they can change," I said, kneeling. "And when they don't, or won't, I have learned patience. Because perhaps they are not the ones who should change; perhaps I am the one who must change. The queen taught me that."

I folded my hands. I looked at the altar. The wise eyes of the Shepherd were on me, as they had been the moment I came squalling from my mother.

"'"Father, I have sinned against heaven and before you, and I am no longer worthy to be called your son. Make me like one of your hired servants." . . . But when he was still a great way off, his father saw him and had compassion—'"

Beside me, Laura was weeping. "'And ran and fell on his neck and kissed him. And the son said to him, "Father, I have sinned against heaven in your sight, and am no longer worthy to be called your son."'"

"'But the father said to his servants, "Bring out the best

robe and put it on him, and put a ring on his hand and sandals on his feet. And bring the fatted calf here and kill it, and let us eat and be merry."'"

We finished my mother's favorite parable in unison: "For this my son was dead and is alive again; he was lost and is found."

"I'm sorry." Laura wept. "I'm so, so sorry."

"It's all right." I helped the Antichrist up from her knees. "I didn't ask you here to shame you. Only to show you."

"You don't even know." She fumbled in her pocket, found a napkin, and gustily blew her nose. "You don't know what I've done. I'm sorry."

"To Elizabeth?" I asked sharply.

She shook her head. "Betsy's safe."

"And so am I. And so are you. The rest can be for another time."

"You. Are not even gonna believe. What's going on in here." I looked; Marc was openmouthed, the phone nearly dropping from his fingers. "I don't have the words. Which sucks for you, since you're in my car trunk and can only rely on my narration to know what's happening. But this incredible thing you're missing is friggin' incredible!" His last *incredible* was nearly shrieked.

"Shush," I scolded. "Remember where you are." I rarely saw people in this church on a weekday in the middle of the day, but it did not follow that disrespectful noise was acceptable.

"Somebody's been keeping secrets," Detective Berry scolded. "How long have you been a vampiric Presbyterian?"

"By kidnapping Betsy, you outed him!" Jessica told Laura. "So you can feel good about that. But stop crying now, or you'll get me started."

"Ah, give her a break." Detective Berry hurried down the aisle, but I had already helped Laura to her feet. "How often does someone's faith in humanity get restored? Let her have her moment."

"Laura's crying," Marc narrated, "but everybody else is in pretty high spirits. Okay, I'm muting my phone for a minute." He pressed something, took the phone away from his face, and said to me, "God, God, *God*!" At my raised eyebrows, he turned to the others. "See? I knew he was off!"

"Off?" I asked.

"I slipped a couple of times the last few days and apologized, and Eric was always 'no problem my good man' about it. I *thought* it was bothering you less."

I could not hide my amusement. "Less?"

"Well, no. That's not right. I thought you were hiding it better," he admitted. "Usually you and Tina react to a God comment like someone lashed you in the eyebrows. Lately you've been a little less flinch-ey. I just figured hiding it better was a king-of-the-vampires thing, since Tina's a lot older but it sure bugs her."

Something beyond the sun, I remembered. I had been lost in Elizabeth, drowning in her, and thinking that she had not just given me the light. But that was nothing I wished to share; it belonged to me as did the queen, and as I belonged to her.

"I had no idea you were so observant," I teased.

"Hey, if Betsy didn't give a shit about shoes or TV or the movies, she'd be really observant, too. It's just, she spends a lot of her brainpan focusing on shoes. Hang on, I gotta get Tina back in." He touched another spot on his phone. "Hey, I'm back. Just had to test a theory. How's the charge on your Kindle . . . ? It is? Okay, good." He looked up. "You know, the only thing we need for that extra bit of TV drama is for Jess to instantly go into labor." He paused and stared at her. We all stared.

"What?" she replied testily. She'd refused to sit in one of the pews and, given how they appeared to be designed to enrich chiropractors, that seemed wise. "I feel fine. Go get your drama somewhere else."

That seemed as good as any indication that it was time to take our leave.

CHAPTER
THIRTY

My shoes ex machina *dumped me on my front porch.*

"Yes!" I was so pleased I hugged myself. But not for long! My poor husband and bereft friends, likely worried to death about me, would be hugging me soon enough. And soon after that, Sinclair would be hugging me naked while I hugged him back while we moved up and down a *lot*. Sex: hugs, only better.

I seized the doorknob, only to find it locked. Eh? Their cars were in the driveway. They hadn't been here long, either; it was snowing lightly but their windshields were wet and snow free: they'd been driving with their wipers on until very recently. Alas, when Laura dumped me into the hellfog, I hadn't grabbed my keys. And although I could eventually kick in our enormous ancient front door,

I had no interest in spending the time or, ultimately, the money.

Side door? Sure! They were probably in the kitchen comforting themselves with sadness smoothies, so that door was probably unlocked, and if it wasn't, they could take a break from their mourning long enough to let me in.

"Guys?" I trotted through the side yard and up the walk to the kitchen door. My silver shoes had surprisingly good traction. Also, now that I was out of the hellfog, how long would these shiny shoes stick around? Something perhaps to ask my wise husband. If I ever found the mournful s.o.b. "I'm back, so you can start with the rejoicing!" I couldn't hear anything, but the door was unlocked. "Guys? Time to swap out the sadness smoothies for smoothies of triumph—guys?"

Nobody in the kitchen.

WTF?

Argh! Reason #26 I hated texting: texting invaded the language, infecting even those who did not text. Invading even my thoughts! What I meant was: *What the fuck?*

Nobody in the kitchen. Recently driven cars in the driveway. Nobody was looking for me, nobody was listening for me. Tina and Sinclair should have both heard me by now. Ergo, they were in trouble or they weren't here. The third option, that they were here but somehow their every thought *wasn't* bent on finding me, didn't bear considering.

Were they in trouble? Oh, jeez, while I was blundering through the hellfog restraining myself from strangling the Watsons with their own spinal cords, had my family been in trouble? Dying forever trouble?

Call for them or sneak around hoping to get the chance to brain any would-be bad guys? There were advantages to—

"Ow, Goddammit, ow!"

Jessica. And this probably wasn't her standard bitching about taking a room on the third floor.

I ran at the stairs. Really ran, because there was something like forty stairs on two floors apiece but in next to no time I was ready to bash in her door (it was a day for me to be confronted with doors I couldn't open, I s'pose) except her door was open.

Her door was open and she was on her bed and Marc and Not-Nick were also on her bed and at first I had the horrified impression it was some sickass "Dear Penthouse Forum" insanity, except—

"No, it's okay, now you get to push! Go ahead and push!"

"*Get* to? What, like it's a fucking prize I've won? I swear to God, Marc, I *swear* it, if you weren't dead, I would fucking kill you."

"Hey, guys." I waved. Multiple heads—Jess's, Not-Nick's, Marc's, Sinclair's, and Tina's—all swiveled toward me. "I'm back. I guess."

CHAPTER
THIRTY-ONE

!!

(That was Sinclair's first thought. Which was touching and also weird.)

"My own, never has your face been more dear to meeeeee." Sinclair was holding one of Jessica's hands and apparently, the girl could squeeze.

"You okay?" Jess panted. I'd seen her more wild-eyed, but not when she was sober.

"Yep."

"Any demons on your heels or some scary-ass vampire coup we've gotta worry about right this minute?"

"Nope."

"Well, *good*!" Then somehow she scrunched her beautiful face into the approximate size of a golf ball. "Nnnnnnnn!"

"I told you, the dramatic yelling on TV actually just saps oxygen in real life. Put the noise into your pushing."

"Uh . . ." I took a few tentative steps closer to Marc. "She's letting you deliver the babies?"

"You know it's twins?" Tina said, startled. I hadn't quite figured out her function yet. Nick was standing at Jess's right playing "you can do it, rah-rah, you've never been more beautiful and we both know I'm lying!" labor coach, Marc was kneeling at the foot of her emperor bed (wider and taller than a king bed; it was like going to sleep in a football field) either delivering the babies or on the hunt for newborn braaaains, Sinclair was letting Jessica pulp his knuckles into jelly, and Tina was playing stereotypical dad, wringing her hands and pacing and occasionally saying something sharp, but not to us. "I wasn't talking to you!" she barked into the phone. "I called for an ambulance thirty-two minutes ago!"

I brightened. Not about the late ambulance, which I suspected was gonna be problematic for all sorts of reasons, but because I remembered a way I could be helpful. "Hey, Jess, don't worry about the twins. You're fine and they're fine. The reason nobody's been able to keep track of your pregnancy is—"

"Because the babies are shifting through parallel universes, yeah, yeah," Marc said without looking at me.

"Laura told us all about it," Not-Nick added.

"Oh." The bitch bushwhacked me, then came calling to chitchat about Jessica's pregnancy? And they hadn't removed her head from her shoulders *why*? "Well, glad you're in the loop." I *guess*.

"Nnnnnnnnnnnnnnn!"

"Sorry, was that a no or a—"

"Okay, okay, good job, good job, last one, last one."

"Did you say last one?" I'd sort of assumed she was in labor, not actually—

"Here we go here we go here we . . . *are*!" Marc held up a writhing octopus. No, it was a purple baby. A hideous writhing purple baby, but at least it was—

"Nnnnnaaaaahhh! Nnnnaaahhh! Nnnaaahhh!"

—*not* mute. Tell you something else: those sheets would never be the same.

"Okay, it's a girl! Gorgeous, Jess, good job!"

Frankly, neither Jessica nor the purple thing was especially gorgeous. Maybe Marc's zombie brain was getting his adjectives that start with *g* mixed up. Did he mean gruesome? Grotesque? I appreciated his tact. There was no tactful way to say, "Wow, you've just birthed the most hideous baby in the history of human events."

Ah! One of Tina's jobs was supplying clean towels for the purple thing. I noticed for the first time that on the bed with Jess, on the chair next to the bed, and piled beside

Marc, there were several towels, dish towels, sheets, sponges (?), and two rolls of paper towels. All clean (thank goodness), but not for long, I bet.

Silence fell as everyone looked at the purple wriggling thing, and I decided to fill it. "So, I'm okay and all."

"She *is*," Tina cried, peeping at the baby while still clutching her phone. "She *is* beautiful!"

"This sucks," Jessica gasped, up on her elbows, "but not as much as I thought it would, I gotta admit."

"This is the easiest birth I've ever seen," Marc told her. "Well, from my perspective." He smiled when she managed a laugh. "You're doing great. My mom was in labor with me for less than half an hour. Sometimes it's like that. About one percent of labors, the mom thinks her contractions are just another backache, and the next thing she knows—whoops!"

"We'd barely got back from going to church with Laura when my water broke," Jessica told me.

WTF? Was it possible they'd forgotten Laura had kidnapped me in front of their horrified gazes? Were they faking the horrified gazes because they were secretly glad to be rid of me for a couple of days? (How long had I been stumbling around in the hellfog, anyway?) Or did they figure the best way to bend the Antichrist to their will was to go to church with her?

Meanwhile Tina had engulfed the purple thing into one of the good emerald green bath sheets while pinning her phone to the side of her head with an upraised shoulder. "They're fourteen minutes out because some idiot drove his semi into a ditch to avoid decimating a school bus," she told the room at large. Feral killer vampires had been after her—I'd been there and seen them—and she hadn't been this upset. "The kids are all safe, as is the truck driver, but traffic's blocked. Yes! Yes, they are! All the children are alive and the ambulance is less than ten minutes away! Yes! Yesyesyes!" She nuzzled it and the purple thing subsided; probably it didn't like being cold. I crept a little closer to it.

"Ask me how glad I am you're here."

"Thanks, Jess," I said, touched. "I'm glad—"

"I was talking to Marc. Jeez, Bets! I know it's all about you but right now? It's all about—"

"You?" I guessed.

"—my babies!"

Well, I'd had a 50/50 shot. Except it was twins, so it was a 33.3/33.3/33.3 shot. Wait. Was that right? Note to self: ask later.

"I'm lucky I don't need a C-section, right?" she asked anxiously. She'd collapsed on her back, but now struggled back up on her elbows. "I don't, right? For the other baby?"

"No, no. Actually, just over half of twins are born vaginally, so your odds were good anyway."

"I don't feel much right now," she said anxiously. "Is the next one coming?"

"Actually, there's an average of about seventeen minutes between twins," Marc replied. "So you guys have time to get a Coke or something."

I looked around the room. "Anyone want a Coke?"

Nobody did.

"You're saying 'actually' a lot," I told him.

"I've been doing lots of reading. Okay, I'm gonna check you again, this time to make sure the other baby's in an okay position . . . sorry again . . ."

Jess winced while Marc did unspeakable things to her unspeakable. I was impressed it was only a wince and not a yowl of agony. "So you guys got back from church and all this started?"

"Yeah, and welcome home, by the—ow! Jeez, Marc, time to trim the nails!"

"Actually, they don't grow anymore since I—never mind." *Good call,* I mouthed at him. Women in labor don't need to hear the fingernail pedigree of the zombie delivering their parallel-universe babies. "Okay, your other bag's broken, so this one's—"

"Nnnnnnnnn!"

"—yep, coming now."

"Well, it had to come out eventually, right?" I had a ringside view, which I never wanted less. Not-Nick had the smart view: the top of her head. "So, uh, sooner rather than later is okay, right?" Never had I been more out of my depth. And I'm including the vampire queen thing in that.

"Jessica, your upper-body strength is impressive." Sinclair had been so quiet on the other side of the giant bed, holding her hand, I'd almost forgotten he was there. "I have lost all feeling in three of my fingers."

Good, was my unworthy thought. (Unworthy = bitchy.)

"Okay, okay, looking good—this one's in a rush to say hi to the world—it's perfect, you're perfect, keep it up, keep it up—here we go—Bets! Get your ass over here!"

Oh, now he remembers I'm here? That was only in my head, though; Marc in doctor mode was no one to sass. By the time "ass" was out of his mouth I was beside him, taking the towel he'd grabbed with his spare hand and thrust at me.

"Twelve minutes out and *you are worthless,*" Tina said to the phone (I hope it was the phone), then shrugged her shoulder so the thing she took to bed with her every night fell to the (carpetless) floor. She didn't even look to see if it fell into pieces. Marc didn't dare look at me and I didn't dare look at him, but we were freaked. Gollum wasn't as fond of his "precious" as she was of her iPhone. "Yes they are!" she cooed to the purple thing. "EMS is overrated yes they are!"

"Oh, come on, like we really want some poor EMTs in here with a zombie, three vampires, a—" Never mind. That was incredibly dumb. Of course we wanted EMTs, of course Jessica wanted EMTs. She wanted a labor and delivery suite at Fairview, too.

And was that so much to ask? She had to put up with vampire politics and fallout from same and werewolves dying and coming back from Hell and zombies and the Antichrist and Ancient Me and that was just the stuff off the top of my head. She *should* have a suite, and nurses who were nice because they were good nurses and doctors who were sucking up because their bosses knew she was worth billions, and a plasma screen in her delivery room so she could be skeeved out by *American Horror Story* between contractions. She should have the best hospital food available, which was still awful, and one of those warmer things full of blankets for her and the purple things when they came because one of them for sure didn't like being cold, and a NICU ten steps away if something was wrong with one of the purple things.

And it sucked that she didn't have any of that; it sucked that she had a drafty old mansion with a zombie delivering purple things, a Southern belle pissed at her phone and possibly the City of St. Paul, an off-duty homicide detective doing his best to pretend the zombie and the mansion and the lack of epidural were all part of a perfectly viable plan B, and a vampire queen thinking about herself instead of her friend and her friend's purple things.

First Marc had thrust the towel at me; now here came another purple thing. Yuck-yuck-yuck! "Okay, okay, got him, got him," Marc chanted. I obediently opened my arms and he dropped the thing into the towel. "Wait, wait—" Marc did something to its head, and then it made the same "Nnnnnaaaahhhh!" sound the other one did. Actually, it was sort of cute; it sounded like he was wailing "Naw! Naw!" over and over. Like he was saying no-no-no to the room and maybe the world.

Heh.

"Jeez, take a breath before you pass out," I told him. "Your sister's not being such a baby. Which is pretty good for a baby. Hey! Jess!" I bent over, rubbing Naw with the towel (which he didn't like) to make him warmer (which he did), and looked at Other Naw in her towel in Tina's arms. "They look like you!" And they did, little tiny pissed-off replicas of Jess. "But they're really pale!" And they were. His sister's yucky purple color was wearing off; must have been a newborn thing, I realized as they got warm and dry their color got lighter. Jess's face; Not-Nick's coloring. Depending on how it all shook out, the Naws would be gorgeous or hideous.

Not my problem. It was for Jess and Nick to worry about how ugly their freakish offspring might get. Me, I thought they'd turn out pretty cute. Now that they were warm, Naw and Other Naw had quit with the bleating and were yawning and going to sleep. Well, they'd had an exhausting twenty minutes. Babies: nature's slack-asses.

"Hey." I nudged Marc, who was up to his elbows in bits of Jessica. "Good job."

"Oh, *man*, am I glad you're back," he muttered. "It's been nonstop around here. Not that you being back will make it less nonstop."

"Thanks. Do you need, uh, help?" *Please don't say yes. There's no one less qualified than me.*

"No, I think it's—Jess, you've got a little more pushing to do. I'm not sure how, but the placenta didn't come between the babies, so you've gotta push it out now."

"No! I'm on vacation as of the second the babies were out. The babies have vamoosed from me. See?" She pointed at the towels Tina and I were holding.

"It's just a little push, nothing at all like earlier," he coaxed.

"Nope. I'm closed."

"Maybe when the paramedics come—" I began, as if I had the vaguest idea what I was talking about.

"She thinks me defeated so easily? Ha!" Marc shook a fist slick with baby goo. "She'll come to regret that."

"Are you all right?" Not-Nick asked with real concern. He had been stroking Jessica's face while they murmured to each other, but now he looked up. "Because you sound like you're channeling a Bond villain."

"I don't want you to pass your placenta. I want you to *die*." He stared around the room. "Where's a big fluffy evil white cat when you need one?"

"No cats!" I almost screamed. I still got the creeps when I remembered what he'd done to Giselle's corpse. I knew why he'd done it, and under the circumstances it wasn't wrong, but it was still yucky. As was this moment. I was in a world of yuck. "Do you want some Wet-Naps or something? I think all the towels are gross or holding babies or both."

"No. Jess, will you please—"

I cocked my head, looked up, and caught Sinclair's glance. *Finally.*

"The ambulance is almost here," I said, and Marc sagged with relief.

"Excellent." His tone made me break Sinclair's gaze and stare at him. He was scared. He was *really* scared, and he'd done a wonderful job hiding it. I felt such a rush of warmth for him I nearly staggered. I loved my zombie so much! (Argh. Marc. I loved Marc.) "In a couple of minutes, you're officially their problem."

"I know!" she agreed, happy. "I can't wait. No offense to you." She reached out and caught his mucky hand. "Couldn't have done it without you." She looked the worst I'd ever seen her look, with sweat-matted hair and her eyes almost bulging from deep sockets; she looked bad and she smelled worse. I don't know how she managed it; I don't know where that beautiful smile came from and how she could look so luminous. But she pulled it off. "How can I ever, ever thank you?"

"Same goes for me, buddy," Not-Nick said hoarsely. "The next time you need a favor, you better come see me first."

(I liked how even Not-Nick's warm gratitude came out like a vague threat; it must be a cop thing.)

"Really, really good job," I said. At first I'd been annoyed to get here in the middle of it. But now I saw how foolish that was. What if I'd gotten here earlier? *I* might be the one with Jessica up to my elbows! "Really, really great, good, excellent job. Nice work. Really. Just outstanding."

"She's right," Jessica said, and it was only now that I could see how scared she'd been, too. Her face had that funny blotchy look it got when she'd been terrified but then realized things were going to work out. "You were great. Thank you for not eating my babies' brains."

Don't laugh. This is a touching moment and she probably wasn't making a joke. Don't you dare laugh.

"You're welcome," he replied. "Thanks for not freaking out more about me having to deliver them."

"No chance."

Meanwhile, Tina sort of scooted Sinclair out of the way with her butt as she bent over so Jess could see Other Naw; it occurred to me I should do the same with her brother.

"What, no chance?" I asked, showing Jess her second-born. He'd warmed up and depurpled, and was now sound asleep. Lazybones I and Lazybones II, that's what they oughta name them.

She put her hand on the top of Naw's tiny head, took her hand away, kissed her first two fingers, and put the hand back. The gesture—so tender and so unconscious; she didn't think about it, she just did it—brought a lump to my throat. I had to look away before I made a bigger fool of myself than usual.

"Like I said: no chance." She reached up and Tina gently handed Other Naw down, towel and all. Jessica snuggled her daughter for a second, then turned back to me. "Okay, yeah. I was nervous about Marc being around if I went into labor at home, and I thought about making a fuss and we even talked about moving out." Not-Nick nodded, startling me. She'd never said a word. And Marc was suddenly very busy peeling off gloves and trying to clean up. He wanted to be long gone before the EMTs got up here; we'd have to think about just what to tell them. But first I wanted to hear this. "But then I remembered every single movie and TV show where someone's pregnant. They always go into labor when it's least convenient or safe or fun. Friggin' *always*."

I nodded. She was dead-on. You could almost set your watch by it.

"So I figured with all the paranormal nonsense in our

lives the last couple of years, wherever I was, whatever I was doing, something would happen so that Marc would be the only one to help me. My plans would be for shit. So when the babies started coming super fast I was scared, but not—you know—*surprised*."

Tina cleared her throat. "As there has been a happy outcome, it might be time to confess I also have been running obstetrical errands for Dr. Spangler."

"I don't know what that means," I confessed.

"OB books," he explained. "Figured I better study up. Just in case. Because, yeah. *Every* TV show. *Every* movie. Tina's been helping me track down the stuff I needed to bone up on."

That must have been when he started making her cozy nests in his trunk as they drove around the Twin Cities on the hunt for OB books, and probably solving mysteries on the side. It was like a Pixar flick. A vampire and her zombie! A zombie and his vampire! Egad.

I felt Sinclair's gaze and looked up. And for a few seconds the chaos and blood and sweat and stress and relieved tension went away; for a few seconds the only thing I could see was him.

My own, my own, how I wish I could have you in my arms at this moment.

Yeah, sure, now all of a sudden you're glad I'm here? You haven't said two words since I walked in.

Dreadful neglect and I should be shamed to dare hope you still cherish me as I do you. And I would show you just now, would stride across the room and make you mine in front of all, but I doubt I will be able to break Jessica's grip. I am her prisoner until she releases me. It makes you all the more beautiful to me, since you are as yet unattainable.

I started laughing; I couldn't help it. Yeah, I was piqued that they hadn't been worried about me, and it was annoying that the annoying babies were here to begin stealing my thunder annoyingly early, but the babies were cute and, even better, okay. (And much less purple!) And my family was okay. And I was okay.

Asking for anything past that was just greedy.

CHAPTER
THIRTY-TWO

After love, I flopped over on my back. "Now I have to call Laura and get her to come over, or meet me somewhere, because she's got her Big Girl Apartment and won't tell me where it is."

"One-three-one-one West One Hundred Forty-third Street, Burnsville, Minnesota." At my astonished silence, he reeled off, "Five-five-three-zero-six."

"You suck!" I jerked the roll pillow out from behind me and smacked him with it. Right around the time he'd been raining kisses on my inner thighs, I vaguely remembered grabbing the small log-shaped pillow and shoving it into the small of my back, and then my brain blew up. Or something.

But now I was back in my body, ready to wreak havoc

with crimson-colored and gold-tasseled throw pillows. "Wait, did you go sheet shopping while I was gone? I don't recognize any of this linen. No, let's get back to Laura— how'd you find out where she lived? Did she tell you on the way to church? Which, by the way, was gonna be our little secret for a while."

"Circumstances," was his dry reply, and I had to laugh. I was teasing him now, but the moment we were alone he'd shown me the despair and loneliness that had whirled through his brain the minute I left our dimension.

"The word of the week," I agreed. "Spill!"

"On one of my walks I put a tracer on her car. Tina keeps track of your sister's hithers and thithers. It's how she knew Laura was at your mother's." I must have looked as surprised as I felt, because it was his turn to tease. "Why, my own, did you think all my fun in the sun was only about fun?"

"Kinda," I admitted. So sneaky of Sinclair to be sneaky even when he wasn't trying to be sneaky! That . . . that was the *definition* of sneaky. "I assumed your main objective was al fresco sex, sure."

"And it was," he replied sagely. "But there were occasionally other goals."

I made a fist and thumped his chest. "And I meant it about church. I thought you wanted to keep that under your immaculate vest for a while."

"And so I did." He reached for me and drew me down

beside him. I ran my hand up his ribs and snuggled into his side. "But I saw an opportunity to make a point without scaring or angering her. I must say, it was rather theatrical." The badass king of the vampires giggled like a little boy pulling off a prank.

"I'll bet." *So* bummed I missed it. Sneaking off to church had been our little secret for days. Apparently back in the day, the Sinclair family was big on regular churchgoing. His church was a whole other community, a little town (townlet?) of people who looked out for each other and stuck together when shit went bad. I had no idea he'd missed it so much. So when he realized he could reclaim that part of his boyhood, he did, and I helped. It was wrong that it made us super horny, right? A morning of God-bless-us-everyone followed by outdoor sex, then drinking blood after the sun went down. Just your average big-city married couple. "And Laura didn't need to be pressured into doing anything, so it worked out. How'd you know I'd figured out how to come back from the hellfog by myself?"

"I realize I only gave you a chance to recount 'the Cliffs-Notes version' before taking you to bed—"

"To dining room, actually, then to parlor sofa, then to stairs—ow, by the way—and then to bed, technically speaking." After the ambulance had taken Not-Nick, Jessica, Naw, and Other Naw to the hospital for at minimum an overnight, Marc had disappeared to spend the next few hours cleaning up, and not just Jessica's room ("Out, out, damned purple things and their spots!"), and Tina had likewise vamoosed, to do what I couldn't bring myself to care. Which was about when my husband fell on me, with all that entailed.

"Always a stickler for the technical details, my love. But since you have not had sufficient time to recount what you endured, I must ask for a definition of 'hellfog.' But before that, what did you mean?"

Since parts of me were still numb, I was having trouble following the conversation. "Which time? About what?" Now I was stroking his abs: one, two, three, four, five—yep, a six-pack. A genuine six-pack! In elderly men, such things were mythological, like a horny unicorn.

"You wondered how I knew you could come home without Laura. I did not know."

"So you dragged her to church to—what? Threaten her with more tithing if she didn't produce me?"

"I had no plan," my man-with-a-plan spouse admitted. "Laura had assured us you were safe and would shortly return. I believed her, and I cannot explain why."

"She never lies," I suggested. "That might be one reason."

"She was so . . . despairing. Not because she grieves for the Morning Star, I think. Because she felt—feels—trapped. And for good reason. Now, don't look like that, my queen. Of course you were quite right to kill the devil. But the consequence of that, as you knew, as you explained to me, is that it effectively trapped the Antichrist into taking that job. For the next million years, most likely."

"Yeah." I let my head flop back onto Sinclair's biceps. I loved it when a man put his hands behind his head after love; I loved lying on biceps. I know. It's odd; I can't explain it. "Yeah, and I still have to figure out what to do about that. About her. Because nothing's been solved, you know? She was pissed and she took me and I put up with Thing One and Thing Two and then figured out how to come home and the babies came. Stuff happened, but nothing's been resolved."

"The wisdom of a serpent, the gentleness of a dove."

"The irritation of a wasp stinging my ass. Yeek!" I knocked his fingers away. "So I guess I'd better start by calling her. See if she'll meet me somewhere so we can work this out."

"She will."

"Oh, you two are best friends now?"

"Hardly. But now she trusts me a bit, I think." *The fool.*

"Caught that one," I said. "Be nice."

No reply to *that* but a stubborn silence, and who could blame him?

"She's young." I could hardly believe I was making

Laura met me in the lobby of Burnsville's Fairview Ridges just before suppertime the next day. "This was perfect since I was already volunteering here this week," she told me, adjusting the collar of her volunteer smock.

I groaned. "You're the worst Antichrist ever."

"They normally only let college students volunteer in the summer, but Mrs. Greeley said I did such a good job, I could come during the holiday break, too."

I put my hand on my forehead like I was an undead psychic. "You're majoring in religion with a minor in . . . let me see . . . social work. Right?"

"Not once I switch majors to philosophy," she said with a dignified sniff.

"Thanks for setting me straight." Ridges was pretty nice

as hospitals went. Nobody was screaming, anyway. The place smelled more like flowers and less like antiseptic. Maybe that should be more worrying. Not to me, though; I always hated the sting-ey smell and since I had the nose of a thousand bloodhounds, places like hospitals made me *very* nervous. Give me a hospital more greenhouse than surgery drive-thru any day. I could hardly make out the blood over the poinsettias. "You want to go see Jess with me?"

"Already did," she replied brightly. "The babies are *so* cute! She told me they're keeping the three of them at least one more day, but you know it's so they can pitch her for a donation to the new birth center. And Dick's been running around handing out bubble-gum cigars!"

"Adorable. Walk with me."

"You want to talk here?" She fell into step beside me, eyeing the other visitors meandering through the lobby and in and out of the hallways. "About . . . about stuff we need to talk about?"

"Safe as houses," I assured her. "Most people here are too wrapped up in their own problems to care about what two random blondes are babbling about. The ones who aren't—what are they gonna do? Grab a roving shrink and tell them two random blondes they've never seen before are talking about vampires and the devil and, jeepers, they were here just a minute ago so somebody should *do* something? *If* they could convince anyone and track us down—with who and for what I've got no idea—we're not exactly gonna rush to corroborate their story. Also: nobody cares, Laura. I promise."

She still looked doubtful, but shrugged and started walking through the lobby with me. "Are you thirsty? More than usual?"

"No worries. Stopped at Caribou and quaffed two large half white chocolate, half milk chocolate hot chocolates. I'm feeling a little sloshy inside, but I'm good for now."

We walked in silence for a minute. I couldn't speak for my sis, but I was basking, lizardlike, in the greenhouse effect. Big glass windows + winter sunshine = mmm, toasty. Sure, we were wrecking the planet, but at least we'd be warm. Laura broke my surprisingly contemplative silence with, "I'm glad you made it back okay."

"That's my cue to snap 'no thanks to you, bee-yotch!' except nobody says bee-yotch anymore, so I'll just stick with 'no thanks to you' and that'll be that."

"Er . . . yeah."

"Don't bother." She'd been peeking at my feet and I couldn't help being amused. "The silver shoes disappeared between Naw and Other Naw showing up in the world. I've got no idea where they went—back to the hellfog, maybe." Or maybe not. I was pretty sure I could make them appear just by thinking about them. And I was pretty sure that a few months from now, or weeks or days, I wouldn't need them to go back and forth. But that was for me to know. For now, anyway.

"I hope you understand why I left you there. If I wanted you to truly understand, I didn't have any choice but to—"

"Don't!" I said it so sharply a few other visitors in the hall looked up. I did the patented Minnesota Nice Apologetic Head Dip and Shoulder Shrug, and they went back to their business, and I went back to mine. "I hate 'I had no choice.' D'you know why?" At Laura's head shake, I continued. "It's always a lie. Just because the choices other than the one you want to go with are *bad* doesn't make them nonexistent. 'I had no choice' always, *always* translates to 'I had two choices, but one sucked. So really, I had no choice. Except I did.' So it's fine that you decided to ditch me—okay, not fine, but you know what I mean—but at least own that. Don't go with the anthem of the pathetic, 'I had no choice.' Because you absolutely did have a choice, every step of the way. You just didn't like most of them."

"All right. So. I chose to leave you there. And I hope you know I was never going to leave you there forever. But what I don't understand—"

"Because this is all about answering *your* questions." I heard the acid and decided to dial it back. If the point of our meeting was to show each other our claws, I could have done it over the phone or, even better, via bitchy e-mail.

"Sorry. Go ahead." Wow, for a second there it was like *I* didn't have a choice! Except I did.

"Why didn't you tell me your . . ."

She trailed off, and though it could have been any one of a dozen unfinished thoughts, I took a stab that it was the big reveal.

"Why didn't I tell you Sinclair could go to church? Can sing Christmas carols?" Oh boy, could he. And as much as Sinclair loved church? He loved Christmas and everything about it a hundred times more. I've never had sex while my lover was singing "It's Beginning to Look a Lot Like Christmas" before. Erotically surreal doesn't begin to cover it. "Can freely wander a mall without fearing his ears will implode from Christmas Muzak? Although that's a risk everyone takes this time of year."

"Yes! Why didn't you? Why didn't the both of you shout it from the rooftops? Betsy, that's so huge!" She'd seized my arm in her excitement and—yow! The Antichrist needed a mani in the worst way. Long *and* unpolished *and* jagged. It was like being grabbed by a blond wolverine sporting a volunteer smock. "You should have seen him. No fear, and he was so—so happy to be there! I could see him bathing in the light of God's love."

"Okay." Bathing? In love? Hyperbole much? Wait, was that right? Either way, she was happy for him and I was glad to see it. "The reason I didn't tell you—didn't tell anyone—is because Sinclair asked me not to. He wanted to keep it between us for a while. But I was bound to tell you sooner or later, because it kind of leads into my point about your mom wanting to die and how I'm kind of the victim again."

She shook her head and, even better, removed her daggerlike nails from my arm's tender underside. Ah! Ouchie! "I don't understand."

"Then here it is again. The devil granted me one wish. She didn't do it because she was afraid of me and she didn't do it to hurt me—it wasn't a Monkey's Paw kind of wish. Why would she do that if not to do something nice for someone who was going to give her what she wanted?"

Laura didn't say anything.

"I didn't even know what to ask for at first. It's not like I lie awake in the morning trying to think of what I'd ask for if Satan granted me a wish. Plus, she gave me a *time* limit! That was soooo her. Anyway, after her insistence that I play beat the clock in Hell, I managed to come up with something. And it was a close call between getting something for Sinclair or bringing back my beloved Christian . . ." But I couldn't talk about that without worrying about bawling in the Fairview hallways while the Antichrist patted my shoulder. "But I didn't wish he could go outside and work on his tan. I wished he could bear the light."

She frowned, thinking it over. "Any light? So even . . . the light of God's love?"

"Ask the guy who plays Christmas carols in our bathroom now." Not that vampires had much use for bathrooms. But I still liked to make sure my layered eye shadow looked as terrific as possible. And we showered together. Now we showered together while he belted out "All I really want for Christmas . . ." in his soapy baritone. I . . . I don't understand why my life is like this now.

"But we were talking about wishes, and Satan, and how she's dead now. I think we decided before my vacay in the hellfog that I wasn't going to apologize for killing your mom."

"Yes. And during your vacay I explained to the vampire king that I wouldn't apologize for your vacay."

"Now look at that! We're agreeing on so much already." I smiled, and I guess it wasn't a very nice one because the corners of her mouth turned down. I reminded myself that I wasn't here to score points. *If you've ever had to keep your mouth in park and your temper under control, it's probably now. It's also been other times. Learn, dammit! Learn from your thousands of mistakes!* "I thought you had some good points amid all the whining and shrillness."

She snorted. "Sure you did."

"About what's fair and what's not. I thought about it and you're right. Your situation is unacceptable." Oh boy. Was I gonna do it? The vague idea I'd formed between Thanksgiving 1.0 and 2.0, the notion that solidified in the hellfog, the thing that was about to come out of my mouth . . . I was about to change my life—again—and not just mine. Everyone's life, and I wasn't going to take a vote or pretend to be interested in what the others would think. "Totally unacceptable."

"Thank you for that." Laura grinned. "Did I get that out without whining or shrillness?"

"Yeah. Remember, practice makes perfect. Anyway, I'll help you."

Wow. I was—was I? Yep. I really was doing this. I'd have some explaining to do when I got home. I hadn't told Sinclair what I was going to do, but he knew my mind and hadn't tried to talk me out of it. He hadn't insisted on coming with me, either. I'd like to credit that to the strength of our marriage, but I think it was more about the postcoital coma I'd left him in.

She groaned and covered her eyes. "And now you're going to ruin it with one of your bitchy—yeah, that's right, I said *bitchy*—one of your bitchy asides."

"I'll help you run Hell. I mean, take the hellfog and turn it back into Hell and then help you run Hell." *I'm sorry. I made the mess. I've got to clean it up, no matter what it means for our marriage and our future and even our—groan— kingdom.* How could I always think of what to say when the person in question wasn't anywhere near me? This, also, was something I probably shouldn't spend a lot of time pondering.

"This!" More visitors were looking, and Laura didn't care. "This is what I don't like about you!"

"To be fair, there are lots of things you don't like about me."

"It's all a joke. For you there's a hilarious side to everything, and if not, you just hide behind your ignorance. 'Hey, guys, I didn't know better, can't help being a moron and now I'm off to another midnight madness simple sale.'"

"Sample."

"I know." She was screaming in the middle of a hospital, which is better than screaming in the middle of a library. I probably shouldn't have blown off her suggestion that we talk about this somewhere else. "I was being sarcastic!"

"Okay, but you suck at it. Listen again: I'll help you run Hell. Everything you said is right. I created the problem and it's shitty to leave it in your lap while I traipse off to a simple sale."

I glared around at the looky-loos until they fled in a restrained Minnesota Nice manner, which is to say they slowly turned and walked away while murmuring in low voices to themselves that we should be ashamed while not addressing our rudeness directly. I was distracted from their restrained fleeing by the Antichrist saying in a small voice, "It's sample. Sample sales."

"Right. Sorry. Thanks for correcting me."

"If you're joking I'll—I'll do something awful. Burn you or—or kill someone. Something. I'll do something."

"I know." I reached out a hand and took one of hers, except it was a fist. So I patted her fist. "I'm sorry about your mom."

Too little too late, I figured. Laura would see it as a half-assed Band-Aid when it should have been a full-on life support system. (My analogies had never sucked more.) But I could at least put it out there. Worst case, Laura would— actually, there were so many worst-case scenarios, so many hideous things Laura could do to me or mine, I couldn't even think of them all. Which was too bad for me.

So I braced myself as best I could, but was still unprepared when one of the things I couldn't think of happened: the Antichrist burst into tears.

CHAPTER THIRTY-FOUR

"I'm in the hospital for three days and get home to find you're the codevil?"

"To be fair, you only needed to be in for two d—"

Her glare cut me off cold. "Did you squeeze two humans out of your body under conditions that can be best described as fucked up?"

"No, ma'am."

"Then I advise you to shut your undead piehole."

"Yes, ma'am." And so it began, the thing I'd been dreading since I came home from a long day of changing the timeline to find my best friend pregnant. The 'you're not a parent so you will never be able to know my torment/angst/ pain/hilarity/agony/insanity' thing. The irony was, I *should* have known. I was BabyJon's parent, dammit. And now that I was going to help run Hell, what was that gonna do to our already-iffy mother/sister/brother/son relationship? Did I now have the power to implement Take Your Child to Hell day? Hmm. Maybe that wasn't as nuts as it sounded.

"And Laura went along with that?"

"Laura was delighted to go along with that." Laura was delighted about everything. Me, not so much, but it wasn't as though I'd been *sent* to Hell (like the millions of souls I'd now have partial dominion over). I'd volunteered. "It wasn't a coup, Jess."

"It's pronounced 'coo,' like 'your breathy coo made the Antichrist think running Hell with you was a great idea,' not 'coop,' like 'but you'll end up turning it into a chicken coop of the damned.'"

"Thanks. Besides, it was a suggestion she was free to—"

"Yeah." My friend, who looked a thousand times better than she had when I'd last seen her in her bedroom, let out an elegant snort. (I know. But she pulled it off!) "Like she'd turn you down after bitching about how awful she had it since her mama bit the big one? Also, are you gonna hold a funeral in Hell for the devil?"

"Nooooo. Maybe?" I was appalled and didn't bother hiding it. "I never thought of that. Please don't suggest that when Laura comes over for supper."

"When's that?"

"Tonight. Sinclair's picking her up at the church in Hastings."

Jess shook her head. She'd been going back and forth between her room and the nursery, the bedroom next door she was converting for her purpose. The babies were asleep in their cocradles downstairs in the kitchen. Fur and Burr were also in the kitchen; they'd frisked about the cradles, ate their weight in puppy kibble, then collapsed into puppy food comas. Tina was keeping an eye on all four of them while running a spreadsheet, God help that poor bitch.

Jessica, ever practical, had wanted to hire a nanny. Tina, ever practical, had suggested that with the varied sleep schedules of so many in the house, hiring a nanny was unnecessary at best and a potential security risk/headache/ lawsuit at worst.

It also helped that Not-Nick told (*told*, mind you) the Minneapolis Police Department that he was taking six months of paternity leave. They reminded him it would have to be unpaid. He reminded them that he was rich and his wife was richer. They congratulated him on the marital *coup* (apparently you don't pronounce the *p*) and on the twins.

"Your hub really likes that church."

I had to smile. "After all this time I think he'd like any church. But apparently First Pres burned down in 1907 and his grandpa raised the money to fix it."

"That's so cute." She'd been folding baby clothes and

had stacks of them all over her bed, which had been made with clean sheets. I assumed the old ones had been burned, or shot into space. I also assumed "so cute" had applied to my husband, but since she said it to a pea green onesie, it could go either way. "What'd he say about you running Hell?"

"The usual 'if you want to work outside the home I'll support your decision' stuff. Which is an improvement over a couple of years ago." Before we were married, he'd actually stomped through Macy's and forbidden me to work. I'd laughed so hard I almost fell down. "But he knows I'm going to be coming to him for advice about every eight minutes, so that's all right."

"Speaking of jobs, has Dick talked to you about this shoe design website thing?"

I was startled and let it show. "He didn't drop that? We were in my room a couple of days ago, before I went to hellfog in a handbasket, and he was saying I should get in the shoe-designing business."

"He told me. He's got this idea where people come to your website and pick out what kind of shoe—suede, patent leather—and style—pump, sandal, flat—and color and such, and your staff artists crank them out to order. You could run it on your vampire schedule."

I couldn't believe it. With all the insanity going on, with Jessica's belly and the ensuing babies, he'd found time to look into his idea to help me cope with the loss of the genius Louboutin?

"Are you okay? You look like you just smelled something awful."

"If you must know, I'm trying not to cry," I said with what little dignity I could manage. "I can't believe he's been working on that."

"He feels bad that Christian guy is *no más.* He's been trying to think of how to cheer you up."

"I'm just not used to him liking me." It wasn't the first time I'd had the thought that the addition of a well-adjusted Dick (heh) and a happy Jessica more than made up for the lack of Christian Louboutin, but it was the first time I'd had it and not felt like an utter traitor to my first love: designer shoes.

"We should have hired a nanny," Jess replied, which made no sense. Another thing I dreaded about her impending mommyhood. Except since Naw and Other Naw were here, it wasn't impending anymore. You could be having a perfectly normal conversation about Hell and former time-line boyfriends hating me, and the mommy in question wouldn't be thinking about anything but her spawn. "We'll need it."

"I think Tina had a good point about everybody's schedules—" I began.

She finished folding her thousandth onesie and looked at me over her shoulder. She'd magically shrunk; it looked like she would be one of those annoying moms who get their prebaby body back about a week and a half after giving birth. "Not for that," she said. "But between the twins and BabyJon, we're running an honest-to-God nursery here, a day care! And who knows what the future holds?"

"You probably meant that to sound hopeful, but it just sounds terrifying."

She chuckled. "Now that's too bad, Bets." She started stacking piles of baby stuff. "Wait'll they find out the new coruler of Hell has no imagination."

"Not only that, I've seen too much. Also, I'm kind of hoping Laura's gonna let me phone this in. With any luck, pretty soon someone will stage a *coop* and overthrow me."

I made it out the door in time to hear a pile of li'l baby T-shirts patter against the door. Ha! Motherhood was slowing her down.

Then I heard the knob start to turn, and fled in terror. Maybe it wasn't too soon to start winning the babies over to my side. We could form an alliance: Naw, Other Naw, and Betsy Taylor: vampire queen and co-overlord of Hell.

Things had come to quite a pass when this was my plan! Was it too soon to win them over with pureed peaches? How long was Jess planning on breast-feeding? I should probably read a book about babies or something. Maybe applesauce? I'd be their Fun Aunt Betsy!

Jessica had gotten me thinking, and I didn't appreciate it at all. But she had a point, and it wasn't a minute too soon to introduce them to BabyJon. He'd be the oldest, kind of their big brother. As they grew they'd form alliances against the adults in the house. *Survivor: Bad Babies! Outthink, Outlast, Outdrool.* Already I could see how Marc would always be the one to take their side, the softie parent. Sinclair and I'd have to be the disciplinarians, along with Jess. Not-Nick would be another softie. Tina would be what she'd been to Sinclair all his life, the kindly old auntie with spectacular legs.

If my mom was home, I could go pick up BabyJon right now! Filled with new purpose, I bounded down the stairs.

The minister, a charming, clear-eyed woman with wavy red hair and green eyes, had welcomed me into the sanctuary with a warm smile. Ah, if my grandfather could have lived to see such a sight! Knowing the old bounder, he would have jettisoned my grandmother and wooed the lovely reverend to his side. He had made no secret of his unfashionable love for strong women, and no apologies.

"So nice to see you again, Mr. Sinclair." This came as no surprise, as I had recently donated twenty thousand dollars. But I liked to think I would have gotten the smile and the welcome if I'd been a penitent, come to the Lord's house in rags. The prodigal son, so to speak.

I had briefly explained my business: "I am meeting my sister-in-law here. May I await her upstairs?"

She said of course, of course, and now I thought about parables and waited for the Antichrist. It did not take long; the spawn of Satan was unfailingly punctual.

"Hello!" She greeted me with a big smile. She looked beautiful, as she always did, though why she settled for dungarees and a "Fairview Ridges Volunteer" T-shirt when dark slacks and a navy turtleneck would have set off her coloring to far greater effect was a puzzle. "I apologized to the reverend for how I'm dressed," she whispered, shrugging out of her peacoat. "I didn't think you'd be up here again."

"I quite like it up here."

"I can imagine."

"You cannot."

"I'm sorry?" Her eyes widened.

"You cannot imagine. Not any of it."

"I don't—"

"You cannot imagine being cut off from your Father for decades longer than you lived and scurried on the earth as a bug among bugs. You cannot imagine the life—of sorts—of desolation and hopelessness you lead after being denied the Kingdom of Heaven. You cannot imagine what it is to come to terms with the darkness and then meet someone who drives it out, someone to whom the light is so ingrained she *does not know how she does it.* And you cannot imagine what it is like to realize there are others just as powerful, others who will snatch that light out of your life to indulge a tantrum and then expect everyone to be chums when the tantrum has passed."

She'd been staring, openmouthed, through my discourse, and when I had finished she raised an eyebrow and said, "So that's how it is now, huh?"

"Yes."

"Okay. I'm supposed to come home with you for dinner. Should I cancel?"

"Why?"

"Right, I almost forgot," she muttered. She had retrieved her purse from the floor and was rummaging through it. "You're one of those."

"I see no reason why antagonists cannot share a meal. Not that I will eat, of course."

"Of course. Don't worry, I never forget you don't eat. I keep it in mind all the time."

"Lovely. Are you planning to tell the queen what you and your accursed mother have done?"

"Uh . . ." She had retrieved a Kleenex and wiped her nose. I did not flatter myself that I had moved her to penitent tears. It was cold outside; it was warm in the church. The Antichrist was as prone to a runny nose as any living mammal. "What have we done, exactly?"

"How you trapped her into agreeing to help you run Hell. Except that was never the plan, was it, Laura? Elizabeth is to run Hell alone. Leaving you free to do whatever it is unemployed Antichrists do."

"Okay, I'd like you to explain that, please. Because I didn't even know my mother was doing that until after she was dead. She left me some papers and—and things."

"No doubt." *And things?* I was suddenly consumed with curiosity. What things? Written things? Artifacts? Instructions? I made a mental note to ask my queen for a tour of Hell very soon.

"I didn't get it at first," she was explaining as if I would be moved by her distress. "I was upset, and scared, and it took me a while to figure it out."

"Elaborate."

"That she hadn't ever been grooming me to take her place. She'd been grooming Betsy. Once I did figure it out, I could *see* it, you know?" She was as relaxed as I'd ever seen her, one denim-clad leg primly crossed over the other, her right arm resting along the back of the pew as she turned to face me. "Why would she have stuck me with a job she hated? I don't know if she loved me, but I know she liked me, and I know she wanted me to be happy."

"Satan, a doting mother," was my dry comment.

She shrugged off my sarcasm. I did not care for the changes I saw in her. I had expected her to be intimidated when I revealed what I had surmised. I had not expected the relief . . . or the self-confidence.

"I realized the last thing Mother would have done was stick me with the world's first thankless job. And most enduring thankless job. So if not me, who? Who shared a bloodline with me, and so had the potential to go back and forth? Betsy. Who liked me, which was something my mother knew she could exploit? Betsy. And who did my mom never like, not this Betsy or other timeline Betsy or future Betsy? Who could she stick with it and also not care if that person got stuck with Hell?"

She waited, and I realized she was waiting for me to say my line. "Elizabeth, clearly."

"Right! Okay, but how to even start to prep for the change of management? Offer Betsy things she wants. Who in the history of *anything* would be better at offering some-one what they wanted so my mother could get what *she* wanted?"

"She had a gift," I allowed.

"So when we went back in time, it wasn't so I could learn how to control 'porting through the dimensions . . . or not entirely. But it gave Betsy an idea of how to use the ability, too. Because she watched me learn, she was able to pick it up much faster once I'd left her in Hell. And if I needed any proof that my mother's plan was working, I had it when I found out about the silver shoes. I mean, come *on*! Silver slippers from *The Wizard of Oz*? Pure proof that Betsy's already starting to bend the place to her will."

"Yes, how clever." She was still lovely, but I could have cheerfully stripped the skin from her face and fed it to her. My beloved, manipulated into—what had her Judas sister called it? The first, most thankless job ever?

"Once I figured out what my mom had really been up to the last couple of years, I knew what I could do to help her work—her last work!—along: dump Betsy in Hell so she could see what Mother's death had stuck me with. And it worked. She saw and she offered to help me and now she thinks we're going to be running it together.

"And I'm not such a fool—

Wrong.

"—that I think Betsy's only in this to help me. She can see the potential as well as the harm in getting in on the ground floor. And it's a terrific way for her to keep an eye on me. That's the other thing she thinks would be an advantage." Unspoken: she *thinks.*

"Such a clever girl."

She was studying me as if she'd never seen me before. I likely had the same look on my own face. "You're not fooling me, you know. You're sitting here in the pew with me and the sun's shining through the windows, but you're just as capable of ripping the reverend's throat open and showering in her blood as you are of writing her a check. God's grace doesn't mean you're incapable of the evil you've been perpetuating for the last hundred-some years."

I made no comment, but wondered again what it was about me that made people think I was well into my next century. Perhaps Elizabeth had a point: I should dress younger. And perhaps she did not.

"It was a touching moment the other day. The prodigal son returned and all that. But you forgot about the other son."

"Oh?"

"Sure. No surprise; you're out of practice. The man had two sons, and the eldest—remember?—was the good one. He'd always done what his dad wanted, never gave him any trouble. And he had a *huge* problem with his little brother coming back after burning through their inheritance, coming back after pissing away all his money and cavorting with whores and basically being a real asshat—"

"I'm sorry," I said, struggling to hide my mingled horror and amusement. "Did you say 'asshat'?"

"Never mind! The point is, the little brother pulled all that crap and was *still* met with open arms. And fed fatted calf, too! 'Lo, these many years I have been serving you; I never transgressed your commandment at any time; and yet you never gave me a young goat, that I might make merry with my friends. But as soon as this son of yours came, who has devoured your livelihood with harlots, you killed the fatted calf for him.'"

Ah. It was time for me to say more of my lines. "'And he said to him, "Son, you are always with me, and all that

I have is yours. It was right that we should make merry
and be glad, for your brother was dead and is alive again,
and was lost and is found." '"

"Right." She sounded pleased. "You do remember. Well,
my whole life, I've only tried to be good. Her whole life and
yours, you *never* did. You never cared about anyone but your-
selves. You know what that taught me? Being bad made her
a queen; being good almost got me stuck with Hell. I'm
done with it."

"Ah."

She waited, and I was childish enough to be glad to have
disappointed her. "That's it? Ah?"

"What else is there to say? You were a fool a year ago
and you remain one still. You still believe people will not
change." I paused and shook my head. "Not quite right:
you have *decided* you believe that to justify setting a trap
for your sister, who only ever tried to help you. Congratula-
tions: you fooled someone who loves you. A feat worthy of
Machiavelli himself. Or any teenager."

She was watching me through narrowed eyes. "I don't
expect you to take my side."

"At last, you have said something intelligent."

"And when you tell Betsy—"

"You know I will not tell the queen."

More surprise. *I* was surprised . . . and gratified at how
much I enjoyed that look. "I do?"

I looked at her, unblinking. "Tell the woman I love that her cherished sister tricked her into a job out of laziness *and* selfishness? Explain to my queen that she has been manipulated for years and, after dispatching the Adversary, the author of all sin, the deceiver and the destroyer, the father of murder and the liar from the beginning—after ridding the earth of your blight of a mother—her reward is a job her enemy died to escape rather than accept the consequence of starting the war in Heaven? Of course not, never in life could I crush her with that. As you must have known."

She considered that and nodded. "Yeah. I did know."

"I shall do something much worse."

"Don't keep me in suspense," she said, trying for a jest and not . . . quite . . . getting there.

"It's quite simple. I am going to let you have what you think you desire. My Elizabeth, your sister, the Adversary's adversary, queen of the undead, will also be queen of the damned, if you'll pardon the obvious Anne Rice reference."

I stood and reached for my coat. Warm for Minnesota was still quite cold for a churchgoing vampire. "Elizabeth will rule Hell. And I shall do everything in my power to assist her." I shook out my coat and slipped into it while Laura gazed up at me from her pew.

"Big surprise. Eric Sinclair sticking his fingers into the power pie."

"Your analogy is almost as dreadful as your coat. I chose this spot so I could pray for you, as I did before you came, as I do now. May God pity you, Laura; may He shelter you from your most dread desire. May He save you from what you will bring to pass. You shall have what you want, and it shall be the end of you."

I left. Places to go, people to stomp, as Elizabeth would say, and both were true of me.

Besides, it would never do to keep my queen waiting.

Addendum

The parable of the lost son can be found in Luke 15:11–32. This version is from the New King James Version, online at www.biblegateway.com.

11 Then He said: "A certain man had two sons. 12 And the younger of them said to *his* father, 'Father, give me the portion of goods that falls *to me.*' So he divided to them *his* livelihood. 13 And not many days after, the younger son gathered all together, journeyed to a far country, and there wasted his possessions with prodigal living. 14 But when he had spent all, there arose a severe famine in that land, and he began to be in want. 15 Then he went and joined himself to a citizen of that country, and he sent him into his fields to feed swine.

16 And he would gladly have filled his stomach with the pods that the swine ate, and no one gave him *anything.*

17 "But when he came to himself, he said, 'How many of my father's hired servants have bread enough and to spare, and I perish with hunger! 18 I will arise and go to my father, and will say to him, "Father, I have sinned against heaven and before you, 19 and I am no longer worthy to be called your son. Make me like one of your hired servants."'

20 "And he arose and came to his father. But when he was still a great way off, his father saw him and had compassion, and ran and fell on his neck and kissed him. 21 And the son said to him, 'Father, I have sinned against heaven and in your sight, and am no longer worthy to be called your son.'

22 "But the father said to his servants, 'Bring out the best robe and put *it* on him, and put a ring on his hand and sandals on *his* feet. 23 And bring the fatted calf here and kill *it,* and let us eat and be merry; 24 for this my son was dead and is alive again; he was lost and is found.' And they began to be merry.

25 "Now his older son was in the field. And as he came and drew near to the house, he heard music and dancing. 26 So he called one of the servants and asked what these things meant. 27 And he said to him, 'Your

brother has come, and because he has received him safe and sound, your father has killed the fatted calf.'

28 "But he was angry and would not go in. Therefore his father came out and pleaded with him. 29 So he answered and said to *his* father, 'Lo, these many years I have been serving you; I never transgressed your commandment at any time; and yet you never gave me a young goat, that I might make merry with my friends. 30 But as soon as this son of yours came, who has devoured your livelihood with harlots, you killed the fatted calf for him.'

31 "And he said to him, 'Son, you are always with me, and all that I have is yours. 32 It was right that we should make merry and be glad, for your brother was dead and is alive again, and was lost and is found.'"